INTERNATIONAL

ALSO BY CAMARA LAYE

The African Child
A Dream of Africa
The Guardian of the Word

THE
RADIANCE
OF THE
KING

CAMARA LAYE

THE
RADIANCE
OF THE
KING

Translated from the French by James Kirkup

Vintage International

Vintage Books

A Division of Random House, Inc.

New York

FIRST VINTAGE INTERNATIONAL EDITION, October 1989

Copyright © 1971 by The Macmillan Company

All rights reserved under International and Pan-American Copyright Conventions. Published in the United States by Vintage Books, a division of Random House, Inc., New York. Originally published in French as *Regard du Roi* by Librairie Plon in 1956. Copyright © 1956 by Librairie Plon. This translation originally published in Great Britain by William Collins' Fontana Books in 1965 and in the United States by The Macmillan Company in 1971. This edition published by arrangement with Macmillan Publishing Company, a division of Macmillan, Inc.

Library of Congress Cataloging-in-Publication Data
Laye, Camara.
    The radiance of the King.
    (Vintage international)
    Translation of: Regard du roi.
    Reprint. Originally published: London: Collins, 1965.
    I. Title.
PQ3989.C27R413   843   88-40528
ISBN 0-679-72200-9

Book design by Chris Welch

Manufactured in the United States of America

10 9 8 7 6 5 4 3 2 1

CONTENTS

PART ONE

ADRAMÉ

1

THE ESPLANADE

When Clarence reached the esplanade he found his way blocked by such a vast, dense crowd that at first he felt it would be impossible to get through. He was tempted to turn back, but he had no say in the matter—he seemed to have had no say in anything for some days now!—and tucking in his elbows, he began to squeeze his way through the crowd.

He made very slow progress. The black people whom he was shoving aside made no protest, but neither did they make any effort to clear a path for him: they seemed to be unaware of his presence, or pretended to be; and Clarence would find himself held up for minutes on end by some strapping torso round which it seemed impossible to work his way, or wedged as if in a vice between two great hips. At such moments it seemed to him as if he was trapped in this crowd as in a liquid that had suddenly congealed, or in a slowly-shifting sand, and he felt unable to breathe, or maybe he was simply falling asleep. An odour of warm wool and oil, a herd-like odour that seemed to dull the senses into a kind of trance, emanated from these men packed tightly together under the African sky. Clarence must certainly have fallen asleep from time to time. Then gradually he began to shake off his torpor— maybe the smell had become less strong, maybe there was some other reason. And he started pushing his way forward again.

The expression "pushing his way forward" must not be taken too literally. In fact his progress was rather crab-like: Clarence would slowly insert his own shoulder between two others and give a sly shove, or else, raising his elbows slightly and leaning on his immediate neighbours, would manoeuvre them like levers. With every shove he gained an inch or two. And he did not seem to be causing any particular inconvenience to the men he was elbowing aside. In any case, they were so deeply ranked that those in the rear would almost certainly be able to see nothing of what was going on in the centre of the esplanade; and even those in the foremost ranks, with the exception of those in the very front, would not see a great deal, because as Clarence pressed forward the black men got bigger and bigger, growing imperceptibly to giant size. This was really very stupid, the exact opposite to what should have been the case, for these giants in the front row could easily have stood at the rear and so have given the smaller ones a chance to see. But perhaps this city belonged to a country in which no chances were ever given—at any rate, Clarence had so far never had a chance in this place.

It was becoming more and more difficult to squeeze through these giants: in spite of the crush, or perhaps because of it, they remained immovably planted there, as if their great limbs had taken root. But Clarence was so persistent that he managed to wriggle his way into the foremost rank.

Once there, for a long time he was able to make out nothing but a huge red cloud that rose to a great height in the sky and which he had already noticed as he was struggling up towards the esplanade. When his eyes had become a little more accustomed to that vapour that seemed to shine like fire, a fiery powder, he realised that it was composed of a very fine red dust, an almost imponderable substance threshed up from the bare earth by the naked feet of a horde of dancers. The cloud which only a moment before had risen like a column into the still air, was now beginning to spread out broadly at the top. Soon, thought Clarence, it will cast its shadow over the whole city. And no doubt this cloud would have been welcome if it could have intercepted the rays of the sun; but the sun broke through it everywhere, the sun clung to every atom of dust, so that the great cloud intensified the light and the heat rather than subdued them: it even gave the heat a kind of tangible presence, a massive and almost unbearable solidity. Now there was nothing to give protection from this heat: the trees at the edge of the esplanade were ancient and as if at the end of their strength, for their foliage was sparse and stunted, and so lacking in density that the sun was able to riddle it with holes like a battered sieve.

As for the dancers, they were young black men who seemed to be performing a very freely-improvised war-dance, each one dancing, as it were, for himself, without paying any attention to his companions. At times there were, it is true, certain concerted movements which carried all the dancers forward, then backwards, rather like waves beating at the foot of a cliff (though here they were beating at the packed crowd of spectators), but these movements seemed to be quite independent of the dance itself, their purpose being merely to keep the crowd from overflowing on to the esplanade.

Clarence watched the dancers for a long while. It was the first time he had witnessed one of the native dances, and the novelty and strangeness of this rather barbaric spectacle were such that he could not take his eyes away from it.

"They are dancing well," he said at last. One of the black giants at his side looked him up and down in an unfriendly manner.

"You call that 'dancing'?" he said bitterly. "I call it 'hopping,' nothing more."

"Well, yes, they *are* hopping," thought Clarence. "They *are* hopping, but they're dancing, too; that must be their way of dancing."

"They don't know the first thing about dancing," the black man went on. "They . . ."

But he did not finish his sentence. He spat contemptuously on the red earth.

"You wait a while, yes, you wait, and you'll see some real dancing," he said, spitting again. "You'll see some real dancing when the king . . ."

"Will the king be here soon?" asked Clarence.

"He will be here at the appointed time," answered the black man.

"What time will that be?" asked Clarence.

"I've just told you: at the appointed time."

"Yes, I know. But exactly what time will that be?"

"The king knows!" replied the black man. He spoke the words abruptly, cutting short the interrogation.

"Can I have offended him?" Clarence wondered. "I don't think I said anything that might have upset him." He looked back at the dancers, but found he could see them much less clearly: the red cloud seemed to have grown considerably denser.

"I came here in order to speak to the king," he said.

"So you want to speak to the king?" said the black man, looking Clarence up and down a second time.

"That is what I came for."

"But it's unheard-of!" said the black man. "It's absolutely unheard-of. Young man, do you think the king receives just anybody?"

"I am not 'just anybody,'" replied Clarence. "I am a white man."

"A white man?" said the black man.

He made as if to spit, but stopped himself just in time.

"Am I not a white man?" cried Clarence.

"The white men do not come here, on the esplanade!" retorted the black man, using the same abrupt tone of voice as he had used before.

"No, this esplanade would not be the place for white men to put in an appearance," Clarence thought bitterly. "They wouldn't let themselves be shoved around by all these black men; they would more likely be sitting in their villas, where it was cool, or else playing cards and sipping iced drinks on the veranda of the hotel."

And he saw again in his mind's eye the spacious veranda with its neatly-arranged tables and its swaying fans, its striped awnings and its black waiters in their white jackets putting bottles of wine to cool in buckets of ice. Only a week ago, he had been sitting on that veranda, playing cards and drinking brandy; he was calling his partners by their Christian names and ordering the black waiters around, free with his tongue, and bitingly witty . . . But now he was no longer at the hotel . . . Would he ever go back there? . . . No, he would never go back there, because if he did, they would all turn their backs on him. There was not one of those white men whom he did not owe money to, money he had lost at cards and, moreover, money he had borrowed at a time when he still had hopes of getting on his feet again, and—what foolish hopes—of breaking his run of bad luck.

Luck! . . . it was enough to make you die of laughing.

But what was it that had urged him to go on gambling? He didn't like cards! He never used to touch cards! But it was like this: all the white men who went to that hotel were gamblers and they had more money than they knew what to do with! . . . What was it to them, the money he owed the white men? They could lose it at a single throw of the dice and never feel the loss! But because he owed it to them, he who had never had very much money, who no longer had any money, they had insisted harshly on being paid, not of course because they set any store by it but merely in order to humiliate him, purely and simply in order to humiliate him . . . That was why he was living now in a sort of negro caravanserai; yes, a sort of caravanserai, that was all you could call it; you couldn't truthfully call such a hovel a hotel. Maybe he was being too generous in calling it a caravanserai, because it was really a . . . No, no! he would not distress himself by calling it to mind again; he felt sick at the mere thought of it . . . The only hope left to him—the last chance!—was to be taken on in the king's service.

"I shall present myself to the king as soon as he arrives," he said.

The black man beside him sniggered.

"Do you really mean that?" he asked.

Once again he looked him up and down, with an even

unfriendlier expression on his face than on the previous occasions.

"The guards won't even let you go near him!" he declared.

"Then what shall I do?" said Clarence. He suddenly felt overwhelmed with weariness . . .

"Perhaps I shall put in a word for you," said the black man.

"What—*you!*" cried Clarence.

He looked at his neighbour in amazement: he was an old man, poorly clothed; a tall man, no doubt, like all those in the front rank, but dressed in rags—a sort of beggar.

"But you are a beggar!!" he said.

"That is true: begging and soliciting—that's my trade," said the black man. "It's not an easy life; I began to learn the trade when I was very young."

"A fine advertisement you would be!" thought Clarence. If the guards were going to stop him, a white man, from approaching the king, with all the more reason they would stop this black man in his disgusting rags from addressing him. The man was obviously nothing more than an old fool.

"Your clothes are shabby," said the black man all of a sudden.

"But they aren't in rags!" retorted Clarence.

"I was especially careful not to say they were in rags," went on the black man. "No, they aren't in rags, yet—but they're already very shabby."

A few moments went by, then he continued:

"It won't be long before they're in rags."

"In rags?" cried Clarence.

He looked down at his clothes, at his jacket and his trousers. They were made of coarse linen. Would the material wear so very badly? Perhaps in this climate and with all this red dust, it would not wear as well as in Europe.

"It's good material," he suggested.

"Listen," said the black man. "I know you don't think much of me but never mind, I'll put in a good word for you."

"*You'll* put in a good word for *me?*"

He felt a quick surge of anger. What! *Him,* a beggar, a negro, "put in a good word" for *me?* The phrase stuck in his throat. He was asking no favours of anyone. He would offer his services to the king; he was willing to do some kind of work, provided it was honest and he received adequate remuneration for his services. *He* wasn't going begging! . . . But he swallowed his rage: he was on his beam ends, and had lost the right—the right or the luxury—to be angry; he owed money even to that native inn-keeper who was in charge of the caravanserai! This creature had more than once cast a covetous eye on Clarence's apparel and had even insinuated that he might accept them in exchange for the price of a bed. "Of course, I wouldn't want *all* your clothes," he added, "only one of the less important items—the jacket, the cap, or the trousers. It's not absolutely essential to wear both a jacket *and* trousers," he added. "Many natives wear nothing more than a shirt!"

As if Clarence would walk round in his shirt-tails after that! At the moment, all his worldly goods were the clothes he stood up in. Of course, he had two trunks full of belongings, but they were being held by the white hotel-keeper who had refused to give them up, and was keeping them as security for the unpaid hotel bill. The only thing Clarence had been able to take away were his razor and a piece of shaving soap: not even his shaving brush—he had to lather his face with his fingers! . . . No, he no longer had the right to anger. "I've still got the right," he told himself, "but I no longer have the means to put my anger into effect." . . . The means! Is that what one's "rights" were? . . . Apparently! And that

was why this black beggar had taken the liberty of saying he
would "put in a good word" for him.

"How ludicrous!" thought Clarence. A fresh wave of anger
swept through him, but this time it was anger against himself,
and anger whose sole object was to castigate his own petti-
ness. Why had he turned on the beggar just now? The man
had said nothing amiss. He wasn't much to look at—with his
ragged clothes, he certainly wasn't much to look at—but he
was certainly someone who had knocked about a bit, and so
must know a thing or two.

"It's not right," began Clarence.

"Well, any child knows that," the beggar said.

"Yes, any child," replied Clarence, "but if . . ."

He broke off. He had been going to say: "But if you had
not pointed it out to me, perhaps I should never have realised
it." And at that moment it suddenly dawned on him that ever
since the beggar had offered to speak on his behalf, the
beggar had not uttered another word, except of course when
he spoke about what any child would know. In the mean-
time, the beggar had kept completely silent; he had made no
allusion whatsoever to any kind of "right" . . . Yet it was as
if he had been speaking at the time . . . Could it be that the
beggar had the power of entering into the thoughts of others?
He might very well have that power! Perhaps he was a bit
of a witch-doctor; lots of beggars are given that way . . . Oh,
no! If this man had really been a witch-doctor, he would have
been in the procession with the king on a day like this
. . . "Are you a witch-doctor?" Clarence rehearsed the phrase
in his head, but just then a louder roar rose from the waiting
crowds and interrupted his train of thought.

This great roar was followed almost at once by piercing
cries: the young dancers, that the royal guards were driving
along in front of them with whips, surged forward rapidly

towards the edge of the esplanade. It did not seem as if their tragic cries were to be taken seriously: it was partly the lash of the whips that caused them, and partly the primitive delight in uttering them. Besides, the dancers had no sooner joined the crowd than they became part of it, adhering to it and falling silent. They were drenched in sweat, their naked bodies were steaming with sweat and spattered with red earth from head to foot. They were panting hard. Their sudden approach had the effect of turning the front rank of spectators into the second rank. This did not affect their view, as these dancers were hardly more than boys, whereas the black men in the front rank were all giants; but from the point of view of cleanliness, it was another matter. This earth, this red dust with which the dancers were caked and their rank sweat, an almost oily sweat, could not be kept off the spectators' clothes. However, no one made any protest at the defilement, apart from the beggar who, dressed as he was in rags which could hardly be made any worse, angrily addressed the dancer who had placed himself in front of him:

"Don't you dare touch me!" he cried, "or I'll give you a good hiding."

The boy drew swiftly to one side, as if the beggar's words had scorched him.

"Stand here," said the dancer who had taken up his position in front of Clarence.

He seized his companion, putting his arm round his neck and drawing him close.

"I trust we are not obstructing your view?" he asked Clarence.

"Not at all," replied Clarence. "But mind you don't press against me: this is the only suit I've got, and you are both covered with dust and sweat."

"Don't worry," the young dancer reassured him, "we'll soon have stopped sweating."

"The sun will have dried us before the king arrives," said the other.

"They're liars, both of them!" growled the beggar, beating the earth with his stick. "A pair of downright liars."

"We can stand somewhere else if you like," said the second of the two dancers.

"No, stay where you are," said Clarence. "You're not in my way."

But his nose was on a level with the tops of their heads, from which gave off a strong smell of rancid grease.

"Does your hair always smell as strong as this?" he said.

"It always smells like this until it gets dry. The sooner we've finished sweating, the sooner our hair will be dry."

"I wonder how they think them up, all these tales they tell you," the beggar said.

Clarence lifted his head, but the odour of grease, the stuffy odour of wool and oil was very penetrating, and he could not escape it. A faint drowsiness came over him: he closed his eyes, and his head lolled forward . . .

"Come on!" the beggar was shouting, "wake up!"

"Is it time?" asked Clarence.

"It's the appointed time!" said the beggar.

But the esplanade was still empty . . . Then it was suddenly alive with galloping horses that came to a halt, rearing up on their hind legs, only a few feet from the front of the crowd. They were strange horses, all caparisoned and panoplied and wearing layers of petticoats and some of them had even been dolled-up in silken trousers. The eye was so much taken up by all these trappings that it was some time before the rider himself could be made out. Yet they were proud figures, seated with almost insolent assurance in their saddles, and bearing lances that whirled and flashed in the sun. They were enveloped in long, flowing robes and on their heads were turbans curiously decorated with acorns and surmounted by high, round hats with broad brims.

Clarence wondered if the king himself might be among them: the king might easily have been one of these magnificent horsemen. But if he *was* there, what were the signs, the insignia, by which he could be recognised? He must surely have some kind of insignia. And Clarence's eyes went from one horseman to another. But how was it possible to make out anything clearly? The cloud of red dust, which had settled a little since the dancers had left the track, had become denser than ever with the arrival of the horsemen.

"Don't get excited," said the beggar. "All these are nothing but petty rulers who have come to do homage to the king . . . The king . . . But how could anyone fail to recognise the king! . . . He is . . ."

He was at a loss for words. Perhaps he realised that there are no words to express what the king is.

"He is . . ." the beggar began again.

But a sound of drums and trumpets drowned his voice. Kettledrummers were marching towards them, in splendid array, drumming away bravely on their drums, the male drum on the left, the female drum on the right. They were followed by trumpeters, who, with grotesquely distended cheeks, were blowing long ivory horns. Their vehement music seemed to be utterly without meaning, as if it were simply a loud din that had to be flung against the barrier of heat, against the sky; but it was obviously more than that, more than just a queer, haphazard noise, for the beggar announced suddenly:

"They are heralding the king's approach!"

"Yes," said Clarence, "that's what I gathered."

"No you didn't!" said the beggar crossly. "You didn't know *what* it was. Those drums are talking drums. They announce the king's approach and they say that he is king of kings . . . It's only the white man's music which is devoid of meaning."

He was speaking again in his old abrupt manner.

"The king of kings?" asked Clarence. "Well, he must certainly be the king of kings, after all this display, all these horsemen, this red and radiant cloud of dust, this vast crowd . . . And yet, and yet . . . he couldn't really be the king of kings: he would only be a negro king, a ruler of one of the negro tribes . . . Yet this cloud, this vast assembly . . ."

And suddenly the whole crowd—and it was immense, stretching all along the edge of the esplanade and reaching almost certainly right down to the centre of the city; perhaps it had even, like the great cloud, overwhelmed the city itself—the whole crowd suddenly began to shout and jump up and down, though what they were shouting and why they were jumping he had no idea at all. But perhaps it was simply the back rows which had begun to jump up and down in the hope, the vain hope, of catching a glimpse of part of the esplanade above the heads of the nearer ranks, and then their agitation had communicated itself to the entire crowd in the end, for it was such a homogeneous gathering and so densely packed that the slightest movement would make itself felt throughout its length and breadth.

"The king!" shouted the beggar, his voice rising over the tumult.

It was then that Clarence saw an adolescent boy dressed in white and gold, mounted on a horse whose caparisonings trailed on the ground—a caparison of green velvet embroidered with silver flowers. An attendant, with a drawn sword in his hand, was leading the horse by a bridle; this seemed quite indispensable, because the horse's head was so laden with flossy plumes and pompoms that it must certainly be able to see nothing at all. A second attendant, walking slightly in the rear, held over the sovereign a huge parasol with deep fringes. Then, at a respectful distance, came a band of pages, or rather dancers, for at a sign from the attendant with the bared sword, their group unexpectedly spread out in the pattern of a star around the king.

Each of these dancers then began to repeat the same movements as Clarence had seen performed by the boys before the guards drove them away from the track with their lashing whips. But this time all the movements were coordinated: each section of the great star took the lead from the dancer who was at the point. The movements, performed in this fashion, lost much of their barbaric nature, but unfortunately the dancers set up another cloud of red dust on the esplanade, and soon the king was completely hidden from the spectators.

The two boys in front of Clarence had difficulty in keeping still: they kept shaking their heads and wriggling, their muscles reproducing every gesture the dancers made. With this new excitement and the heat it engendered, their heads soon began to give off an even stronger smell of rancid grease. Once more Clarence felt himself growing drowsy.

"For pity's sake . . ." he murmured.

"What's the matter now?" asked the beggar. He looked at Clarence, then at the two boys.

"Didn't I tell you to send those two good-for-nothings packing?"

"You told me no such thing," said Clarence.

"Was my own example not sufficient indication?" queried

the beggar. "Why do you think yourself more clever than me?"

A smart slap over their heads made the two would-be dancers stand still.

"That's the way to treat them!" he snapped.

From then on, the smell, though never disappearing altogether, became less overwhelming.

Now they were able to see the king descending from his palfrey; or more exactly, the dancers who had gathered round him gradually disengaged him from the saddle by making him slide off sideways and receiving him in their arms which had previously been wrapped in white cloths for that very purpose. This unconventional method of dismounting gave the impression of extreme heaviness, but apparently it was only an impression, and a false one, for everything about the prince's person gave on the contrary an impression of miraculous lightness; yet the first impression lingered on with the second. As soon as the king reached the ground, two of the pages or dancers placed themselves at his right hand, and two at his left, and slowly lifted his arms. It was only then that Clarence discovered that these arms were encircled with so many golden bracelets that the king would never have been able to lift his arms without help: and it was this extraordinary profusion of gold bracelets that gave the impression of heaviness. At the same time as the pages were lifting the king's arms, the royal robe was falling open to reveal the slender black torso of an adolescent boy.

"How young he is!" thought Clarence. "And how frail he seems!"

But it was his fragility that was most striking; it was even more striking than his youth, and painfully so. One wondered how the king, such a slender boy, could bear the weight of all those bracelets, why his arms were not broken by such a load; and one understood that he could not have taken a single step without the support of his pages. He was so extraordinarily frail that he seemed utterly defenceless—yes, defenceless, in spite of his innumerable pages and drummers and trumpeters, in spite of the superb warriors who had ridden so proudly before him, in spite of the reverence of the immense crowd that stood all round him.

"He is young and he is frail," remarked the beggar, "but at the same time he is very old, and very strong. . . . If he were not so heavily weighed-down with gold, there would be nothing to keep him among us here."

"Why should he want to leave you?" asked Clarence.

"Why should he not want to leave us?" retorted the beggar. "Do you suppose he was intended for the likes of us? But the weight of all that gold holds him captive here."

"Gold . . ." said Clarence, bitterly.

"Gold can also be something more than just gold," the beggar proclaimed. "Among you white men, is gold always just gold and nothing else?"

"We scramble greedily for the smallest grain of gold dust."

"Yes, in the beginning, when you first came to this country we thought you must use gold for food. But gold may also be one of the signs of love, that is, the purest kind of love. That is the sort of gold that holds the king a prisoner, and that is why his arms are so heavily laden."

"Love . . ." said Clarence, very softly.

He began to think about love . . . Yes, it seemed that it might be possible to love this frail adolescent, yes, it would be possible, despite the pitch-black night of his skin . . . But why "despite the pitch-black night of his skin"? . . . What has the colour of a person's skin got to do with love? . . . Perhaps the midnight of those limbs would help to lift love to its purest peak; yes, it kept love at an ideal remove, it prevented it from being changed into one knows not what, or only too well . . . into a hurtful bestiality . . . And these darknesses were absolute, blacker even in the king than in the blackest of his subjects; more absolute, and more profoundly black, too, perhaps because of the vivid contrast with his white robe and the twisted rope of gold that was his turban. As for the features of the king . . . It seemed as if there could be nothing to say about those features: they were regular, and, apart from an almost imperceptible smile that hovered round the lips, they were quite impassive. But was it really a smile that played round the lips? Was it not rather . . . And Clarence was afraid to pursue the thought: it was the sort of smile which one sees on the faces of idols—remote, enigmatic—and which is composed perhaps as much of disdain as of benevolence; the reflection of an inner life, no doubt, but—what sort of inner life? Perhaps of that very life which lies beyond death . . . "Can that be the sort of life I have come here to find?" wondered Clarence. Yes, perhaps it was that life. "When all is lost, and everything departs out of our hands . . ." But such a life seemed so infinitely remote, so fraught with uncertainty . . .

"What kind of life could it be?" he asked himself.

A sort of abyss opened up under his feet as he thought of it.

"Can't you keep quiet for a minute?" the beggar said. "Look at the king!"

Supported by his pages, the king had taken a few steps forward. At once, in this great crowd massed along the edge of the esplanade, massed along all the thoroughfares of the city, massed—Clarence felt certain of this now—far beyond the outskirts of the city and standing reverently before this vast red cloud as if it were the insignia of royalty itself, an immense surge made itself felt. It came, this surging force, from a long way off; and it certainly came from the rearmost ranks, those at the farthest extremity of the esplanade: but it must also have come from those standing even farther back, far away from the esplanade. But where it came from was of little importance; what was really extraordinary was the force, the violence with which it swept through the ranks. As it advanced, and its advance was like a tidal wave's, the spectators found themselves knocked over on top of one another, all except the front rank, of course, whose members found themselves measuring their length upon the esplanade's red earth.

The beggar at this moment must certainly have regretted the removal of the young dancer who had come and stood so close to him; the old man's chin was now ploughed deep into the red earth and his noisy grunts were raising clouds of dust in front of him. Clarence, however, had had a soft fall, and was lying on the backs of the two boys. "I mustn't crush them," he said to himself. But his own weight was the least of it: Clarence could feel the weight of the numberless masses behind him all pressing on his back, his loins, and his legs, and he soon found he could hardly draw breath. Did you have to stop breathing in the presence of the king?

"I can't breathe," he said.

"You are not allowed to breathe," said the beggar. "The king is making his salutation!"

The pages were slowly raising the king's hands to his forehead and then no less slowly lowering them, with the palms turned out towards the crowd. This gesture, though a very simple one, seemed to take an eternity to perform; but the king's arms were so delicate, and so heavily burdened with their weight of gold, that it was obvious they could not be bent or extended without infinite precautions. Moreover this extreme slowness of gesture was inevitable, for no one could have understood or even accepted a rapid or negligently-executed salutation. The exercise of royalty makes certain demands upon kings and princes which it is not permissible to scant in any way, and which a king—and how much more so the king of kings!—would never allow himself to perform carelessly or incompletely, even when no one of his subjects has the right to demand such perfection, but simply waits in the hope that such a favour may be granted him.

As soon as the salutation was completed, the crowd, in spite of the unbelievable disorder it had been thrown into by its adoring prostration, leapt as one man to its feet. Then, in a further surge of adoration, it carried itself forward towards the king and once again fell prostrate. The king, supported by his pages, made his way towards the palace. Clarence caught another brief glimpse of him, and then saw him no more, for as the procession proceeded the crowd rose and with uplifted arms gave vent to clamorous cries. Only the parasol, held very high, gave any indication of the royal progress.

During all this tumult, Clarence had hardly moved a step from his original position. When the crowd, in a concerted movement, had rushed towards the king, the beggar and the two dancing boys had covered Clarence with their bodies and so had protected him during a stampede in which, through lack of experience, he might easily have been injured. On the whole of the esplanade, their group alone had formed a small oasis of stability. But this stability and immunity were not without their unfavourable points: though Clarence had indeed escaped unharmed from the uproar, and was naturally congratulating himself on his escape, yet never before had he been so far from his goal as he was now, for as soon as the procession reached the palace, the king would disappear again for an unpredictable length of time—no one could say just how long that would be, but everyone knew it would be a long time: two years, three years, perhaps longer.

"We must reach the king at once," cried Clarence.

"Reach the king? And will you tell us how you propose to do that?" asked the beggar.

He indicated the sea of uplifted hands and woolly heads, the sea of waving hands and yelling heads, above which the royal parasol swayed languidly.

"You're not going to fight your way through *that?*" he said.

"But I've absolutely *got* to speak to the king!" shouted Clarence. "If I don't speak to him now, who knows when I'll get the chance . . . Or would you like me to wait three years?"

He watched the parasol departing and stamped his foot with vexation.

"There are some who wait longer than that," said the beggar.

"But I *can't* wait as long as that. D'you hear, I *can't!* I haven't time. I've no more time to waste."

"Then throw yourself in front of the crowd!"

Clarence cast his eyes over the crowd and gave his foot a final stamp. That immense crowd . . . It was too much for him.

"Well, what are you waiting for?" the beggar inquired.

"Is the king always surrounded by such a tempestuous sea of people?"

"There are always certain obstacles."

"Obstacles, obstacles, that's the only word you know!" cried Clarence. "I come here, I let myself be shoved around and trampled on and crushed and half suffocated—I put up

with all that, and in the end it's still not enough: there are
certain obstacles!"

"Well, is that *my* fault?"

"If you had not kept me here, we should have reached the
king by now," said Clarence. "Don't forget, we were in the
front rank."

The beggar shrugged his shoulders.

"You are never satisfied," he said. "Why don't you make
your way towards the South?"

"And what would I do in the South?"

"Didn't you say you wanted to speak to the king? The king
is bound to go South some time or other. On this occasion
he has been paying a visit to his vassals in the North; in all
probability, he will go South next time. There are a few
vassals in the East, but they are all very minor ones. As for
the West, it's hardly worth considering; it's only a thin strip
of land bordering the ocean and enjoys the rule of the king
himself."

"When is the king likely to visit his territories in the
South?" asked Clarence.

"I don't know," replied the beggar. "No one knows. And
it isn't even certain that the king, on his next progress, will
take the road to the South rather than any of the others.
However, there's a good chance that the king may choose
that particular route, rather than the one to the North or the
one to the West. Wouldn't you like to try your luck?"

"My luck?" echoed Clarence. "Yes—my *bad* luck!"

"And what if there's no other kind of luck?" he asked
himself. "If . . . Oh! I've got no choice. And I can't afford
to waste time hanging about." He began thinking about the
black inn-keeper: every day the man seemed less willing to
give him credit, every day he cast an even more covetous eye

at his clothes. "I've only bad luck and I'll make a bad choice, then there'll be more delay. I must go. If I don't want to part with the shirt on my back to that foul toss-pot I must set off at once!"

He mopped his brow; the sun was beating cruelly on his head. Here, in the North, the heat was hardly bearable; what would it be like in the South? And he wondered what would be the final result of the fresh trials that awaited him. Perhaps there would be no result. Would he, once he had reached the South, be able to approach the king more easily than in the North? The people of the South must be even more exuberant than those of the North. He watched the parasol waving over the black crowd, the black sea-swell. Would a white man ever be able to battle his way through such seas, such waves? The beggar himself had hesitated. And what proof was there that things would be easier in the South than in the North? As he watched the parasol moving farther and farther away, Clarence felt all hope draining from his heart. It seemed to him now as if that parasol was taking away his final chance. It had never been much of a chance, and when the crowd had rushed on to the esplanade, it had grown much smaller, but now it could not be called even the slightest chance: it was nothing, it had vanished, and it had even lost the name of chance.

He felt more than ever sorely pressed. Even more so than when he had had to leave the hotel, when he had been more or less hounded out of the hotel. More so than when the negro toss-pot had reckoned up the value of the clothes on his back.

"All is lost," he said to himself. "Everything's against me . . . As soon as I set foot in this place everything turned against me."

He thought of the reef which protected this red earth from

the outer world and of how difficult it had been to get across. At first he had thought he would never get across; the tide had carried his boat at least twenty times towards the shore, and as often had drawn the boat away again towards the high seas; finally the boat had reached land. Clarence had thought at the time that he was in luck and that everything had happened as he had wished and that he was on the brink of great good fortune. But what a mockery of luck and what precarious happiness that had proved! It would have been a thousand times better if the boat had never crossed the reef.

"I'm going to see what I can do for you," the beggar was saying.

"For me?" said Clarence, surprised.

Then suddenly he remembered. But would the old beggar really be able to put in a good word about anyone? Was he anything better than an unbearable braggart? Clarence looked at him for a moment. However destitute he might be, and however ragged his clothes, he had an air of authority; and perhaps a beggar would have access to places where others would have met with only curt refusals. But was his the kind of authority that was needed at this moment? . . . A beggar with an air of authority? And for this sort of business? No, it didn't make sense . . . "So much the worse," thought Clarence. "So much the worse, or so much the better!"

"With things as they are . . ." he said.

"Yes, with things as they are," said the beggar. "Nevertheless, I shall put in a good word for you."

This time Clarence did not even protest; he had fallen so low, and looked on everything with such a worm's-eye view that this phrase from the lips of a negro beggar no longer exasperated him.

"I am much obliged to you," he said.

It was not entirely out of politeness that he said it; however faint the ray of hope appeared, he could see it shining,
and looked eagerly towards it. What did it matter after all
that it was a favour, when it should have been his by right?
Could there be any question of "rights" in the sort of world
he found himself in now? "Not in this world, nor, perhaps,
in any other," thought Clarence. "Viewed from the pit where
now I lie, there are no such things as 'rights.'"

"These two scamps will stay beside you to protect you
from the mob," said the beggar.

He made as if to go, then suddenly turned back.

"Do you two understand what I said?" he said sternly to
the boys.

"You talk loud enough—we must be deaf if we don't," said
one of the two boys. "I don't like that sort of thing."

"Oh! you don't like that sort of thing?" said the beggar.
And he lifted his stick.

"Don't you dare touch us with that stick!" said the other
boy.

"We won't stand for it!!" said the first. "You," he said,
turning to his companion, "did it ever enter your head to
abandon the white man?"

"I should never have dreamed of doing such a thing,"
replied the other.

"Do you hear that?" the former went on, once more addressing the beggar. "Who do you think you are? Do you
really believe everything will go to pieces just because you
aren't here? Do you think you are the king?"

"And there is no need, either, for you to speak to us all the
time in such a threatening manner," added the other. "We're
not little boys."

"Stop!" cried the beggar. "That's enough! I won't have

you bamboozling me like this. I need to have all my wits about me for what I'm going to do."

He looked at the palace at the end of the esplanade, and his face had a worried look.

"I can't think why I don't give you both a good trouncing," he said.

But he strode swiftly away, roughly beating a passage through the crowd with his stick.

Meanwhile, the king must have returned to the palace, because the fringed parasol was no longer swaying above the heads of the crowd, and besides, the excitement which only a few seconds ago had made the spectators dance and scream had suddenly subsided. Even the great red cloud had disappeared from the sky: it had either been dispersed by the wind—though there was very little wind, almost no wind at all—or else its vanishment had coincided with the king's withdrawal.

The palace reared against the sky its tremendous mass of red stone. At first sight it looked like a long, crenellated wall surmounted at intervals by thatched roofs, as if various main buildings were attached to it. The whole was dominated by a central tower whose staircase, constructed on the outside, seemed to give access to the sky itself. Not that the tower was exceptionally high, but the platform to which the staircase led seemed in a curious way to be level with the sky. This illusion—and it could be nothing more than an illusion—was almost certainly created by the fact that the stairway had no hand-rail and the platform no discernible parapet.

In the middle of the wall, a row of more or less perpendicular tree-trunks, roughly shorn of their bark, made a kind of colonnade, though it was difficult to tell whether they were there for ornament or support to the roof which at that point projected some distance from the top of the wall. With the exception of a door that was actually very low and narrow, there was no opening, but as there were frescoes running the whole length of the wall, one would have hesitated to say that the wall was a blank one. One would have been more inclined to say that the palace disdainfully refused to look down upon the esplanade or the crowd, and was concentrating all its attention on the interior, on the courtyards or the buildings inside, on the vistas and the edifices which, judging by the dimensions of the wall, were perhaps no more impressive than the esplanade and certainly less numerically overwhelming than the crowd. Yet in total impressiveness it surpassed by a long way both the esplanade and the crowd upon it, perhaps by reason of its dignity, or its mystery, or some other fact with which it would have been quite useless to acquaint the crowd. The general impression was one of sturdiness and strength. The building had more the air of a fortress than of a palace, and its proportions even gave one the feeling that it was a fortified city rather than a mere fortress.

From where Clarence was standing, it was difficult to make out the frescoes. They seemed to represent battle scenes which probably commemorated the mighty deeds of former kings. But as he drew nearer, Clarence realised that this was not so. What he had taken for battle pictures were purely religious scenes depicting a series of sacrifices, a long procession of captives being led to altars where priests—perhaps kings—were cutting their victims' throats. Clarence felt they were kings rather than priests, as all the slaughterers were wearing twisted turbans similar to the one he had seen on the king's head.

"What do those frescoes mean?" he asked the two boys.

But almost at once he regretted the question: how could these children be expected to know?

"They depict the king punishing his unfaithful vassals," said one of the boys.

"No, Nagoa," said the other, "you are mistaken. If such was the case, the king would have no vassals left; he'd have to cut all their throats!"

"You're joking," replied Nagoa. "Look here, my man . . ."

"I am not your man: I am Noaga."

"Well, Noaga, you can take it from me that the frescoes were put there as a warning to those vassals who might be led astray by rebellious thoughts. What other meaning can they have?"

"I can tell you," Noaga retorted.

"What is it then?"

"The king is turning away from his unfaithful vassals: he considers them sufficiently punished by their own infidelity. Only the most devoted of his vassals are being immolated, because they alone are worthy of the altars. It would profane the sacrificial altars if guilty blood were spilt upon them."

"What sort of nonsense is all this?" said Clarence.

He did not understand how the king could sacrifice his most devoted vassals, or how such a sacrifice could be a reward. Yet when you came to think of it, the boy . . . the boy perhaps . . .

"What do they call you?" he asked the boy who had spoken last.

"Noaga."

Yes, when you came to think of it, this Noaga's interpretation was . . .

"Your interpretation is the right one," said Clarence.

But he at once regretted having said these words. No, that

interpretation *couldn't* be right . . . it's . . . it's not common
sense! . . . Or rather it was "right" without being right at all
. . . "How silly!" he thought. "If something is *not* right, how
can it be right? . . . It's just silly!"

"As for you," he said to the other boy . . . "But first tell
me what they call you."

"Nagoa."

"Why have you both got the same name?" asked Clarence.

"We have *not* got the same name!" the boy said. "I'm
Nagoa; he's Noaga."

"Really?" said Clarence. "And you say . . ."

But he broke off. Similarity or would-be similarity of
names seemed to him just as silly as the business of the
vassals.

"Listen!" he began.

He was addressing them both, but he no longer knew quite
what he had been going to say to them: the similarity in their
names must have upset and confused him. Had he been going
to ask them to choose names that would not give rise to so
much confusion? Perhaps. But he had no time to get this
clear or to say anything further. For at that moment, piercing screams were heard, the screams of a wounded beast. Yes,
it was as if the frescoes had suddenly come to life, as if all
these men stretched out on the altars had suddenly begun to
scream.

"What's that?" he asked.

"It's the vassals," said the boys in one voice.

"What do you mean, the vassals?" Clarence asked.

"Why, the unfaithful vassals!" Nagoa said.

"No, the faithful vassals!" said Noaga.

Faithful! Unfaithful! Clarence wondered how much longer
that particular joke was going to last. This was no time for
joking, was it? If the beggar had been there, these two

scamps . . . But fresh screams were heard, as piercing as the
first. This time they were accompanied by rolling drums.

"Now they're cutting their throats," the two boys said.
They spoke in animated tones.

"Their throats . . . are being . . . cut . . ." said Clarence.

He was thinking to himself: "I'm dreaming. I'm dreaming,
but I'm going to wake up soon . . ."

"Can't you hear them?" Noaga asked. "The drums are
announcing it . . ."

"The drums are speaking . . ." said Clarence.

"This is just a bad dream," he said to himself. "Who would
have believed such nightmares were possible!"

"Yes, they are announcing that the faithful have been
judged worthy of . . ."

"No!" shouted Nagoa.

"Yes!" shouted Noaga.

"Oh, shut up, for God's sake!" said Clarence.

They were silent, but the screams then sounded more
piercing than ever . . . Why were the drums beating? . . . They
were raucous screams, screams that rose from the back of the
throat; yes, despite the paralysis of fear, the screams were
rising from the depths of the throat, and they were screams
that were not allowed to finish. A knife stuck in the throat
gave them no chance to elaborate their suffering: for then
they changed to a kind of breathless gargling.

"We must go and see about this!" said Clarence. "They
can't just . . ."

He wanted to dash away towards the palace, but found he
couldn't move. He was trembling. He was shaking from head
to foot.

"Isn't there *any* way of stopping this butchery?" he asked.

He was wringing his hands: these screams seemed to be
tearing at his vitals.

"The vultures!" cried the two boys.

Vultures were hovering in the sky, attracted obviously by the smell of blood.

"Now the king is bathing his hands in the vassals' blood," said Noaga.

"Yes," said Nagoa, "his hands are crimson with blood."

"But how dare you tell us that he's bathing his hands in the impure blood of the unfaithful?" said Noaga.

"Once and for all, will you two shut up?" cried Clarence.

He felt at the end of his strength; his patience was running out. Those cries, and this argument on top of everything! He stopped his ears: he did not want to hear anything more. He shut his eyes, too, so that he would not see the vultures. But the screams went on echoing through the very depths of his being, and although his eyes were shut, he could still see the vultures, he could see the king's hands, he could see the knife, he could see the blood spurting from the victims' gaping necks, he could smell the odour of blood, and he could taste this odour on his lips, the taste of blood, a little sugary, a little insipid, as if his own lips or his gums had begun to bleed . . . No! . . . as if it were his own blood spurting up into his mouth from his slit throat! . . . He spat; he felt sick . . . He was shaking more than ever. In an attempt to stop his shaking, he let his head fall on the heads of the two boys; but then a heavy fetid smell rose from them, strong and overpowering, and he felt he was going to faint, he was actually fainting . . . He was suddenly jolted out of this state of torpor: the two boys were pulling at his arms.

"The king!" they were shouting. "The king!"

"What do they want with me now?" wondered Clarence. "Couldn't they leave me alone for just one moment?" He clenched his hands even more strongly, he squeezed them tightly against his ears: he did not want to hear any more.

No! He wasn't going to listen to any more! But the shouts
of the boys finally penetrated his stopped ears and he let his
hands drop, he opened his eyes.

Supported by his pages, the king was slowly ascending the
stairway of the central tower. The stairs were lined by vassals, one standing on each step. Each one held his drawn
sword in front of him, the handle turned towards the king
and the point resting on the vassal's throat, as if patient for
sacrifice. But the king did not even look at them. He as-
cended the stairway with faltering steps. He seemed exhausted. "Exhausted by that butchery whose story, whose
abominable and age-old story, is impudently displayed in the
frescoes," thought Clarence. But perhaps it was only the
height of the steps and the weight of the bracelets that made
him stagger. And not only did he have the bracelets on his
arms to contend with: there were the bracelets on his legs,
encircling and weighing on his heels, for the king's legs were
almost as heavily laden with gold as his arms. The cloak
which, on the esplanade, had concealed them, now fell back
revealingly at every step, and his legs were as slender, as frail,
as painfully slender and frail as his arms.

When the king reached the platform he made his salutation. But this time it was not the crowd he made it to; he
turned his back on them and raised his face to the sky: he
was making his salutation to the sky. Then the pages who
until then had been supporting him withdrew, and the king
seemed in a curious way to be moving forward alone into the
open sky. Was it because the platform had no parapet, and
was, as it were, set directly against the sky? Perhaps. Perhaps, too, it was more than just an illusion. But how could
they tell? As the king moved forward, the edge of the platform gradually hid him from sight. Could it be that the
platform was so spacious that someone walking from one side

to the other would become entirely hidden from the sight of the spectators on the esplanade? It was most improbable, but there was no way of knowing. And perhaps there was simply another stairway at the far end of the platform, which the king would walk down, supported by his pages. Yes, perhaps . . . But nevertheless one still had the impression that the king was walking off into space, as if the bracelets and the rings of gold, as if that gold, and all that love had suddenly became powerless to hold the king to the earth. . . .

The vassals who had formed the guard of honour now descended the stairway very leisurely, with their swords under their arms; and soon, above the surrounding wall, all that could be seen was the central tower, with its empty steps. Then the tower itself seemed to fade away, obliterated somehow, and becoming a kind of anonymous vapour which, like something which has been used and will not be used again, died away into nothingness. All that was left was the long wall with its frescoes. But now the frescoes seemed less legible, and represented one could hardly say what . . . sacrificial scenes, no doubt. Perhaps they were simply pastoral scenes, perhaps nothing at all: in other words there was nothing but vaguely interweaving shapes. Everything was gradually becoming blurred, as if night were already beginning to fall. There were no longer any guards at the palace door. But was it really the door, that reflection on the wall? One would have said that there was no longer any door, only the reflection image of a door. And the palace itself seemed to have been moving imperceptibly away: the dark ditch that separated it from the esplanade was rapidly growing deeper, and filling up with darkness. Was this the grave where midnight lay, and where the night was born?

The silence had grown very strange. The black men began to run from the esplanade. They went by like fleeing shades;

their feet, treading the red dust, made no sound. Thus silence
after tumult, this great sheet of darkness along the side of the
palace, and the palace itself, slowly fading away, becoming
quieter and quieter; this festival and this disintegrating
crowd . . . it was a kind of agony, a slow dying.

Could it be that all this splendour, the king, the procession, then the utter horror, the screams and deathrattles of
the victims had been nothing but a mirage? And was this the
end of the mirage? Not a single scream, not a word, not one
roll of the drums . . . nothing more than a deathly stillness.
But the horror had certainly not been a mirage: the vultures,
perched on the battlements of the wall, were preening their
glittering black feathers, as if at the end of a funeral banquet.
Clarence shivered. "Alone!" he thought. "I am alone!" And
he forced himself not to shout.

"Are you still there?" he asked.

"We have not stirred an inch from your side," replied the
two boys.

"No, I see you haven't," thought Clarence. "But what are
you? Two kids! Two kids, that's all! . . . I am alone, just as
much alone as when the white hotel-keeper showed me the
door. I was in the street, standing in front of the door. I could
hear the black servants poking fun at me because my luggage
had been confiscated and also perhaps because it was the first
time they had ever seen a white man thrown out on the
streets. And I could not bring myself to leave that door: I just
didn't know where to go." At the same time, he remembered
the reef that barred the coast of Africa—a great foaming line
like a festering weal. "Why did I want to cross that reef at
all costs?" he wondered. "Could I not have stayed where I
was?" But stay where? . . . On the boat? Boats are only
transitory dwellings! . . . "I might have thrown myself overboard," he thought. But wasn't that exactly what he had

done? When he had agreed to play cards—and he had always hated cards—he had thrown himself overboard! . . .

Someone touched his shoulder. The beggar had returned without giving any warning of his approach.

"Excuse me for disturbing your thoughts," he said.

"You are not disturbing me," said Clarence.

He was trying to read the beggar's face, but he could make out nothing at all: he had been too short a time in this country to be able to decipher the expressions on the black men's faces.

"Well?" he asked.

"I'm sorry," said the beggar. "There is no post available for you."

"But I would have accepted any post whatsoever!"

"I know. But there are no posts available."

"I should have been satisfied with the humblest situation," said Clarence.

"Alone," he said to himself. "Each time I find myself a little more alone!" And he realised that he had in spite of everything cherished a last fond hope: standing there on the esplanade, he had been in despair. Yet in the depths of his being, and despite the rebuffs he had already received, there had always been a faint hope. And it had been this shadow of hope—this pallid reflection—for one could not decently grace with the name of hope this obscure remnant which was all that was left of hope—it had been this poor shred of hope, become now a wretched phantom, that he had been pursuing.

"I could have . . ." he said.

But what could he have done? Had he the least idea?

"I could have been a simple drummer boy . . ."

"That is not a simple occupation," said the beggar. "The drummers are drawn from a noble caste and their employment is hereditary. Even if you had been allowed to beat a drum, your drumming would have had no meaning. You have to know how . . . You see, you're a white man!"

"I know!" replied Clarence. "There's no need for you to remind me of it all the time . . . I've known it longer than you. Oh, you get on my nerves!"

"Yes, but the white men think they know everything," went on the beggar. "And what *do* they know, when all's said and done?"

"Anyhow, I know that the king was cutting his vassals' throats a short while ago," said Clarence.

"This old rogue treats me like one of his own kind," he thought. "Well, I'll make him sing a different tune!" A hideous joy filled his heart: if it became known what horrors had been perpetrated, the white man might seize the pretext, and the king, even though he were the king of kings . . .

"Do you really think that after all that I would want to enter the king's service?" he went on. "I was looking for honest work."

"Are you out of your mind?" said the beggar. "What's all this about vassals having their throats cut?"

"Do you suppose I didn't hear their screams?"

"The screams?" said the beggar.

He suddenly turned on the two boys.

"What have you been telling the white man?" he asked sternly.

The two boys hung their heads.

"There was no need for them to tell me anything," said Clarence. "I've got ears."

But the beggar took no notice of his interruption.

"If I catch you two making up stories again," he said to the two boys, "I'll tan the hide off your backsides with my stick!"

The two boys had not raised their heads or uttered a single word.

"And do you mean to say you've swallowed it all?" the beggar asked Clarence.

"Were those screams 'made-up'?" Clarence replied.

"I don't know what screams you are talking about," said the beggar, "and I don't want to know. All I know is, these two rascals have been pulling your leg . . . But can't you see they're simply two talkative and lying brats trying to give themselves airs? . . . Come on, let's go! . . . Everybody's going . . . We mustn't let the darkness overtake us when we're so close to the palace."

He looked round him with frightened eyes. "Why is he afraid?" Clarence wondered. "He said these children have been making up stories, but he himself . . ." He too looked along the esplanade. It was deserted now, and looked even vaster than before: it was ten times, a hundred times vaster than when the crowd was there. The palace . . . But Clarence could no longer make out the palace; the sun was going down, and was level with the crenellated edges of the long wall: it cast slanting rays that prevented him from seeing anything. The stillness now was absolute, and one had no desire to break it: one would have been afraid to waken who knows what dreadful echoes . . .

"Well, are you coming?" said the beggar impatiently.

"Don't speak so loud," said Clarence.

The beggar growled something that Clarence only half caught, something like: "First you shout, then you whisper . . . never anything in moderation!" But it didn't matter.

They began walking, all four of them, down towards the city. They met no one in the streets. All those crowds . . . But where had all those crowds disappeared to? . . . They could not all have found shelter in the houses. Besides, there

was no sound at all coming from the houses. The stillness
preserved its defenceless nudity . . . a chilling nudity . . .
Sometimes, on the edge of a roof, a vulture would peer,
stretching its neck and tilting its head, watching with great
curiosity as Clarence went by. Perhaps it was surprised to see
him with such an incongruous escort . . .

2

THE INN

"Here you are at your destination," said the beggar.

"Yes," said Clarence, casting a scornful look around the caravanserai. "Here I am, as you say, at my destination."

"But if this is my only destination . . ." he thought. "If this is all destiny has in store for me . . ."

"You're not pulling my leg, are you?" he asked.

"Why should I do that? It's dark."

"I don't see what that has to do with it."

"There's no fun in pulling people's legs when it's dark; you can't see how they take it."

"All right," said Clarence. "I'm not going to argue with you."

He was worn out. The long wait on the esplanade, the futility of his efforts, and then the victims' screams and the smell of greasy sweat had all worked upon him more than he had realised, and his arrival at the caravanserai—and the thought of bed, no doubt—suddenly made him conscious of how tired he was.

"Not that I feel any less grateful to you," he went on. "Even though my destination were the most forsaken place on earth, I do not know how I should have found my way if you had not guided my steps."

He raised his eyes and looked at the sky for a moment. Walking back down the esplanade, they had been overtaken by night, that had fallen with that suddenness which is usual in the tropics and that in contrast to the dazzling radiance which precedes it, makes it appear at first so dense a darkness.

"I don't think I've ever known such a black night," he said.

"The night after the king has gone back to his palace is always a very black one," said the beggar.

"Yes," continued Clarence, "a black night it is, and the city a never-ending maze of narrow streets . . ."

He was thinking of the thousand and one alleyways of the native town, the twisting, narrow, little streets, crisscrossing at the most unexpected angles, and many of them ending in cul-de-sacs. No, nothing was ever made easy in this town.

"Aren't you coming in?" he said.

He had said it mechanically; it was a phrase which committed no one, unless it was taken literally. But he suddenly had the idea of letting the beggar see the sort of shameful hovel that was run by the black inn-keeper.

"Come in!" he said. "I would very much like you to step inside."

"Well, I can rest my bones for a moment," said the beggar. "But only for a moment, for I've still got a long stretch in front of me to-night."

"I shan't detain you any longer than you wish," said Clarence. "Would you be so kind as to step inside?"

He drew aside to let him pass. He was very pleased with his scheme. This beggar had expressed rather too often his scorn for white men; now he would see what the "nigger quarters" in the caravanserai were like, and he would have to eat his own words.

"And what are you two waiting for?" Clarence asked the two boys. "Do you want the old toss-pot himself to invite you in? You seem to think that if you stand with your mouths open, the larks will fall into them ready cooked!"

"Larks?" said the beggar. "Larks for rogues like these?"

"Don't worry," said Clarence. "I shouldn't think a lark has ever flown in here. And I very much doubt whether a lark has ever winged its way across these heavens."

He turned to the boys.

"Go on in!"

He used the same tone of voice as if he had said: "The more the merrier!" But the two boys apparently were not interested in his tone of voice; all they were waiting for was the invitation, for they dashed inside and shoved each other about as much as possible in the vestibule. Actually it was a ridiculously narrow vestibule and was more of a covered way than a vestibule. At the end of the passage there was a courtyard which was covered with piles of filthy rubbish from which a great swarm of flies arose: they were as angry as wasps and greedy as grasshoppers.

"This way, and be quick!" cried Clarence. The flies had so little to eat, they were quite capable of devouring you!

He ran towards a crack of light which denoted the entrance to the main room. On the threshold a dark shape stood out, a man with arms akimbo and legs wide apart, who seemed to be barring their way.

"And here's the old toss-pot in person!"

He had suddenly forgotten his tiredness and had regained courage; he felt full of courage. He forgot that this courage was no more than foolish bravado which only a few days ago had urged him on to play for high stakes, when all he had to lose was his honour. And because he had recovered that feeling of reckless courage, he was no longer the man who had been expelled from the white men's hotel, nor yet the man who had not been able to get himself the wretched little job of drummer to the king; neither was he that wreck of a man who owed money to this negro inn-keeper whom he addressed publicly as "old toss-pot." No, he was that man no longer, he wasn't the same man at all! But this insolent man, this blown-up blusterer, this would-be hero—was he any better? Wasn't he like a creature that has reached the depths of despair, a creature who cared as little for others as he did for himself, a creature whose only defence is sarcasm? . . . Is that what you call a man? . . . And supposing all men were like that? . . .

"I have brought you some guests," he said to the negro.

"Try, if you can, to treat them a little more decently than you've treated me so far!"

"Are you paying the bill?" asked the inn-keeper.

Now his face could be seen in the lamplight, and it was distorted into a horrible grimace.

"Don't make such a fuss about trifles like that," said Clarence. "What's settled is settled. Get back to your dirty
dishes!"

"What I mean is . . ."

"Go on, when the white man tells you to!" cried the
beggar.

"Excuse me," the inn-keeper said to the beggar, "I didn't
see you there."

"Well, you see me now! What are you waiting for?"

"I'm going!" said the inn-keeper. "I'm going at once!"

He plunged into the darkness of a corridor; and almost
immediately there was a great clattering of pots and pans.

"Pray, gentlemen, be seated," said Clarence.

He indicated a corner of the room that was no dirtier and
no cleaner than the rest and they crouched down there
among all kinds of bits of rubbish.

"Most comfortable, isn't it?" asked Clarence. "The last
time it was swept was ten years ago."

"Pooh! A caravanserai!" exclaimed the beggar, shrugging
his shoulders.

"And just about the worst-run, and the filthiest, that ever
was."

"It's a fact," said the beggar.

He was looking at the litter-strewn ground. He seemed to
be counting the bits of rubbish.

"But perhaps this is all I have a right to?" said Clarence.
He smiled at the beggar.

"What right?" asked the beggar, as if the word had startled him.

"Wasn't that more or less what you told me? Wasn't that
what you were hinting at, at least?"

Clarence was now speaking with great bitterness.

"I spoke only of 'favours,'" said the beggar. "You are

quite wrong to think I said anything about 'rights' of any kind. As far as I'm concerned, I have never claimed any kind of 'rights.' I have always restricted myself to soliciting favours. I'll say no more than that I expect these favours to be granted."

"But you look upon those favours as your rightful reward?"

"I must confess that I do on occasion use a more peremptory tone than I ought to. Is that what you are trying to insinuate?"

"I'm insinuating nothing," said Clarence. "I'm stating facts."

"But I always regret at once having used that peremptory tone," went on the beggar. "It is not suitable for a person like myself."

"But it's only after you use it that you feel regret."

"What meaning do you attach to the word 'regret'?" asked the beggar. "Would you like me to feel anticipatory regret? And what meaning then would you attach to the word 'impudence'?"

He gave Clarence a piercing look.

"Do I understand that you have never felt true regret?" he continued. "If that were so, it would indeed be a misfortune."

"I regret only one thing," said Clarence, "that I did not throw myself overboard before I landed on these shores. If only the reef had been less easy to cross . . ."

"But at that moment you thought it was too difficult."

"That's true," said Clarence. "And besides I thought I'd had great good luck in getting across . . ."

"Good luck!" exclaimed the beggar. "You never talk about anything else—it's always on your lips and in your heart, and you dare to reproach me with talking about 'fa-

vours'! . . . Why do you make such a great distinction between 'good luck' and 'favours'? . . . I must own that sometimes I find it hard to follow you."

"Good luck . . ." said Clarence. "Good luck is . . ."

He was wondering how to begin his explanation when he
suddenly realised that this "good luck" which he never
ceased thinking about was in fact nothing more than a 'favour;' either one received it, or one did not receive it, one
kept it or lost it, and there was no more point in receiving
it than in not receiving it, no more point in losing it than in
keeping it. And he stopped short. As short as the two boys
after their dressing-down, he felt. Can it be that my own
reasoning is as stupid as theirs? . . . And he was ashamed. He
was glad when the entrance of the inn-keeper created a
diversion. The latter had just placed on the ground between
them an enormous stew-pot full of rice and fish seasoned with
red peppers. The two boys, their eyes shining, were digging
each other in the sides with their elbows.

"Pray help yourself," said Clarence to the beggar.

The beggar dug three fingers into the pot and helped himself as skilfully and as plentifully as if he had been using a
large spoon. Clarence in his turn used three fingers, but the
rice slipped off, and all he could put in his mouth were the
few grains that had stuck to his fingers; he cast a puzzled look
into the pot. The two boys burst out laughing.

"Look, this is how you do it!" they cried.

They dipped their fingers in the pot, but a couple of sharp
clouts over the head made them draw back their hands.

"Are you so famished, so starved with hunger that you
cannot wait your turn?" said the beggar. "You shall have
your share when we have finished."

"There, you see!" the boys said to one another, licking

their fingers. "In the end we got even less than the white man."

"Will you be quiet!" said the beggar.

And to Clarence: "They're what I call a saucy pair."

"You know the customs of this land better than I do," said Clarence. "I thought they could have eaten with us. But if you think it's not proper, I shall respect your point of view."

"It is not proper," said the beggar. "The young should serve themselves only after the older ones have finished. They may count themselves lucky if I leave them a few scrapings at the bottom of the pot."

"You're not going to empty the pot yourself?" cried the boys.

"I'm going to eat my fill!" the beggar proclaimed.

"I wonder if eating, too, is considered as a favour?" Clarence said to himself. "It must surely be one; and it must be a double favour, a double stroke of good luck, when one has the money to pay one's share!" He wanted to dismiss the thought of the inn-keeper presenting his bill, the bill for his own portion and for those of the three others whom he had so capriciously invited, but the thought was not of the kind which allow themselves to be pushed to one side at will. "I go on from one folly to another," he thought. "This is the least of them; the most extraordinary one was to put my fate in the hands of a beggar. And what a beggar! If I had approached the king myself . . . Oh, yes, I know, the guards, or the pages or the attendant with the drawn sword would have driven me back, but at least I should have been noticed by . . . by the king . . . Surely the king would have wished to know what had brought me to him. Perhaps . . . Yes, perhaps he would have asked me to state my case, myself . . ."

"Aren't you eating?" asked the beggar.

"Of course!" replied Clarence.

He dipped his fingers in the pot and succeeded in snatching a bit of fish. "Good luck!" he said to himself. "Good luck, at last! . . ." But was it worth anything? "If this is the only kind of good luck I'm to have . . ." But perhaps these little bits of good luck were all he would be allowed at first: perhaps one didn't get into the way of big slices of good luck until one had grown accustomed to the little bits. Clarence looked at the beggar. "Perhaps he, too, began by having just such a humble piece of good luck . . ." He examined a little more closely the rags in which the beggar was clad, and he came to the conclusion that this man had never got past the first stage of good luck. "Probably he's just waiting for that stroke of good fortune which will allow him to rise above the mire . . ." Yes . . . unless of course the man rejoiced in his lowly state; many beggars . . .

"What does one do with the bones?" he suddenly wondered. But one just threw them on the floor, of course! That's the way there was all this filth in the inn—the greasy floor, the swarms of flies, the vermin, and, in the yard, those piles of muck. Clarence watched the beggar spitting out his bones and wondered what he had been thinking of to invite such a character to supper. "And yet this is the man I asked to present my request to the king! . . ." He was absent-mindedly chewing his bit of fish. "And now I'm surprised because I have no luck with anything!" He pulled a bone out of his mouth and held it in his hand. "Success would be the surprising thing!" He was staring fixedly at the bone he had pulled out of his mouth. "What am I doing with this?" he wondered. "Is it any better to pull a bone out of one's mouth with one's fingers, or to spit it out? Is it any better to keep it in one's hand and then to put one's fingers in the pot?" He abruptly threw away the bone on the rest of the rubbish littering the floor.

"Have you any plans?" asked the beggar.

"Plans?" said Clarence. "What on earth makes you think I would have plans?"

"I don't know. You seem to be constantly lost in all kinds of thoughts."

"How do you expect a man like me, at the end of his tether, to have plans?" asked Clarence. "This morning, now, when I went to the esplanade, then I had plans. But since then . . ."

He raised his hand and waved it about as if to brush away for ever all the plans he might ever have had.

"Take another morsel of fish," said the beggar, "then you'll feel better. You're talking on an empty stomach. If you had something inside your belly you'd be talking in quite another way . . ."

"No," said Clarence. "I can't . . . this messy stuff makes me sick."

"You've been poking your fingers in it long enough!" he added to himself, though he knew this was not true.

"Then do you really not want any more?" the beggar asked.

"I've had enough," said Clarence. "I've had enough for to-day and for to-morrow, I've had enough to last me for weeks, months, years!"

"Well, I won't press you any further, then," said the beggar. "Come on, it's your turn now!" he went on, addressing the boys.

He did not have to repeat the invitation: the boys threw themselves greedily upon the pot. "There are bones in it," thought Clarence. "They'll choke themselves. Why does the old fool not restrain them?" But the beggar was watching them with the utmost indifference. "He's filled his belly and now he doesn't care what happens to anyone else. Why should he have bothered to see that my request was transmitted to the king?"

"Did you actually give my message to the king?" he said.

"I never forget anything," said the beggar.

He got up, drank a mouthful of water, gargled his throat, rinsed his mouth out, and spat.

"It's only a caravanserai, but the food's good," he said.

"Well, you're not hard to please," retorted Clarence.

He thought disgustedly of the gluey concoction they had been eating. Was it really necessary to eat rice or millet with every meal? He watched the beggar massaging his gums, in which a few wretched stumps of teeth were planted askew.

"Don't these sticky mixtures make the teeth fall out?" he asked.

"Sticky mixtures . . . what do you mean?"

"Well, these concoctions we eat with fish or with meat, or even with nothing at all."

"It's the red peppers that make the teeth fall out," the beggar said.

He had finished massaging his gums and was giving himself a cat's lick of a wash. Then he drank some water from the water-bottle. "Perhaps I ought to have offered him palm wine," thought Clarence, watching the beggar's Adam's apple bobbing up and down as he swallowed, bobbing wildly, as if in protest against all this water, when there was excellent palm wine to be had which was perhaps even now fermenting, perhaps going sour, in the cellars of the caravanserai . . .

"Hey, toss-pot!" he shouted. "Bring some palm wine!"

"It might give me some new ideas!" he said to himself. He watched the two boys for a moment as they attacked the remains of the food in the pot. "Now there's two who don't

bother their heads about anything! Or if they do, they think
nice things, they have rosy thoughts, dreams of soft, melting
flesh, enough to make your mouth water! Why can't I be like
them?" But he could never have been like them; and even
if he'd been able to share their thoughts, he could never be
as skilful as they were—their fingers were literally flying.

"They don't lose a second," he remarked, turning to the
beggar.

"If only they could dance as well as they stuff their bellies!" said the beggar. "But there's no need to be so extrava-
gantly surprised: it's always like that if you don't know when
you might get a decent meal again."

"I suppose so," said Clarence.

"Yet I've hardly eaten a thing," he thought. "I just
pecked at it, and I don't know if I'll get anything to eat
to-morrow." He drank some palm wine. "If I could get
drunk . . ." But could one get drunk on palm wine? The
liquor seemed to have very little body—perhaps you had to
drink a large quantity. "Well, why shouldn't I try it?" he said
to himself. He took a lengthy draught: perhaps he would get
drunk in the end.

He could see that the beggar, too, wasn't losing any time.
His Adam's apple was still bobbing up and down as wildly as
ever, but with a strange alacrity; it no longer jibbed at each
mouthful, but rather seemed almost over-eager to send them
down.

"I did well to order this wine," thought Clarence. "A meal
without wine . . . And when you think of the sticky mess they
served to us! . . ." He drank again: the thought of that gluey
greyness forced him to drink. Already he was feeling a little
less depressed. "First you don't want a thing, then you do.
Does one ever know really *what* one wants?" And to tell the
truth, what *did* he want? . . . "Don't bother your head about

that!" He took another drink of the wine. Knowing what he wanted would do him a fat lot of good; wanting and having were two different things. The two boys, now, they knew what they could have; they were gorging themselves, having a real blow-out! "And yet if I hadn't invited them, they mightn't have had a bite to eat all evening." But perhaps they knew perfectly well what they wanted, perhaps they had only conducted Clarence so obligingly to the caravan-serai because they had thought they might get a good feed. "Oh, well, let them eat their fill! . . . If they get too full, the wine will soon wash that away." This wine really wasn't at all bad: a little lacking in body, yes; and, of course, it bore no comparison with what the white men drank. All the same, it wasn't too bad.

"It's quite drinkable," he said, clicking his tongue.

"A little . . . *inexperienced*," said the beggar.

"Inexperienced? . . ." thought Clarence. "I'll give you 'inexperienced'! I notice you're lapping it up all the same!" He looked at the old man's neck: in front, between his chest and his chin, there was like a skein of slack strings—muscles, nerves, sinews, God knows what—and whenever the beggar threw back his head to drink, the skin which only an instant before had been dangling rather dismally was suddenly tightly stretched, and the Adam's apple would give a great jump. It kept jumping at every mouthful, running joyfully to greet it and accompanying it all the way, guiding it into the right channels, and then rushing back to greet the next arrival. In this way it kept coming and going under the skin like a great marble, very busily full of its own importance. It kept rising and falling unflaggingly, possessed with a strange animation that did not seem to belong to the body; it was part of, yet detached from the body, and bounded up and down like an automatic pump. And the old man was, in fact, pumping vigorously away.

"Pump!" said Clarence to himself. "Pump away! . . . Come on, faster, faster! . . . There won't always be as much as this. But to-day, you can drink till you can drink no more. There won't always be as much wine to drink. And the bill will have to be paid."

But the thought of the bill made him laugh, as if it were part of a great joke. Clarence followed the old man's example.

In fact, he had already begun to imitate him. The fumes of the wine were mounting to his head. But now he began to imitate every movement. If there had been a mirror in the place, he would have watched himself in the glass, but there was no question of finding a mirror in such a pig-sty. He had to imagine what the spectacle looked like, but it was easy to imagine it—he could step outside of himself and observe himself quite easily. His Adam's apple was bouncing up and down, bouncing and falling, and bouncing up again and falling down again. He deliberately took small amounts in order to speed up its movement. "In a pump," he thought, "it's the mechanism that counts . . ." As he was drinking in this way, with quick little gulps, concentrating on the gurgling of the liquor in his throat, he heard one of the boys say to the other:

"Try a little harder!"

And the other answered: "I *am* trying a little harder! Can't you see I am?"

"But really try very hard indeed," went on the other. "If you try very hard indeed, we'll finish it off."

Clarence looked over towards them. They had turned pale and they were breathing heavily. They were still stuffing themselves, and their hands were still travelling from pot to mouth and back again, but now a certain weariness was making itself felt, and perhaps the mutual encouragement they were giving each other was not altogether unnecessary.

"Will you be able to finish it?" asked Clarence.

"We've nearly got through it!" said the boys. "We . . ."

But they were unable to finish what they were saying: they seemed depressed, as they had been when they were driven off the processional route by the whips of the royal guards, and their faces had grown even greyer. "Perhaps that is what they would call 'a heightened colour,' " thought Clarence. He did not think they could be blushing at their own greed: it was such an innocent greediness. "Oh, why shouldn't they eat!" he thought. "Let them stuff themselves till they burst, if they really don't know where their next meal is coming from!" But just as he was about to warn them not to scrape a hole in the pot and not to stuff themselves till they burst, he saw to his great surprise that the pot was really empty.

"Would you like some palm wine?" he asked them.

He held out the calabash without waiting for an answer. He was thinking of all that gluey matter now forming a compact mass of stuff in their stomachs; of the abundance of pepper which would now be making their throats burn: and he felt himself overcome by a powerful thirst. While one of the boys—was it Noaga, or Nagoa—was drinking, the other said, stroking his distended belly:

"Keeps you warm!"

"Won't it make you ill?" Clarence asked.

The boy shrugged his shoulders.

"The main thing is to eat—then you can be as sick as you like."

It was his turn to drink. He only took little sips, and did not bring to the emptying of the calabash the same urgency as they had displayed in cleaning out the pot.

"I haven't much room left," he said, as if excusing his lack of application.

"No, not much room left," said the other regretfully.

Whereupon they fell sound asleep.

"Why don't I do as they do?" Clarence wondered once again. And he heard himself reply: "There's nothing to stop you doing as they do!" But the difference in age . . . yes, perhaps that's what it was. It was some time now since he had been their age . . . He took the calabash and raised it to his lips . . . "Oh, sleep, sleep! . . . Sleep! . . . Forget! . . ." But he was not forgetting? He was forgetting . . . yes, he was forgetting it all now . . . Perhaps he only took a short nap, and that may have been the total extent of his oblivion: but it was oblivion all the same. In any case, there came a moment, probably very brief, in which he lost consciousness of what was going on around him.

When he opened his eyes again, he saw the inn-keeper standing over the pot. He was looking down into it as if he could hardly believe his eyes.

"Empty!" he cried, when at last he was able to bring himself to speak. "It's empty!"

"Well, then?" said Clarence, "are you not satisfied?"

"Satisfied?" groaned the inn-keeper.

And he looked as if he was going to tear his hair.

"Perhaps you were hoping to get some of it back?" asked Clarence. "Perhaps it was not a purely disinterested generosity that lay behind the large helping you gave us?"

But then he saw that the inn-keeper was looking at him very suspiciously.

"What are you looking at me like that for?" he asked.

"The left-overs!" said the inn-keeper. "Where are the left-overs?"

He turned towards the beggar. Then, suddenly, as if inspired, he bent down and felt the boys' stomachs.

"Oh! the little pigs!" he exclaimed.

And as he watched them his brows became furrowed, as if he was pondering heaven knows what gruesome way of getting all the food back: they could hear it rumbling and gurgling through the boys' distended bellies.

"You're too late!" said the beggar. "You've come too late!"

"How was I to know?" said the inn-keeper.

And he lifted the pot.

"You should be glad," said Clarence. "You won't have to clean it out."

And he broke out into a noisy laugh.

"That is, if you ever *do* clean it out, of course," he went on, "and I very much doubt it."

And he began laughing again more wildly than ever. For a second it looked as if the inn-keeper was going to turn nasty. But the beggar stopped him with a look.

"Very well," said the inn-keeper, "I'll be quiet. Don't worry, I'll hold my tongue. I know this isn't the moment to speak . . . I know what the fumes of palm wine do to a man's head. But there will come a moment when those fumes will have cleared away and then the reckoning will come. Then there will be many things to be explained away. Yes, many, many things!"

He wagged his head. Now that he had found his tongue he was ready to go on speaking for hours. But on another look from the beggar, he suddenly stopped speaking and wagging his head and disappeared with his stew-pot. He seemed to disappear so rapidly that it was as if he'd gone through a trap-door.

"That's funny!" said Clarence.

He looked at the beggar's stick. Had the beggar used this stick to make the inn-keeper disappear?

"That's funny!" he repeated. "I thought you just used it to belabour people's backs, but . . . Oh! it's really very funny!"

He was feeling better and better. "This palm wine grew on you in a very pleasant fashion," he thought. This wine went down to your stomach and took root there, and then grew up straight as a palm-tree and when it reached his head it spread out, wreathing itself in leaves, in beautiful, broad, shining leaves. Clarence pictured himself sitting in the shade of these leaves and imagined someone climbing up his trunk for his own especial benefit, to draw a calabash-full of wine for him.

"Is it your stick that does it?" he asked.

"Does what?" . . . asked the beggar.

"I mean: is your stick really a magic wand? . . . There are magicians, sorcerers . . . There's one called Carabosse! . . ."

But he felt his explanations were becoming too involved, he couldn't get his tongue round the words, so he didn't go on.

"I am going South," said the beggar.

"Oh, good!" said Clarence.

"It's not only fishy and peppery rice that keeps the stomach warm," he thought. "Palm wine keeps you warm, too! . . . Henceforward I'll drink it at every meal!" It was only after he had made this observation that the beggar's last words penetrated his consciousness: till then, they had re-

mained as it was on the threshold of his ear. But now he
heard them distinctly.

"You are going South, you say? . . . Isn't the king going
South too on his next visitation?"

"Yes, he will be moving in that direction; or anyhow, it
seems likely. And is that the road you yourself are thinking
of taking?"

Clarence shrugged his shoulders, as who should say: "That
as good as anything . . ." Then he remembered: "Oh, no!
That would be far better. Better than the caravanserai or the
streets, certainly! Yes, the streets . . . I can't expect to be
allowed to stay much longer in this wretched hole. The black
inn-keeper will soon be showing me the door; already he's
behaving almost as badly as his white counterpart. If it
wasn't that he has designs on my clothes, he'd have put me
out long ago!"

"I'm going South," he said.

"We could make the journey together," said the beggar.
"That is, of course, if you have no objection . . . I'll . . . Yes,
that's it, I'll show you the way."

"That's it, all right," thought Clarence. "You will show
me the way, we'll make the journey together, and you'll
do yourself well, at my expense! I shall be ordering the
meals in the caravanserais where we lodge at night, and
you will be eating them while I look on and feel my stomach turning at the sight of the gluey mess and your filthy
habits. And in the morning, of course, I shall be the one
who foots the bill! Perhaps you'll even suggest that we
should pool our resources? Yes, I can see what you've
got in mind . . . But when you find out—and that won't be
long!—that I haven't a sou, and when you receive the joy-
ful tidings . . ." He started to laugh uproariously at the
thought of the sou, that miserable little sou he did not have;

it was partly the wine, too, that had really gone to his head by now.

"Right!" he said. "We'll make the journey together."

"He's an old fool," he said to himself, "but he's an old rascal all the same . . . This time, however, he's met his match!"

"Beware of your imaginings!" said the beggar, in a baleful voice.

"What!" said Clarence.

"I mean that if we are to make the journey together it is I who will see to things. You won't have to worry about either food or lodging."

"And you'll—as it were—keep the pot boiling?"

"I thought I told you that begging favours was my profession."

"That didn't get you very far with the king."

"There is only one king," replied the beggar, "but the number of his subjects is infinite. Don't you know that? If it is true that on this occasion I did not obtain what you desired, it does not mean that it will be the same next time. Moreover, yours is no ordinary case: you were making a request for employment, any kind of employment, but you have no qualifications whatsoever. Yes, I know that you would have been satisfied to undertake the humblest task, but that was simply because you couldn't very well ask for anything better. Humility has never been the outstanding quality of your race."

"And is it *your* outstanding quality?"

"No, I'm not outstanding in that respect. I can't always stop myself from saying disagreeable things, I must confess. But when the occasion calls for it, I can give proof of outstanding humility. This is one of those occasions, I admit."

He was silent a while.

"Perhaps I made a mistake when I presented your request. In spite of all the experience I've had in my profession, I am not infallible. And besides it was the first time I had ever handled such an extraordinary case . . . Perhaps I should not have announced that you were ready to accept any kind of employment whatsoever; perhaps they were suspicious of a man who was ready to accept just *any* kind of employment, feeling that such a one would be incapable of doing anything. The fault, if there is one, is mine, I avow; and that my mistake should have been unintentional is no excuse—the mistake is there, with all its consequences! I know that by advising you to go South I shall not retrieve my mistake—for how can one retrieve a mistake?—but I shall at least have gone some way towards repairing it by the mitigation of its consequences. If, then, you accept my offer—my *offer*, mark you, not the promise of an unlikely atonement, you will be doing me a great service, and you will not be beholden to me for anything. It is I who shall be your debtor. Perhaps I am just an old rascal—I most certainly *am* an old rascal!—but at least I won't have led you up the garden path. This confession, believe me or believe me not, has been very hard for me: my professional honour as a seeker of favours is at stake!"

He raised his hand to brush away a tear, but found his eyes were dry.

"I don't know how to weep," he said. "I can weep buckets when I want to arouse someone's pity, but I can't manage real tears."

"Well, I'm glad it's like that. I really am," said Clarence. "Your frankness has convinced me, and I accept."

"Oh, you have given me back my self-respect," said the beggar. "You've saved my life, and more! Never shall I forget your kindness."

"If that's the way things are, let us arise and go!" cried Clarence. "Let us arise and go, with your self-respect and your life and everything! And let us go without regrets, without tears, since you are unable to shed any. And why are we waiting in this wretched hole where the food stinks and the flies are eating us up?"

He had risen to his feet, and suddenly felt his legs all pins and needles.

"Not so fast, my fine fellow," said the inn-keeper. "Don't be so anxious to be off all of a sudden: you have not paid your bill!"

"His bill? . . ." repeated the beggar. "What's all this about a bill? Am I the sort of man in whose presence bills are mentioned? You ought to be ashamed! . . . Where's your hospitality? . . . Was not the white man your guest?"

"But I am running a hotel!" cried the inn-keeper. "No one has ever accused me of lacking in hospitality. But my hospitality is the sort of hospitality you *pay* for."

"Have you the effrontery to call *that* hospitality?" the beggar asked.

"Call it what you like," the inn-keeper said. "You won't find anything like it anywhere else."

"No. Your kind of hospitality is a paying concern," the beggar remarked bitterly. "Oh, you are right: there's nothing like it anywhere else. Even the flies here are more voracious than anywhere else, and your money is made from the left-overs of other people's meals. And believe me that's nothing to be proud of."

"Who says I'm proud of it?" asked the inn-keeper. "I am not proud of my profession, though it's like any other profession, neither better nor worse. But the white man knew the terms when he came here."

"Can you prove it?" countered the beggar.

"You knew them, didn't you?" the inn-keeper asked Clarence. "Did I ever try to pull the wool over your eyes?"

"I have always intended to pay my bill," said Clarence. "I still intend to pay it. But the thing I was banking on to pay my debts let me down."

"Then why did you bank on it?" asked the inn-keeper. "Why should the payment of one's debts be turned into a gamble?"

"Shut up!" said the beggar. "Don't prejudice your case. The white man is not interested in your remarks, and I don't wish to take any notice of them either. The white man will pay. In any case, if you attack him, it will be the worse for you in every way. Can't you see that?"

"He promised me his clothes," grumbled the inn-keeper.

"I didn't promise you anything," said Clarence. "You looked at my clothes and made some reference to an exchange in kind, but I didn't promise anything."

"Oh, there was some talk of exchange?" asked the beggar. "Well, I think he might be able to arrange that. We do a lot of bartering in these parts, you know."

"I should be quite willing to make an exchange in kind," said the inn-keeper. "I'm not entirely devoid of heart."

"Keep your heart to yourself," said the beggar, "or you'll be prejudicing your case again. Your heart? . . . Oh, that's something I wouldn't care to see!"

He turned to Clarence. "Give him some part of your clothes. You can easily give him something or other. Where we are going, it's not necessary to wear such complicated garments, and if you gave some of them up, you would at once be dressed in a style suited to the country you're in. Moreover, as I believe I have already remarked, the ones you are wearing are already rather shabby. You would probably

get very little more wear out of them anyhow . . . Give him
your jacket."

"My jacket?" said Clarence.

"Yes, your jacket, or any other part of your clothes you
wish to barter," replied the beggar. "That's your affair."

"But you are compelling me to make a choice," said Clarence. "Is there any difference?"

"It's got nothing to do with it. He's the only one who's
compelling you to do anything," said the beggar, pointing at
the inn-keeper. "That hard-hearted man, that heartless man,
and—be honest with yourself!—your own rash words are to
blame. If only you had been more guarded in your speech
. . . But what's done is done. We won't say any more about
it . . . And as for making a choice, please yourself. For my
part . . ."

And with a sweeping gesture of the hand he absolved
himself of all choice and all compulsion.

"You said you would beg favours for me," said Clarence.

"Have I not already done so? And I shall do it again: I'm
a man of my word. But let me warn you—don't be so free
with your tongue. And yet . . . No. Even if you had been
prudence itself, believe me, with this sort of man, when
you're dealing with professional rapacity like that . . ."

He spat at the inn-keeper's feet. "There are leeches in the
marshes that are less bloodthirsty than this man," he added.

"You're insulting me," said the inn-keeper.

"Do you think it's possible to insult anyone as low as
you?" said the beggar. "Go away! You poison the very air I
breathe."

Clarence took off his coat and threw it in the inn-keeper's
face.

"There, take that!" he said.

"What use is the coat to me if I haven't got the trousers?" cried the inn-keeper.

But the beggar had raised his stick.

"Don't!" cried the inn-keeper. "Please don't! Tell him to give me his shirt, that's all I want if he won't give me his trousers."

"Not another stitch, do you hear? Or would you like me to lay my stick along your back?"

"Why are you getting worked up?" said the inn-keeper. "I'm making you a simple proposition. Can't I make a profit? Palm wine costs money."

"Yes, when it's allowed to mature, when you're not in a hurry to make money, it is expensive," said the beggar. "But the wine you gave us was as poor as piss!"

And he turned his back on him, to indicate that the matter was at an end.

"Wake up, you two," he said to the boys, shaking their shoulders. "We're going!"

"Is it morning already?" asked one of them.

"It's still dark," answered the beggar, "and it's time to be going."

The two boys rose painfully to their feet. Their eyes were swollen with sleep.

"I think we must have eaten too much," said one, holding his hand to his stomach.

"You're mad!" exclaimed the other. "We never have enough to eat." He turned to Clarence: "What have you done with your coat?" he asked.

"I paid the inn-keeper with it."

"What!" exclaimed the one who had been holding his stomach. "You gave your coat for that wretched cat's-piss he served us?"

"Sheer robbery!" said the other.

"Do you think it'll do him any good?" asked the first.

"It won't do him any good at all," replied the other sententiously.

"Come on, let's get going!" the beggar shouted. "I've never met such a pair for talk!"

Then they went towards the door. In the hall, Clarence could see the inn-keeper trying to force himself into the coat, but it was obviously too tight for him: he couldn't move his arms. Then he pulled the coat off and tore the back seam open, and tried it on again. This time, he was able to lower his arms to his sides; he walked up and down, smiling to himself. Each time he turned, his pink *boubou* could be seen through the rip in the back. "Like the rosy jaws of a mongrel dog," thought Clarence.

"Well, are you coming?" cried the beggar.

"I'm coming," said Clarence.

"We're coming!" shouted the boys.

They were whispering together; then one of them burst out laughing.

"Don't make me laugh!" he cried. "Not now! When I laugh I feel my belly's going to burst!"

3

THE STOLEN COAT

On leaving the caravanserai, Clarence was not surprised to find that the whole town was in a turmoil. Only a short while ago, as he was coming down the esplanade, the town had appeared deserted and asleep, and rightly so, as night had fallen, though the complete emptiness of the streets was inexplicable. Now the whole place was throbbing with noisy life, filled with a tumultuous clamour, the clamour of the street, and what a street! It was the most animated, the most crowded of all streets: the street of Africa!

Everywhere the drums were rolling and rumbling, sending out their throbbing notes to the reeds and the bamboos of the palisades, to the mud walls, to the very earth and sky, and above all to the crowd which was moving to the rhythm, swaying their bodies even when standing still, crying, clapping their hands and uttering loud cries, both high and low, both deep and shrill, but more especially shrill and violent ones. There were raucous cries from the men, and piercing cries from the women, above all there were piercing cries from the women who would sway forward, frankly offering their naked breasts and rushing, flinging themselves into the dance, where they would abandon themselves naked to an orgy of shaking that should have left them exhausted but that on the contrary seemed to spur them on to wilder and wilder and even more extravagant deliriums of energy, and brought them at last to a pitch of frenzy which transformed the brazier-lighted crossroads into scenes from a witches' sabbath.

These great fires, lighted at every crossroads and on every square, cast on the darkness a radiance that was not unlike that of the crimson cloud on the esplanade. But everyone was too busy shaking to notice this resemblance. It seemed that for the moment only the darker aspect of the festival, the diabolical aspect that is found in all festivals, was in the ascendant. There was nothing here of that superb forward surge which during the preceding day had swept the crowd towards the king.

"Can't you keep your eyes open, just for a minute?" asked the beggar.

"Isn't that what I'm doing?" asked Clarence.

"Every few seconds you keep dropping off!" exclaimed the beggar.

"It's the odour . . . can't you smell the odour?" asked Clarence.

There arose from the crossroads and the squares a sour
odour which was certainly caused partly by the smoke and
partly by the great mass of sweating bodies; it was that very
odour, a mingled smell of wool and oil and sweat, which
always sent Clarence to sleep; the same odour which, on the
esplanade . . .

"Where are the two boys?" asked Clarence.

Now that he had identified the odour it made him think
of the two boys.

"Who knows?" said the beggar.

"They disappeared as soon as we left the caravanserai,"
said Clarence.

"Now don't you worry about them. Now that you've filled
their bellies for them, they won't leave you for long; you may
even see more of them than you want! Look after yourself,
take great care as we approach the centre of the town, keep
your eyes skinned and don't move a step without me, or
you'll get lost yourself. And that would really be serious,
because you don't seem to me to be the sort of man who finds
his way easily again . . . Make way there!" he shouted at the
crowd. "Make way! Can't you see we are in a hurry?"

But as soon as he spoke these words, they were lost in the
throbbing of the drums, swallowed up in the noise and the
tumult. The crowd rarely made way, or did not even make
way at all: their hearts and souls, and their ears, were all
given up to the dance.

"Have you ever seen anything like it?" the beggar asked.

"I have never seen anything like it," replied Clarence.

Now that no one was paying any attention to his shouts,—
even his stick no longer seemed to frighten them—the beggar
would now pursue devious routes through the crowd which
only served to bring him back to the place he started from,
now he would stand grumbling impatiently and waiting for

a pause in the dance in order to break through the circle. But these pauses had to be seized upon at once, because fresh dancers immediately took the place of those whose exertions had made them thirsty and who were hastily, avidly running to the gourds hanging on the lower branches of the trees.

Clarence himself could never seize these opportunities. He would be standing in the midst of the crowd, rubbed and rocked by the swaying of the crowd, and he would fall asleep, the odour of the flock would make him fall asleep. Each time the beggar had to shake him. Then Clarence would cross the circle, rubbing his eyes and wondering where his bad luck had landed him now. Generally, after a moment or so, he remembered. But before his memory returned, he would be like a man who had expected to find himself elsewhere, far from the tumult and far from his own ruin, far from the madding crowd and far from the ruin into which his ill luck, that had triumphed over the reef, had brought him, had precipitated him as if for ever.

"No, I have never seen anything like it!" Clarence echoed. "And I don't think I should ever like to see it again."

"These cursed dancers!" the beggar growled. "We shall never arrive in time."

But none-the-less he was not unwilling to pause under the trees where the gourds were hanging; he would raise these strange new fruits to his lips and gulp down the liquid, as he had done in the caravanserai, with a rapid movement of his Adam's apple.

"Cat's piss!" he would cry, each time he took breath.

Then his Adam's apple would start pumping valiantly up and down again. Clarence, whom the walking and the noise, the heat and the odour had made very thirsty, drank deep too, drank certainly more than was wise.

"If you want my opinion," said the beggar, "I think the dancing girls aren't at all bad."

"Not at all bad," said Clarence, smacking his lips.

"If I don't stop drinking," he said to himself, "I'll soon be talking the most utter nonsense. And this old fool, if he goes on the way he's going, is liable to do anything."

Looking over the curve of his lifted gourd, he was observing the beggar, for as the brazier in the centre of the square was casting a strong light, nothing of what went on in the old man's face escaped his attention.

Clarence could see his eyes shining, he could see a strange fire dancing in their depths, and a kind of lasciviousness; he could see the nostrils flaring, and on the rather too protuberant lips and at the base of the nose a look of greed: yes, caused probably by his delight in drinking, but also perhaps by the growing desire for another kind of pleasure, a pleasure which even now was only vaguely suggesting itself, but which was perhaps not totally impossible of fulfilment: there are men at that age, old fools like him . . .

"Perhaps you would be well advised not to drink quite so much," suggested Clarence.

"D'you think I'll get drunk on this sort of muck?"

"I don't know. Perhaps you've got some other idea in mind . . . But I thought you were in a hurry."

"I *am* in a hurry!"

"Well, no one would ever think it!"

"I am in a very great hurry. D'you hear, it's madness to waste our time like this. Come on, drop that gourd!"

As they prepared to break through the crowd, they found themselves unexpectedly surrounded by a detachment of the royal guards. The guards were staring fixedly at them, not saying a word, not moving a muscle; they were all as tall as the beggar, but unlike him they were bursting with youth and strength. They were standing stiffly to attention, pressed shoulder to shoulder; they were like a wall. Above this wall, all that could be seen was a patch of the night sky, a simple patch of night in the oval of a high window.

"What do these men want with us?" asked Clarence. "Why have they hedged us in like this, as if we were in a gaol?"

"How should I know?" asked the beggar.

"Then why do you not drive them away?" said Clarence.

But barely had he said these words when he saw the black inn-keeper creep into the gaol.

"Got you at last!" cried the inn-keeper, seizing Clarence by the scruff of the neck.

"Hands off!" said the beggar sternly.

"I will *not* take my hands off!" said the inn-keeper. "This time authority is on my side; you're just an old beggar, you don't frighten me! I want my coat! I won't take my hand away until the white man has given me back my coat!"

"But I've already given it to you!" exclaimed Clarence. "Very unwillingly, I admit, but I gave it to you all the same."

"And you took it back!" shouted the inn-keeper.

"Are you mad?" asked Clarence. "I haven't set eyes on you since I gave it to you."

No sooner had he finished this sentence than the guards all round began to double up with laughter, as if they'd just heard the funniest thing on earth. "What's up with them now?" Clarence wondered. But of course they must be drunk. They must have been drinking all the time from the gourds hanging on the trees. They were obviously drunk.

"I'm not joking," said Clarence solemnly.

But they just laughed and threw themselves about all the more.

"Come on, give him back his coat," said one of the guards,

who was wearing a girdle outside his tunic. "Give it back, and we'll forget the matter."

"How can I give it back to him?" asked Clarence. "I've already given it to him."

"Very well, then give it back again, if you prefer it that way," said the guard. "I don't want to discuss the finer points of language; and above all, I have no wish to cause you any trouble."

"But really, I don't see the point of this joke!" cried Clarence. "I don't see anything funny in it!"

He turned towards the beggar and found him drinking peacefully as if what had been happening was none of his concern.

"Why don't you say something?" said Clarence.

"What can I say?" replied the beggar. "Someone has obviously made a mistake. But how can we prove it?"

"Can't you swear that you have never left my side?"

"I swear," said the beggar gravely. And he raised his stick to give more weight to his declaration.

"Don't you dare strike me!" said the guard with the girdle round his tunic. "I'm not one of those gaping idlers you are so fond of beating aside with your stick."

"I had no intention of striking you," said the beggar.

"He attempted to strike me, though," said the inn-keeper.

"Just now, in my very own house, he threatened to strike me. I declare that this man tried to attack me!"

"What if he did?" said the guard. "What is your complaint? Have you dragged me all this way just because he nearly hit you?"

"I won't have him attacking me," said the inn-keeper.

"That's got nothing to do with me," replied the guard. "I'm dealing now with the question of the coat, nothing else. If your backside cries out for a beating, and if this beggar can

lay it on hard, that's none of my business; it's between yourselves, an arrangement between your backside and his stick.
I'm not having anything to do with it."

"Well spoken," said the beggar. Then, turning to the inn-
keeper: "I don't know why I don't give you a good wallop
on your nasty rat's snout of a face," he snarled.

"Let's get back to our business," said the guard with the
girdle round his tunic. "Have you decided to give the coat
back to the inn-keeper?" he asked, addressing Clarence.

"For the last time, I tell you I gave it to him and I haven't
got it to *give* back to him," said Clarence. "I can't be any
plainer than that."

"Too bad!" said the guard. "The king is my witness that
I did not want to use violence, but . . . Guards! Seize him,
guards!" he shouted. "And the beggar as well!"

At once the guards seized the hands of Clarence and the
beggar, gripping them firmly in their own.

"Now follow me to the judge," said the guard. "And don't
attempt to escape; it would only make things worse for you."

The little group formed itself into a procession. The crowd
of people massed behind the guards made way for them.
Clarence walked between two rows of curious faces. The
rumour swiftly spread that he had been arrested for theft.
Clarence felt terribly embarrassed. His confusion was suddenly increased when he glimpsed, beside a fire, a group of
white men who had come to watch the dancers. He would
have liked to speak to them, but what could he say? The fact
that he owed them money was hardly a recommendation. He
tried to make himself as small as possible, hoping to pass
unnoticed, but in vain: the white men had spotted him at
once. Now they were looking at him walking towards them,
their faces full of cunning and malice.

"Look there, they're taking him away!" said one.

"It certainly looks like it," remarked another.

"Ah, that's what should have been done right at the start," a third said, shrugging his shoulders. "Soon as I set eyes on him, I said to myself: 'There's a man on the run.' As for what happened next—well, we all know that story only too well."

He started to snigger, and seemed to be encouraging the others to join in. Clarence felt a terrible longing to tell them that he was being led away by mistake and that when the judge heard the facts of the case, everything would soon be cleared up. But he realised that however clearly he explained the situation it would do no good at all: these men already had their minds made up! He tried to make himself smaller, and kept his head as low as possible.

"Look how he hangs his head," said one of the white men. "Would he hang his head like that if he was innocent? No one will ever convince me that that man isn't guilty?"

Clarence was tempted to raise his head, but it was too late now to make any kind of protest. And anyhow, what was the point in raising his head? Would not everything, in any case, be turned quite definitely against him? If he had gone by with his head high, they would have declared that he was without shame, or that he was undermining the white men's authority, or anything that was no less to his advantage, because it is never the gestures one makes that matter, but the way, the malicious way they are interpreted. "What can I do?" wondered Clarence. "There's nothing I can do! Everything is turned against me, and everything will continue to be turned against me . . . Perhaps I am foolhardy—I am certainly foolhardy—but so are other people, other people are as foolhardy as I am. But it isn't held against them. But everything *I* do is held against me and made to appear twice as bad as it really is!"

He had reached this stage in his reflections when he found himself being pushed roughly into a corridor.

The corridor was narrow and as tortuous as the alleys of the town, but it was extraordinarily quiet, and a great number of doors gave on to it at one point or another. All these doors were ornamented with illegible and pretentious inscriptions—at least, they appeared to be pretentious, for Clarence could only judge by their great length and by their elaborately-formed characters; but these indications were enough, more than enough; they were more eloquent than if the characters had been decipherable. It was obvious that these wordy inscriptions and the great number of doorways belonged to a building used for administrative purposes. They made one think of an army of scribes bent over tables or desks, furiously scribbling away in registers or composing forms to be filled in in quadruplicate. The doors, of course, remained stubbornly closed, but the very last one, at the end of the corridor, opened as if by its own accord, to admit the little procession. Clarence found himself in a vast hall, vaster than any he had seen since he had landed on these shores. At the far end of the hall, a man crouched over a table was telling his beads. This man stared at Clarence a long while.

"So this is the culprit," he said at last.

"I am not guilty!" cried Clarence.

The man raised his hand.

"They all say that when they're brought here. You can't *think* how sick I am of hearing it! . . . The great thing is that you are here, and that no time has been lost in catching up with you . . . And this person," he said, pointing to the beggar, "who may he be?"

"His accomplice," said the inn-keeper.

"I was not addressing you," the man said. "You will speak

when you are spoken to. And so far there's no reason to suspect—no reason at all, mark you—that I shall want to speak to you. I shall interrogate you if I see the need for it . . . Well, who is this person?" he asked again.

"It is the beggar who was with the white man," replied the guard with the girdle round his tunic. "I thought I would be doing right in bringing him along."

"You have done well to bring him to me," said the man. "He shall act as witness to the crime."

"Sir . . ." began Clarence.

"Address me as 'my lord president,' " ordered the judge.

"My lord president," said Clarence, "this man, who is a beggar, has not left my side all evening. He will tell you that I gave my coat to the inn-keeper in payment for the debts I incurred at his hotel, and that at no time have I regained possession of the coat."

"No! No!" said the judge . . . "This man," he went on, pointing to the beggar, "is here as witness for the prosecution; you cannot transform him into a witness for the defence. It would be against the law . . . You must find some other . . ."

"But what do you expect me to find?" interrupted Clarence.

"The coat, my man, the coat!" said the judge. "That's all we're asking of you."

"The inn-keeper's got it," Clarence replied.

"Come, now!" the judge protested. "Think well before you speak. Why should the inn-keeper have run all that way after you, if you hadn't taken the coat away from him? . . . Any child would tell you . . ."

"How do I know?" Clarence cried. "What's to prevent this inn-keeper from accusing me out of sheer spite?"

"That is what we have to look into," said the judge.

He appeared to be taking thought. The beads on his rosary were clicking briskly through his fingers.

"I've got it!" he said, after a moment. "Are you a habitual liar?"

"I never tell lies!" Clarence assured him.

"If you will excuse my interruption, my lord president," said the guard, "when I questioned him, the white man claimed that he had not seen the inn-keeper since leaving the hotel. And all the time, while he was speaking, the inn-keeper was standing right in front of him! So then we all burst out laughing."

"That is something which certainly does not say much for your truthfulness," the judge said to Clarence.

"They misunderstood me," said Clarence. "What I meant was . . ."

"You must remember that the guards are on oath," said the judge. "They are not allowed to tell lies in my presence, even though when off duty they might be the most consummate liars ever known. Did you say anything else besides what the leader of the guard has just repeated?"

"The leader of the guard gave my exact words," said Clarence, "but he has given you an erroneous interpretation of them."

"All right, all right!" said the judge. "We won't concern ourselves with interpretations at the moment; all in good time, you know: this business already seems quite complicated enough, without . . . So you admit, do you, that the leader of the guard has faithfully reproduced the exact words you spoke. That is something in your favour, at least it is a proof of your sincerity, for, of course, as regards your crime itself, we cannot look on that in quite such a favourable light."

He stopped once more, either because he wanted to collect

his thoughts, or simply because he wanted to speed up the telling of his beads.

"When did the white man go to take the coat back?" he asked the beggar at last.

"I can't say," said the beggar. "The white man did not leave my side all night."

"Not at all?" asked the judge.

"Not for a single moment," replied the beggar.

"Good! I deduce from this that you must have been with him when he returned to the caravanserai. Am I to understand that you were his accomplice?"

"I am not his accomplice."

"Precisely!" said the judge. "You are merely the witness for the prosecution. What have you to say against the white man?"

"I did not stir one step from his side."

"Do you still persist in that?" asked the judge. "Be careful: you'll find yourself in hot water if you aren't!"

"I've nothing more to say," declared the beggar.

"What!" cried Clarence. "Do you mean to imply that I *did* leave your side?"

"Silence!" said the judge. "Don't try to influence the witness. He has chosen not to speak; if it's not a very courageous choice, at least he has the right to make it. His silence upsets you, but remember you might be even more upset if he were to speak. So be thankful for small mercies . . . Now! What reasons can you put forward for taking back your coat?"

"He gave it to me much against his will," said the innkeeper.

"That's what the white man told me, too," said the leader of the guard.

"Is this true?" asked the judge.

"Why shouldn't it be true?" cried Clarence. "It is perfectly true that I gave up my coat most unwillingly."

"But he was only too willing to snatch it back," said the inn-keeper.

"It's not your turn to speak!" the judge told the inn-keeper. "If you interrupt us again, I shall have you put out. And it's not your place to make jokes: that is the prerogative of the law, and of the law alone. I shall not warn you again."

"My lord president," said Clarence, "may I presume to ask if *you* would have willingly handed over your own coat?"

"It is not for you to ask me questions," replied the judge. "An accused person, even should he enjoy the benefit of being presumed innocent—but such an eventuality would be so paradoxical that I cannot allow myself to entertain it—should never ask questions: that is contrary to all the rules. It would make things far too easy, as I think you will admit. I might, but only as a very great concession, be prevailed upon to countenance a respectfully interrogative turn of phrase provided that it were the kind of question that is said to 'answer itself,' and that is not the case here. Nevertheless, as I have no desire to be disagreeable, and on the strict understanding that this particular occasion is not to be taken as a precedent, I shall bring myself to depart from custom and provide you with an answer. The answer is: 'No. *I* should have given up my coat neither willingly nor unwillingly, and for a very excellent reason: I never wear one!' Now are you satisfied? Well, now, as I find that you are definitely resolved not to return the coat, will you be so good as to tell me just how you intend to compensate the inn-keeper for his loss?"

"But . . . but . . ." Clarence babbled.

"Do not put me under the painful obligation of having to send you to prison," warned the judge. "Never have I had to put a white man behind bars. I can assure you that such a course would be most repugnant to me."

"I shall compensate the man as soon as I've found some work. That was my intention from the start."

"That was, and indeed still is, a most praiseworthy intention," remarked the judge. "But are you really without any work at all? . . . And if so, when are you likely to be in work again?"

"I had started for the South in order to look for work."

"Oh, really?" said the judge.

"I intend to ask the king for work."

"The king?" said the judge.

He seemed surprised, startled even. He was crouching over his table; it was a good job he wasn't standing up, or he might have fallen, and the shock would have been twofold. He was so taken aback that he forgot to go on telling his beads.

"Look here, my good man," he went on after a pause, "yours is a flagrant case of false pretences. What possible kind of work, I ask myself, could the king entrust you with? And even if he did—which I do not for one moment believe he would—when would you repay the inn-keeper? . . . The king has only just returned to his palace, and he will therefore not be going South for a long while yet . . . But let's say no more about it. Your offence at the moment amounts to little more than sponging on others, so do not imagine you will make your position any better by using false pretences. Now, let us return to the question I asked a little while ago, and which was intended to help you out of this embarrassing situation: what sort of compensation are you going to offer for the loss of the jacket?"

"If the white man would care to give me his shirt and his trousers, I should be willing to overlook the jacket," said the inn-keeper.

"That seems to me a very reasonable proposition," said the judge.

"Reasonable?" cried Clarence.

"Well, yes, of course," said the judge. "As it is, the inn-keeper might very well have claimed your shoes and stockings; but he has very generously confined his demands to your shirt and trousers."

"Can you see me walking naked in the streets?" asked Clarence.

"There is no law against that," the judge declared, "and there is no lack of people who are totally devoid of shame, either. If, as you say, you are going South, you will meet with many such shamefully immodest persons . . . In any case, may I say that you gave no indication of any lack of shame when you took your coat back from the inn-keeper . . . And besides, there is no question of your going naked. White men generally wear, I believe, a pair of pants under their trousers."

"A very short pair of pants, and . . ."

"You'll have to see about fastening them in front," said the judge. "Those are the sort of intimate details which a lord president cannot enter into . . . Guards!"

"At your service, my lord president," said the guard with the girdle round his tunic.

"Instruct the court to rise while I pronounce sentence."

The guard and his acolytes turned to the deserted hall. While he was lining up his men—and their dressing, in the circumstances, had to be impeccable—the beggar crept up to Clarence and whispered in his ear:

"Run for it! At once! . . . We'll meet at the city gates."

"But . . ." said Clarence.

"Make a run for it, I tell you, or they'll rob you of every-thing, underpants and all! . . . Don't you see, the lord president is in league with the inn-keeper? . . . And are you forgetting there'll be the costs of the case to pay!"

It was the thought of these costs, and also, of course, of having to pay for them with his underpants, that decided Clarence. He had become resigned to the thought of parting with his shirt and even his trousers. But what about his underpants? Could he really part with his underpants? . . . He shot off like a hare and found himself outside in the corridor before the others had understood what had happened. When they had finally pulled themselves together—and it appears that the inn-keeper was the first to recover his wits, unless it was the judge . . . but his dignity as the lord president, not to mention the majesty of the law, prevented him from leaving his seat—when they had pulled themselves together, they all collided so violently at the door that it was obvious to everyone that all hopes of catching the fugitive must for the moment be abandoned. They would catch him eventually, of course, but it would take time: the crowd outside was too dense: it would be useless to attempt a search.

"Take your men and scour the town," the judge said to the leader of the guards. "I shall not stir from this table until you have brought back the fugitive. And this time tie him up."

Meanwhile, Clarence had opened at random one of the hundred doors that gave on to the corridor. He now found himself dashing through a maze of empty rooms and deserted corridors. Even in his desperate haste, and urged on as he was by the agonising terror of losing his underpants if he was caught, he could not help marvelling at such a conglomeration of rooms and corridors in a building which, seen from the outside, or at least glimpsed in the murky radiance of night, had not seemed to him to be very much bigger than the other houses in the city. For a moment he had the awful

thought that he would go on dashing through the same rooms
and corridors again and again, but he refused to admit this
possibility. He had other things to think about just now!

First and foremost, he had to avoid bumping into the
incredible quantity of rubbish and debris, some of which
seemed to have been wrenched from the thatched roof by a
violent storm; the rest appeared to be mainly the rubble of
decaying walls. And in these numberless rooms and endless
corridors there was nothing but rubble and rubbish; there
were even excavations, unbelievable mounds of debris, as if
the owner of the place, in despair at the state of the walls and
the roofs, had suddenly given up all hope of repairing anything and had decided to start all over again and build everything anew. Or so it seemed. Otherwise there was no
explanation for the amount of rubbish of all kinds that had
piled up in these rooms and corridors; there was so much of
it, in fact, that one might quite easily have imagined all the
housewives in the neighbourhood had come here to tip their
rubbish. Which was very disrespectful to the courts of justice, or injustice—Clarence was inclined to call it injustice—
in which the laws of this country were supposed to be upheld.

But where, in fact, *was* Clarence? Where was he now, after
running through so many rooms and corridors, after scram-
bling so skilfully round so many obstacles? Was he still in the
palace of justice? Or had he not already reached the other
end of the town? Opening a door like any other, he nearly
shrieked with despair: the door gave on to the very audience
chamber from which he had escaped some hours—or some
seconds—before!

He stopped short, winded, bent double, as if one of the
guards had kicked him or punched him in the belly. Then he
saw that the hall was deserted, except for the judge crouched
over his table; crouched in the very same position as he had

been when Clarence had left, though not in the same state of mind, for now the old villain seemed quite inoffensive. He was sleeping, snoring—and with what majestic sonorousness! "And what a deep sleep!" thought Clarence. "The sleep of the just!" He was tempted to knock the table over, to see what sort of a figure the villain would cut sprawling on his backside. But he might have to pay dearly for the prank, so Clarence tiptoed away. He started down the corridor and went on right to the end without another glance at the innumerable doors.

He breathed a great sigh of relief when he found himself outside again in the red glow of the braziers and the uproar of the street. But almost at once the sight of the dense crowd, as excited as ever, made his heart sink. "However shall I be able to fight my way through this crowd without being seen and recognised?" he wondered. All had gone well up to now, but he suddenly took a gloomy view of his escape. "And even if I succeed in getting through this tumultuous horde of people without being noticed, how am I going to find my way, in pitch darkness, to the gates of the city?"

But the difficulty lay less in the absence or near-absence of light than in Clarence's total ignorance of his present position in relation to the gates. In the circumstances, it was not enough to know that the gates were on the confines of the city, unless he made a tour of the walls and streets. But this was quite unthinkable because of the tortuous nature of the streets and the vast number of cul-de-sacs.

"If only the old fool had waited for me!" Clarence said.

But the beggar was now far away, perhaps at the gates of the city, perhaps not. No, not necessarily at the gates of the town. Certainly the old man was very free with his promises and with advice of all kinds; but it was the over-abundant and incontinent freedom of a tap that had been left running;

and as for keeping his promises or putting his own advice into practice—well, it was better not to count on that. He was an old fool, an old rogue too, and it was not the first time Clarence had made this observation. A little while ago, in the presence of the judge, the beggar had well and truly let him down! . . . It's true the judge . . . Oh, what a mix-up!

"For God's sake!" muttered Clarence.

He walked over to the nearest brazier. "With a little luck," he thought, "I just might be able to reach the gates of the town . . ."

"Excuse me, could you direct me to the city gates?" he asked a dancing girl who had stopped shaking at his approach.

"The city gates?" repeated the girl. "What do you mean? The town hasn't any gates. It gives directly on to the fields."

"Then would you kindly show me the way to the fields?" he asked.

"I've hit on a madwoman," he was thinking. "She doesn't even know where the city gates are!"

"No, you needn't look at me as if I were crazy," said the woman. "I am just a dancer . . . But aren't you the man who stole the coat from the inn-keeper?"

"Well, not exactly . . ." began Clarence.

"What do you mean, not exactly?" she countered. "If you are the man—and who else could you be?—don't deny it. You can trust me: I detest the inn-keeper!"

"Oh?" said Clarence.

"Yes, I detest him," she repeated. "That man is a real pig!"

She was all the time dreamily stroking her breasts, that were naked and irrepressibly luxuriant.

"I shall help you," she went on. "Give me your hand."

And she sped away with him through the narrow streets.

As they passed by, many stopped and turned to stare curiously at them; many were obviously passing remarks about them, though there was no indication that these comments were in any way unfavourable—on the contrary, rather. In any case, no one seemed to be referring to the stolen coat. Was it simply because they did not know? That seemed most improbable in a town where the talking drums seize on the slightest breath of gossip and broadcast it on every wind that blows. "Won't they suddenly turn and denounce me?" Clarence kept wondering. "Even if they haven't recognized me yet, they soon will . . . And then . . . And then . . ."

"There's no need to worry," said the dancer. "It's me the people are looking at. They're looking at my breasts!"

She swung her hips and threw out her chest. "How on earth does she manage to have such prominent and pointed breasts?" Clarence wondered. But he noticed that she was eyeing him in a peculiar way.

"You are very beautiful!" he said.

"Yes, aren't I?" she replied. "Well, come along. We mustn't lose any time."

They crossed a number of streets and negotiated numerous crossroads. Then the thing that had to happen happened: they found themselves face to face with the leader of the guard.

"Got you at last!" he cried, throwing himself at Clarence. "This time you won't get away, my lad!"

He raised to his lips a small trumpet that had been hanging from his girdle and began to blow it, but the noise of the drums was so great that one could hardly hear the trumpet— it was just one of the thousand and one instruments that were making the night hideous with their cacophony. Perhaps the onlookers who were already clustering round Clarence and the leader of the guard had mistaken the latter, in spite of his uniform, for some musician or other from the thousand and one orchestras scattered all over the city. But apparently the sound of the trumpet had carried in spite of everything, because contrary to Clarence's expectations, several guards appeared on the scene almost at once.

"Run for it!" said the dancer. "Quickly!"

She pulled Clarence towards her so violently, the leader of the guard lost his balance and fell flat on his back in the dust.

"Quick!" said the dancer, dashing away. "Faster! Faster!"

She was holding on firmly to Clarence's hand and was plunging determinedly ahead. The streets and turnings, the braziers and the circles of dancers were wheeling by now at an incredible speed. Everywhere the crowd gave way, whether because it was terrified by this thunderbolt rushing upon it, or because it had once and for all taken the fugitives' side against the police, it was impossible to say. Could the guards keep up this mad pace? It seemed doubtful. If the dancer had not hauled him so impetuously along, Clarence could never have kept up the pace, even if the fear of being caught had made him sprout a pair of wings. The guards would surely never overtake them now . . .

At a crossroads, Clarence cast a rapid glance behind him. Alas! the guards were keeping up with them! They were in fact gaining on them, and their hands, grown suddenly enormous, were reaching out, their great, broad palms wide open, ready to seize them!

Clarence ran even faster. This time, a pair of wings had unexpectedly but quite positively sprouted between his shoulder-blades. He suddenly felt himself propelled into a dark and featureless place, whose door was immediately slammed to.

"We're safe!" cried the dancer. "Safe at last! . . . About time, too: I couldn't have gone much farther."

She was panting. Probably her breasts were heaving violently, but the prevailing obscurity made it impossible to tell.

"Have we reached the gates of the city?" asked Clarence.

"Of course not," retorted the dancer. "Didn't I tell you that there aren't any gates?"

"Where are we then?"

Clarence was suspicious. What was she up to? He remembered the rooms and the corridors in the palace of justice, and he was afraid he might in the end find himself back where he started.

"You are in my house!" said the dancer. "Come with me."

Walking on tiptoe, she entered a corridor as tortuous and with as many doors as the one which had led to the courtroom; moreover, all the doors had inscriptions on them, and the inscriptions did not appear any less illegible or less bombastic than the ones on the doors in the palace of justice.

"Are you sure this is your house?" asked Clarence.

"Sh-sh-sh!" she hissed, putting a finger to her lips.

She was stopping at every door; she would listen for a moment, then go on to the next. She never looked at the inscriptions, she would just listen and, after a moment, would go on to the next door, where the same procedure would be repeated—a procedure which did not say much for the legibility of the inscriptions.

"It's just as I thought," she announced suddenly.

She shoved open the door she had come to. Clarence saw a group of people sitting round a table drinking palm wine. The old beggar and the two boys were among the group, but far from making a fuss of Clarence, they barely glanced at him, and it was the most indifferent, the most miserable and the most unseeing of glances; so much so, that one might have thought they were seeing Clarence for the first time in their lives.

"Well," said Clarence, "don't you know who I am?"

"We know perfectly well who you are," said the boys.

And one of them winked at him. Clarence followed the direction of his nod and suddenly saw the judge sitting at the centre of the group.

"Heavens!" he cried.

"Allow me to introduce you to my father," said the dancer.

And she led Clarence to the judge.

"Sit down," said the judge, "and have a drink of palm wine. I can see you've been running: a drop of wine won't come amiss."

"I thank you, sir," said Clarence.

He had almost said: "I thank you, my lord president," but something had stopped him—perhaps the fear of saying or doing something incongruous. He took his seat in the circle next to the dancer.

"Isn't your father a high court judge?" he whispered in the dancer's ear.

"I should think not!" said the dancer. "I wouldn't allow such a thing in my house. My father is an honourable man!"

"Isn't a lord president an honourable man?" asked Clarence.

"Those sort of men have all kinds of dangerous contacts," she replied.

"Drink up!" said one of the guests, holding out a calabash full of wine for Clarence.

Clarence drank. He drank deeply. He did not know he could be so thirsty. He felt his whole body given up to the wine as dry earth gives itself to rain. He drained the calabash to the last drop.

"Did you see that?" said one of the boys.

"I certainly did!" exclaimed the other.

"I was beginning to wonder where on earth you'd got to," said the beggar.

"Well, you see . . ." began Clarence.

But the beggar did not allow him to proceed:

"Didn't we arrange to meet at the city gates?"

"The city hasn't got any gates!" said Clarence.

The whole group burst out laughing, including the dancer.

"Did you hear the excuse he gave?" said the guest who had given the calabash to Clarence. "That calls for a fresh calabash."

Clarence began to drink again. His thirst seemed endless.

"Do you think he's going to drain it?" said one of the boys.

"I shouldn't put it past him," said the other. "At first he pretended to be just sipping it, but now . . ."

"Do you hear what those two are saying?" said Clarence, pausing a moment.

"I hear them," said the dancer, grimly.

"Did I ask if you would scrape the very last grain of rice out of the pot, and the very last fish-bone?" went on Clarence.

"That's right!" said the beggar. "Let Clarence drink in peace."

"As for you . . ." said Clarence.

"What about me?" said the beggar, whose face had at once assumed an expression of amiable virtue.

"As for you, I know what you are," said Clarence. *"You were going to feed me, protect me, give me shelter and God*

knows what else, but you weren't even capable of defending
me before the judge. And when I say judge . . . !"

He was suddenly silent. Then:

"Are you quite sure that your father isn't a high court
judge?" he whispered into his neighbour's ear.

"Absolutely sure," the dancer replied.

"And when I say judge," went on Clarence, "I'm being far
too generous: never have I encountered such an old villain,
or seen such a farce."

"Oh!" cried the dancer's father suddenly.

And he rose quickly to his feet.

"What's the matter, Papa?" asked the dancer.

"Nothing, my dear child," he replied. And sat down
again.

"There's no need to bear a grudge against him or against
me," the beggar told Clarence. "That's his job, to be an old
vil . . . I mean, a judge. My job is to seek favours."

"Couldn't you have asked for my full pardon?" said Clarence.

"Your pardon? Certainly I could have asked for it. For
your pardon or your . . . well, the undergarment, you know
what I mean. But as it happened that was the very thing I
could not ask for, because what you call your 'pardon' is your
'right.' "

"All the more reason, then?" said Clarence.

"No, not at all," retorted the beggar. "Can't you get it into
your thick head that one cannot beg the favour of receiving
something that is one's 'right'? I could have asked for any
favour, I mean something that is *not* due to you; I could not
possibly have asked for something that is your 'right,' something which devolves upon you officially. Anyhow, I never
learned how to beg for 'rights'—that sort of thing can't be
taught. Now do you understand?"

"My head's reeling," said Clarence.

"Look, take this example: there is nothing to prevent my asking our host for a calabash of wine, but . . . Thank you!" he said, bowing to his host who was holding out a fresh calabash for him. "But," he resumed, "I do not ask for it as if it were my 'right,' or even one of the simple rights of hospitality. You must understand that it is highly insulting, to ask for something that is one's 'right.' "

He fetched the calabash to his lips, and contrary to his general habit, began drinking it in tiny sips. His Adam's apple no longer executed the great pumping movements that had agitated it on previous occasions: from which one might deduce that while waiting for Clarence the sanctimonious knave had been drinking until he could hardly drink another drop.

"He's not pumping half as well," said one of the boys.

"No matter!" said the other.

"If we have your kindness to thank for that . . ." began the first, addressing the dancer's father.

"Pure kindness on your part . . ." murmured the second.

Their host gave each of them a calabash. The two boys swung back their heads and drank avidly; at the same time their tunics rose in front.

"What the devil's that you're wearing?" asked Clarence. He pulled at a piece of cloth that was showing under one of the boys' tunics.

"Why, it's my coat!" he exclaimed.

"Your coat?" said the dancer's father.

"No, it's only half of it," said the other boy. "This will make up the pair!" And he pulled the other half from under his tunic.

"Well!" was all Clarence could say.

"Give them here," said the dancer. "Mamma will soon stitch them together again."

She took the two halves to a little old woman who was crouching in a corner of the room shelling nuts.

"What a surprise!" gasped Clarence.

"If only the inn-keeper could have been here . . ." the dancer's father said.

"A nasty shock, a dirty trick!" said the beggar.

"Yes, but a *nice* nasty shock. I might have lost my shirt and trousers."

"Not to mention your . . . honour," said the beggar.

"My honour?" said Clarence. "Oh, you mean my underp . . ."

"Sh-sh! Not when there are ladies present!" hissed the beggar.

"The inn-keeper . . ." said the dancer's father.

"The inn-keeper? Do you know the inn-keeper?" Clarence asked.

"My . . . my daughter knows him."

"Oh! I thought I heard . . ." began Clarence.

"If we believed everything we hear . . ." the dancer's father said.

"And now you have your coat again, and in one piece!" laughed the dancer, giving the mended coat back to Clarence.

"Well, then, we must be moving!" the beggar said. "We've wasted far too much time as it is."

He stood up, and everybody did likewise. The dancer's father led them along the tortuous corridor to a door that was much smaller than the others and had no inscription on it. He opened it. Clarence saw that it gave on to the fields.

The full moon was gently shining on the ploughed acres and on the patches of fenced ground that looked like market gardens. In the distance there was a long dark line: the forest, perhaps, or mountains.

"If you go this way you won't have any unpleasant encounters," said the dancer's father. And he gave Clarence a very obsequious bow.

4

THE ODOUR OF
THE SOUTH

During the whole of that night, or what remained of it, for their various activities had occupied the greater part of the hours of darkness, Clarence and his companions made their way to the South.

The moon was softly shining, and the silence, the rapt silence of the countryside, seemed a very sudden transition from the uproar of the town, and had an infinitely peaceful quality. The road wound through richly-cultivated fields. From time to time a dog's bark, giving warning of the little band's approach, brought to view the thatch of a farm.

There was a chill touch in the air. A little before dawn, the cold became really severe, and if he had not been heated by walking and by the persistent glow of the palm wine, Clarence would have been shivering. But this cold was not unpleasant; it was refreshing after the heavy air of the town.

"I still haven't thanked you for having recovered my jacket," Clarence told the boys. "But put yourselves in my place: imagine my surprise when, without any warning, it turned up again. Pray forgive my oversight, and let me tell you how very pleased I was to have it back; I am even more pleased just now, in the chill of dawn, to be wearing it again."

"But the pleasure was all ours!" cried the two boys.

And their laughter rang out freshly on the calm morning air.

"Of course!" the beggar grumbled. "The pleasure might have been all yours, but we had all the worry! I'd like to know why you trouble to thank them. But perhaps it's not too late for me to knock their heads together."

The boys at once scampered off a little way.

"It's no use running away," shouted the beggar. "It can wait, if you can't!"

The sun had risen on a magnificently cultivated landscape and on fields richer than one would ever have expected. There were fields of millet and groundnuts, of rice and maize, all looking just as they do in other lands. Then there was an abundance of exotic plants whose names Clarence was perhaps not unfamiliar with but which he could not identify exactly. Among them there were some very like cassava and sorghum, as well as corn of a luminous red colour which, even if it was not eatable—and why shouldn't it be?—provided, in the light of the rising sun, a feast of unparalleled splendour for the eyes. Finally, there were whole forests of palm trees, in part certainly, if not entirely, devoted to the wine industry.

A little later, Clarence and his companions halted at a

farm. The air had turned rapidly warmer, and it would have
been impossible to expose oneself to the burning heat of the
sky any longer without grave inconvenience.

It was not a big farm, and the mud buildings were in a bad
state of repair. It really seemed as if the beggar might quite
easily have found a better place, one more comfortable and
more recently built. But the farmers gave the travellers a
most cordial welcome, and they were served with well-piled
platters of food. The two boys stuffed themselves, as was
their wont. After which, as a kind of dessert, the beggar,
taking advantage of the boys' helpless state as they digested
their meal, banged their heads together as he had promised.

By nightfall, they had reached the outskirts of the forest.

They were made aware of its proximity by an odour which
ought to be described, not merely because Clarence was
especially sensitive to smells, and very curiously affected by
them, but also, and above all, because this odour was particularly representative of the whole character of the South.

The odour was a subtle combination of flower-perfumes
and the exhalations of vegetable moulds. It was certainly a
strange and even suspect fragrance, not disagreeable, or not
overwhelmingly so, but strange, and suspect, a little like the
turbid odour of a hot-house full of decaying blooms; a sweet-
ish, heady and disturbing odour, but one which was all-
enveloping rather than repellent, curiously caressing, yes,
and—one hardly dares to admit it—alluring, insidiously alluring. It was an odour in which the body and the spirit, but
above all the spirit, were gradually and imperceptibly dis-
solved. One might have called it, to be precise, an emollient.

"The South begins here," said the beggar, lifting his hand
towards the forest.

Clarence looked at the immense green wall and the
thought entered his mind that it resembled the red wall of

the royal palace. He could not have explained why, because the forest was much higher than the wall, and stretched away interminably to right and left. Was it because there was no entrance? Perhaps that was it—that very same lack of entrance, that inaccessibility. On the red wall of the palace there had been nothing left at the end of the day but the shadow, the mere shadow of a door. Here, too, there were shadows, nothing but shadows. It was no more accessible: there was a network of branches and creepers, but there was not, or did not seem to be, any opening large enough to allow a human being to enter.

It must be this inaccessibility, this common indifference—and perhaps worse: this common hostility—which made the two walls resemble one another; and doubtless also the general impression of two equally disdainful masses.

"We haven't got a machete," said Clarence.

"What do we want a machete for?" replied the beggar. "There are paths . . . I know all the paths in this forest; I've walked along every one of them hundreds of times."

"Where are the paths he's talking about?" wondered Clarence. "He can't see anything, he can't see anything more than I can. All he can see must be shadows of paths, just shadows, and he's making it all up! He calls the two boys idle gossips and liars, but he himself . . ."

"I'm not making it up," the beggar suddenly went on, as if he had once more been reading Clarence's mind like an open book. "There *are* paths. If you can't see them—and why should you see them?—you've only got your own eyes to blame. A white man can't see everything: and he has no need to see everything either, because this land is not a white man's land. But even if this were not the land of the South, there is no reason why you should see things any better.

When we were on the esplanade, you could not even see the door of the palace."

"You're wrong there," said Clarence. "I could see the door perfectly well. It was only towards the end, when the sun began to go down, that I couldn't see it."

"Yes, but actually it was there all the time; it was just as much there when the sun was going down as it was at midday, under the full blaze of noon. And the proof of that is: how could I have presented your request, if there had been no door to go through? . . . Believe me, there's quite a lot you miss."

"And what proof have I that the request was really presented?" Clarence felt like asking. "I've only *your* word for it! But what proof have you ever given me? . . . Yes, I know I miss quite a lot of things, but perhaps this is something I've not been quite so blind to, probably because my very existence depends on it." But he kept his own counsel: in any case, the beggar would think that having the last word was also part of his profession . . .

"Does this forest extend very far?" asked Clarence.

"It covers the whole of the South," answered the beggar, "but it contains broad clearings. In each clearing there is a village. And there are very many villages, though from here you can't see so much as a ghost of one. There are as many villages as there are paths."

"There is our town, too," said the boys.

"There is only one town," the beggar said sharply, "the one we have just left. In the South, there are sometimes very big villages, but there are no towns."

He paused to shrug his shoulders: "It's just impudent bragging, to talk about a second town."

But perhaps there was only one village in the forest. "One

village! Yes, a single village!" thought Clarence, after days
and days of walking in which they seemed to have been going
round in circles all the time. "And each evening," he mused,
"the beggar arranges for us to come back to this same village
and find shelter there for the night. The first time, we go into
such and such a hut; another time, some other hut, but it's
always the same village, and perhaps each time it's the same
hut too . . . How should I know? Who can tell the difference
between huts that are all the same, hosts who are all the
same? . . . In any case, it's certainly always the same path
we travel on in the forest."

This path is like a tunnel; it has the strange half-light of
a tunnel. It is a greenish light, though it is not strictly speaking a light, but rather the reflection of a light. Higher up,
much, much higher up, among the branches which cannot be
seen from the floor of the tunnel, maybe there is a real green
light. But down below, it's nothing but the wavering light of
a cavern. And all along this pathway, the same flowering
lianas twist round the same cankered trunks, the same
thorny underwoods stretch out their claws, and the same
oozy ground goes sliding underfoot. And however far one
walks, it's always the same path, the same tunnel . . . The
same tunnel, and the same vertigo that comes from turning
round and round all the time . . .

"Why are we wasting our strength on these exhausting,
useless marches?" Clarence wondered. "Why? They don't
seem to lead us anywhere . . . And if the beggar really knows
all the paths through the forest, as he says he does, why does
he always choose the same one? . . . Perhaps it's a game. But
what sort of game would that be? It's a stupid game!"

"Is this a game?" he suddenly asked.

"What do you mean, a game?" said the beggar.

"I mean all these comings and goings. These endless comings and goings."

"I don't know what you're talking about," replied the beggar. "We are on our way to the South. We . . ."

"The South! The South! Always the South!" muttered Clarence. "I ought to leave signs," he thought, "to mark where we have been. I could lay a trail of white pebbles, or break certain branches, or notch trees . . ."

But there is no possible means of orientation in this shifting half-light. And even if the light were stronger, how could Clarence recognise the signs he might make? For the greater part of the time he is only half awake, he is walking along in a half-sleep. Scarcely has he entered the tunnel, he is overwhelmed by an irresistible languor; he closes his eyes, he lets his head fall on his chest, he is walking in his sleep. It is the odour, the terrible odour of flowers and decay, that is sending him to sleep.

However, the odour fascinated him at first, for it is not the crowd's herd-like odour, and it is not just an odour of decaying vegetation; it is subtlety itself, a seductive perfume, or rather the seductive mingling of a thousand perfumes, almost too many perfumes, yes, far too many perfumes, all of them far too heady, disturbing, caressing, far too . . . But how can he express it? Clarence hardly knows whether he ought to say it . . . He makes a compromise, and says, under his breath: "far too delectable."

It's not quite the right word, but it has some of the quality he wants, and it is certainly the right word to describe the outermost reaches of this perfumed gulf that is like a real sea: a sea that is already present on the winds and on the lips before the eye has discovered it. But here there is not that livelier and more vibrant luminosity, at once more definite

and more definable, that enlivens the regions of the sea itself.
That peculiar radiance is missing here. Instead there is only
a nocturnal opacity; the glaucous opacity of undersea
depths, and all the confused disturbances of night. And besides, it is not just a tranquil bay or a smooth sea. It is like
that at first, it is like that at first sight. But then it becomes
a mysteriously agitated sea, full of mysterious commotions;
an ocean with its own currents and its secret tributaries, an
ocean that nourishes its hidden life with the breath of flowers
and the exhalations of the fermenting earth. Yes, it is like a
ferment! A fermentation and an insistent calling, an eternal
rising of sap and that most irresistible of all appealing invita-
tions, the appeal of flower-pollen!

Under cover, everything is shifting and moving, yet nothing moves; nothing gives itself to the great wind that does not
exist, yet everything is abandoning itself, everything is moving slowly, everything is proceeding towards some centre of
attraction, with all the torpid slow-motion of a sleep-wan-
derer.

With Clarence's sleep-wandering motion? Perhaps! Yes,
perhaps there is something of that in it, though it is not the
same kind of instinctive motion—not yet the same kind of
instinctive motion—that informs them both. No! It is not,
it cannot already be the same octopus-like writhings and the
same horribly-waving, suckered tentacles guiding them both,
even if Clarence had been moving his limbs rather more than
he was moving them now. No, it is not yet that utter aban-
donment, nor yet that surreptitious exploration and sinister
probing that animate the forest: the forest, where everything
attracts and is attracted, where everything is split open like
a ripe fruit bursting with warm and heavy juices, where
everything is penetrated by everything else.

What can it matter that, from time to time, there are

clearings in this all penetrating and impenetrable languor, in this universal possession; and, in Clarence, as many starts of surprise as there are clearings—the fitful starts of restless slumbers haunted by nightmares of impending doom? The awakenings are too short-lived! Clarence opens his eyes because he feels a fresher air upon his eyelids, because the clearing, like a chimney, is breathing a little of the air of the mountaintops into the very heart of the furnace; but the perfumes, the remains of all those perfumes steal into his lungs like the vapours of a poisonous bloom; they creep even lower, into his belly: and lower still, a burning, glowing, and already far from innocent commotion . . .

"The South! . . . Is this the South?" Clarence asked.

"The South? . . ." the beggar echoed.

"Why yes, the South!"

"The South is everywhere," the beggar said softly.

Yes, perhaps this inferno of the senses is everywhere. Clarence suspects it is true, he has a presentiment of bondage; he senses, rather than feels it, but already he is in a state of subjection. He dozes; and in spite of himself the perfumes of the forest are working within him, the poisonous bloom is opening slowly. There is a slackness in the muscles of his legs and in his spirit, while the rest of his body—but he won't admit it, even to himself . . . Perhaps if the clearing were a little broader . . . But Clarence had no sooner taken a breath of fresh air than the clearing had been passed; and again the green tunnel of the forest opens and swallows him up. And the sea stretches away, the musty smells of earth and the poisonous smells of flowers roll endlessly towards him, and he feels the unthinkable fire stirring again in his loins . . .

"Give me your hand," says one of the boys.

"Not now," replies Clarence. "I'm not asleep yet."

"But you are falling asleep," said the boy. "Already you're

dragging your feet along the ground; if I don't take your
hand, you'll be falling over the tree-stumps. Let me have
your hand . . . I wonder why it is you sleep so much. One
would think you never got any sleep at nights, to look at you
. . . What do you do at night?"

"I sleep," said Clarence. "What else can I do?"

"I don't know," said the boy. "There are lots of women
who come into the huts where we sleep . . ."

Women? . . . Yes, there *are* women who come into the huts.
Well? . . . Those women never stay. They . . . Yes, what *do*
they do? Oh, they bring in platters of millet or rice, they
bring palm wine . . . Do they . . . Do they do anything else?

"That's all nonsense," said Clarence.

But was it really just a lot of nonsense?

"It's just a lot of nonsense!" he said.

But he is longing to speak, to tell the boy that his nightly
slumbers have nothing to do with the sleepiness of the day;
he longs to explain that this sleepiness is caused by the odour
of the South . . . But it would all take too long, far too long
to explain! Clarence begins to feel the unclean and cloying
weakness stealing over him, and he quietly holds out his hand
to the boy.

He walks along like a blind man, and it is of a blind man
one thinks as he stumbles along, his hand holding Noaga's
hand, now Nagoa's. But if one were to look at his face, one
would think it belonged to a child being dragged through
suburban streets by his parents on a Sunday evening, after
a long walk. It is long past his bedtime, and the child is more
than half-asleep already. He is heavy, and allows himself to
be dragged along; he has almost lost consciousness, he is
rather sullen, but not *very* sullen, because he wants to sleep
even more than he wants to sulk.

How could this child, this somnambulist, be asked to leave

signs in the forest to show what path he has passed along? He couldn't be asked to do anything. Perhaps it is already too much to ask him to lift his feet, and to look out for the obstacles in his way.

But Clarence is neither so sleepy nor so oblivious to everything that these warnings are totally lost on him, for he obediently lifts his feet. For quite a while, he goes on lifting them higher than is necessary, and he watches out for obstacles in his path. Sometimes, too, these warnings awaken unexpected echoes in his mind. "Wasn't it round about this time yesterday and the day before," he says to himself, "that I was warned about this tree-stump in the middle of the path, or that tree which has fallen across the track?"

And the conviction that he is following the same path day by day becomes stronger. "But what's the use of all this struggling? Why take all this trouble?" he asks himself. "Why? Why?" He can't understand it. He has no difficulty in believing that it would be far better to spend the rest of his days in the darkness of a hut—this hut, that hut, any hut in the one village he was sure of.

"Oh, if I could sleep!" he groaned. "If only I could sleep!"

"Aren't you asleep now?" said one of the boys.

"Is it sleep, when you are walking in your sleep?" asked Clarence. "Do you call that sleep?"

"If that's not sleep, it's a very good imitation," said the boy. "What do you say, Noaga?"

"I'm surprised he doesn't snore," said Noaga.

"Look here! . . ." Clarence began.

But once again, he feels he cannot go on; he does not feel equal to starting an argument. All he wants is to sleep; and he would give a great deal, he would give the whole of the South, he would even give what he had once, during the long winter nights, fondly imagined the South to be, if only he could stop—not just pause a while, but really stop for good, and rest his feet, rest his eyes, rest his feet for a long while in the cool waters of a pond, rest his eyes for a long long while in the blue of the sky, and sleep . . . sleep . . . not just a doze, not just a succession of restless naps as he wandered from one clearing to the next, but a real sleep, a long deep sleep. What he means is, he would like to sleep far longer than any one night, he would like to sleep a whole day and a whole night, or two days and two nights, perhaps even longer . . . Who knows? . . . But *he* knows what he really wants, which is to be able to sleep until the day of deliverance, until the day the king comes on a visitation to his vassals in the South.

But perhaps that is exactly the sort of favour which cannot be granted if one sleeps all the time. Perhaps it is a favour which can only be granted after one has wandered for a long time in the forest. And perhaps it is not even a real favour, since it has to be paid for.

"Is it true that favours can be bought?" Clarence asked the beggar.

"What a question to ask! Have you ever seen me gain a favour without having to beg for it? Everyone gets what he deserves, according to his merits."

"Well, perhaps I'm completely lacking in any kind of merit," thinks Clarence. "But when I've got to the end of this path and passed through the tunnel, when this infernal vicious circle has been broken . . ." And he wonders what sort of people they are who live in the South. Perhaps they too are people who look upon it as a duty to acquire merit of some kind. "It may not be much fun living there, after all," he thinks. "Will I one day regret having left this narrow path?" But this last reflection seems so absurd that he bursts out laughing.

"What's the matter with you?" asks the beggar.

"What sort of people are they in the South?" Clarence inquires.

"Oh, they are just like all those we have met in the forest: not very bright."

"Like all those . . ." Clarence doesn't finish what he has to say; he no longer has any desire to laugh. "The same old joke!" he says to himself angrily. "Does he still think I can't notice that we're going round in circles? . . ." But he keeps his temper: he *wants* them to take him in, for there is nothing he can do about it, and after all the time might be spent in that way just as well as in any other, though there *were* more amusing ways of passing the time. But however low he had fallen, he hadn't fallen quite so low, he hadn't yet fallen quite so low as to admit that he knows he is being taken in. Better to pretend he is a guileless innocent.

"They do not resemble the people of the North," the beggar goes on.

"No, of course they don't," agrees Clarence. "All the same . . ."

"You mean they might dress a little better—wear more clothes?"

"No," says Clarence. "I know only too well, I feel only too well, how stiflingly hot it is in these regions. I was merely wondering why they sharpen their teeth with files."

"They aren't going to eat you."

"I hope not," replies Clarence. But his voice is a little shaky.

"The king would never allow it," the beggar adds.

"The king, oh, yes . . . You see, your words are quite convincing when the day's march is over and we've had a good meal and are sitting with a calabash of wine in front of us. Or else in the afternoon, sitting in the shade of a tree and well away from the forest. But we can't always have a good meal inside us, and we can't always be lying in the shade. And then . . . obviously it's not the same for you as for me—you are a native of this country."

"I am not a native of this country," the beggar suddenly breaks in. "May the king preserve me from ever being a native of this country! . . . The two boys, now, they are natives. Haven't you noticed that? It's because they come from the South that they are such rascals."

Rascals? . . . Yes, it's quite likely they *are* rascals; in fact, they certainly are. But are they the only ones? . . . Clarence feels that the beggar who has been leading him down the same old garden path for days and days, for weeks even, is still more of a rascal . . . But it's not the sort of thing he can allow himself the luxury of saying out loud: he is in the old man's hands. "After all," he consoles himself, "as hands go, there could be worse. If the pact I made with him on returning from the esplanade didn't seem very reliable that first night, it has been worth its weight in gold ever since. It's still worth it: this beggar is a past master at asking for favours."

The pact, of course, doesn't commit me to anything more than providing him with board and lodging; but never a day has passed without them, and the board has never been less than generous. And what quantities of wine! More wine than we could drink. "More than ever *I* could drink," Clarence admits, "and yet I'm a heavy drinker, may the king help me!"

This evening, again, sitting under the hut's thatched eaves, Clarence is drinking; the calabash never leaves his hands. And it is not so much a liking for the wine—although he does, of course, enjoy it—as a desire for the oblivion it provides: he drinks in order to precipitate oblivion's club-like blow, and beyond it, the death which haunts oblivion . . . Death, and something more: everything that lies on the other side of that door, one might say, that shadowy door . . . "The king, and my repose . . ."

"To oblivion!" he says, lifting his calabash.

"Oblivion it is!" replies the beggar.

"Oblivion . . . Will the South bring me oblivion? . . ." Clarence wonders, watching the beggar's Adam's apple bouncing gaily up and down. But he is not quite sure that the South will bring the oblivion he desires; he rather fancies that oblivion is a myth. "Perhaps I ought never to have left the North," he thinks.

"The South!" he says scornfully.

"The South?" echoes the beggar.

"Yes, the South," Clarence goes on bitterly, talking to himself. "They talk of 'The South!' and I keep talking of 'The South!' and they think that there is no more to be said. One imagines a happiness one has never known before, an indescribable, gentle happiness; and so as not to appear completely ignorant of what it is, one adds, dreamily: 'And there is such happiness there . . .' Only it isn't happiness, it's not really happiness; it's a terrible violence. If on the other hand there *is* a little happiness, it is of the most disconcerting kind: a caressing, furtive happiness, exciting as a hand that knows no shame; a diabolical happiness, and an infernal violence . . ."

"Still 'to oblivion'?" the beggar asks, lifting his calabash.

"To oblivion or to the devil!" cries Clarence.

He looks at his calabash and is tempted to smash it against the wall of the hut.

"The South!" he mutters.

And he grips the neck of the calabash, as if, for want of anything better, he would strangle it with his bare hands.

"What! Still on about the South?" the beggar says.

"Yes, the South!" Clarence mutters to himself. "Oh, the

South, it's marvellous, the South, when you live in the North! You sway gently, you are warm, at times you even get over-heated: it's like being in front of a great log fire in the dead of winter. And what do you see? A hammock hanging between a pair of coconut palms at the edge of a lagoon! And then there's that vanilla fragrance, almost imperceptible, which makes the eyelids quiver and the nostrils faintly flare, and which is called the trade winds. And the foliage greener than anywhere else, and the flowers more brilliant—flowers like birds, and plants like fountains; and a sea that was of a profounder blue—more transparent, more intensely blue . . . What could you *not* see? But you see it only because it is drizzling, or because there is frost on the window-panes, because you think you will never see such things!"

"And you should never see such things, or go to see them," he goes on, talking to himself. "The foliage is no greener; it's even rather grey, rather ashen. And the sky? . . . But you can hardly see the sky! And the flowers? . . . What does it matter? It's the blueness of the water that is the most wonderful thing. But where is the azure limpidity of the water? There is the stagnant water of ponds and the muddy water of the rivers. If you drink it, it's like a mouthful of mud that . . ."

"Have you ever drunk much water?" asks the beggar.

"Water?" Clarence says.

"Yes, the stagnant water of ponds, for example, the muddy water of . . ."

"I never drink water," Clarence roughly interrupts him. The two boys burst out laughing.

"Ha! Do you think I hadn't noticed that?" says the beggar. "I'm not blind and I don't go around half asleep. You drink . . ."

"And what about yourself?" Clarence breaks in.

"I drink too. You drink, and I drink! . . . And so do these two young scamps who never miss a drop."

"Your two young scamps are very cheeky."

"Have I ever tried to hide anything from you?" asks the beggar. "You can't hold that against me . . . In one sense, it's a good thing they are cheeky; it's part of their apprenticeship."

"Really?" says Clarence. "I shouldn't have thought that effrontery was a branch of knowledge."

And he indulged in a protracted snigger.

"And supposing it was," he goes on, "it's not necessarily a set subject; there's no need to give it more importance than it deserves."

"That's just your way of putting things!" says the beggar, shrugging his shoulders. "You're like all the white men—you speak lightly and hastily, without thinking. You're incorrigible, all of you. But I'm telling you these two boys will never be cheeky enough. And the reason is: they've taken it into their heads to join the order of dancing pages in the service of the king."

"I suppose it was through you they obtained that employment?" says Clarence, and he laughs wildly.

"They did not come to me for it," says the beggar, "and they don't have to, either. They may make their applications direct."

"Oh?" says Clarence.

"Yes, direct. And don't let that surprise you: *they* won't offer to do 'any kind of work whatsoever.' "

"Then why are they not already working in the palace?" Clarence asks.

"They don't know how to dance!" replies the beggar. "They hardly know how to hop up and down. Didn't you hear me say, on the esplanade, that all they were doing was hopping up and down? . . . When they've learned their job, then they'll be taken on at the palace."

"Queer sort of job!" says Clarence.

"Don't look upon it in such an abstract light; everything is relative. Isn't there a saying among the white men to the effect that it's no sin for a man to labour in his particular vocation? There's nothing sinful about this occupation. It allows access to the king . . . Of course, as a job, it hasn't the same status as my own vocation—there's none of the loyalty . . ."

"Loyalty?" says Clarence.

"Do you know of any other occupation in which one offers nothing—at least, nothing important—in exchange for what one receives?"

"Well, if you put it that way . . ."

"That's the only way to put it," says the beggar. "If therefore the profession of dancing page is not as good as mine—even though it merits the supreme favour of seeing the king every day—if it does not require for its performance as great an aptitude as my own, it is, nevertheless, a very charming occupation; and it's no job for a fool. It might even be the ideal occupation, if the king was not so passionately fond of the dance; I mean, if the dancers did not have to dance so much. Then, I admit, it would be the sort of job for which I would have willingly exchanged my own . . . Now, take me, I have to walk, I have to go from village to village and from hamlet to hamlet. If I stayed too long, if I was seen in the same place too often, people would soon get tired of giving me things. People are generally very willing to give, but they don't always want to be giving things to the same person; as if, after all, it wasn't the same thing, the same gesture and the same expense, the same hope of reward; as if they felt less virtuous after being charitable to the same old

beggar all the time. But there you are: where is the man who
would admit to feeling virtuous every day? He would consider himself insulted and deceived! . . . That is why I walk
about all the time. Yes, that is why the soles of my feet are
like leather. And yet no one could say I'm a lazy person, even
though it does seem, at first sight, as if I'm doing nothing
. . . Only just now and again, one would like to rest awhile,
one would like to rest one's feet a while . . ."

He stares for quite a while at the two boys.

"My own feeling is that those two are rather lazy, all the
same," he says. "Later on, their profession will seem more
arduous than they think . . . And of course they eat too much,
far too much. Do you realise what they put away at each
meal? They would try the charity of a saint . . . I know it's
not polite to look into someone else's calabash, but I can't
always help it, no one could help it."

"After all, they eat only what is given them," says Clarence.

"Yes, I am given enough for them as well as for you and
for myself. That's how you look at it, isn't it? . . . Well, let
me tell you I'm given enough only for myself! It's because
of me that people give the stuff. They give more, because
they see that you are with me; but do you suppose they would
give you anything if you were on your own? They would give
you hospitality, but you'd have to pay for it. You do not
inspire pity: white men never inspire pity. If only people were
more aware of the true state of things! . . ."

"The two boys inspire pity," says Clarence.

"Yes, children always inspire pity. But how could those
two inspire pity? They're as fat as porkers . . . From the point
of view of beggars, they're completely unsuccessful. In our
profession, you need a little discretion; one can ask for a lot,
and eat a lot, but one must not make an exhibition of one's

piggish greed. Now *they* are pigs. Not consciously; perhaps it's just a pose, just sheer effrontery, and in that case—but *is* that the case?—it's their apprenticeship, you'll say, their professional training. No matter! They eat far too much. That's my opinion. And that's no better for dancers than it is for beggars."

He gets up and feels their bellies, just as the inn-keeper had done in the caravanserai.

"I told you so: fat as porkers!"

And he pulled a face.

"There's no need for you to feel us," says one of the boys. "It's our own fat, after all! And anyhow, you tickle!"

"Do we feel *your* belly?" asks the other.

"Don't you dare," said the beggar sternly. "Don't you dare feel my belly, or tickle it either!"

"But you do it yourself," says the other, "and then you pull a nasty face. I don't altogether like that."

"If you want my opinion," says the other, "it's just sheer effrontery on your part."

"Do you hear that?" the beggar asks Clarence. "You just wait till we get to your village, you two! Then you'll have to tighten your belts. Then you'll begin to realise where all that fat came from."

"Their belts?" Clarence thinks. "The way we're going on in this forest, they're not likely to put them on for a long while yet!"

"Do you know the road to their village?" he asks.

"Have I not told you that I know all the paths through this forest?"

"You have!"

"But if you hadn't told me, I should never have thought it!" he goes on, to himself. And he remembers, in spite of his sleepy head, that he had more than once caught the beggar

out. Yes, on more than one occasion the beggar had been
brought up short against a wall of thorns, and each time—
but shouldn't Clarence say "each day"?—the old man had
to decide to retrace his steps. And Clarence suddenly has the
idea that it could be at this point, in front of the wall of
thorns, that the beggar, day after day, has been leaving the
road to the South and going round in circles in the forest,
bringing them back finally to the village.

Yet each day the beggar sets out again on the very same
path—perhaps there is no other path?—each day he comes
and looks at the wall of thorns. But perhaps he doesn't really
come to look at it: perhaps he comes simply to see if the wall
is still there across the path; and when he has seen with his
own two eyes that the wall is still there, and that the obstacle
is neither higher nor less dense nor less insurmountable than
on the preceding days, he retraces his steps. But what is his
idea? . . . Does he imagine that the thorns might suddenly
disappear? Is it a miracle he is expecting? . . . And perhaps
he really is expecting a miracle . . . Because he has learnt to
beg for favours, because he goes, making a poor mouth, from
door to door, because he makes his tongue go as well as his
feet, because he hopes everything will be accorded him as a
great favour, perhaps he also feels he is worthy of the even
greater favour of a miracle. But God is not as gullible as his
creature Man.

"Don't you think it would be advisable to take a bill-
hook?" suggests Clarence.

"We've had no need of bill-hooks so far," the beggar replies. "Why should we clutter ourselves up with that sort of
thing? They're neither use nor ornament."

"But I didn't mean it that way," says Clarence.

"How am I to know what you mean?" the beggar asks.
"First you make general, then specific references . . . How

can you expect me to know where I am with you? . . . All I know is, we haven't needed bill-hooks up to now."

"We haven't needed bill-hooks because we've always turned back at the very first obstacle we encountered," says Clarence. "It couldn't be that you are too bone-idle to handle a bill-hook, I suppose?"

"I am not bone-idle. I thought I'd already told you that. In any case, I would not advise you to compare the soles of your feet with mine."

"But you walk for the sake of walking," objects Clarence. "What sense is there in walking in circles in the forest?"

"I do what everyone else does," replies the beggar.

"So you admit it?" cries Clarence. "You have the cheek to admit it?"

"I admit nothing," says the beggar. "I merely indicated that I have nothing in common with the bone-idle. Do you call that an admission of guilt? . . . The two boys, now, either because they come from the South or because it is their nature, are bone-idle . . . What about yourself? You never stop grousing yourself . . ."

"Now that's taking things rather too far," says Clarence.

"Much too far," the boys echo.

"You mind your own business, you two," the beggar warns them.

"But you're accusing us of being bone-idle," complain the boys. "And it's not the first time, either."

"Supposing we forget what I said; maybe I said more than I intended," says the beggar to Clarence, using a gentler tone of voice. "But I am not bone-idle! . . . And as for these two here, I'll show them that, even if I *am* bone-idle, I'm not so bone-idle that I can't give them a good beating."

"No, perhaps he isn't bone-idle, after all . . . Then what

is he?" Clarence wonders. "Or does he think so much of his own talents that he wants to have the last word with everyone, even with God Himself?"

He walks for a long time in the forest, struggling against the odour, and against his desire for sleep. He has never tried so hard to keep his eyes open: he would like to see the wall of thorns. And he would also like to get to the roots of another mystery—why the beggar behaves as he does. He would not like to fall asleep before solving this mystery.

But the mystery is very hard to solve. Each time Clarence is on the point of solving it, sleep plunges everything into darkness again. Yet Clarence is never nearer to a solution than at the moment before he falls asleep. Then there is a moment, only a second perhaps, or perhaps infinitely less, in which it seems that everything is going to be made clear at last. But then slumber intervenes, and Clarence falls asleep before he has had time to grasp . . . And when he wakens, at the first clearing, all he has left is the very vague memory of something that was being brought to light, and which had perhaps been made quite clear while he was asleep, but which at present is again proving obstinate and refusing to let itself be known.

Or could it be that there is nothing at all mysterious about the beggar's behaviour? That he is simply stupid? That all he has is a stupid obsession which makes him walk and walk and walk . . . Hoping for a miracle that can never happen! Just a stupid obsession! . . .

"The wall of thorns will have to be overcome by a frontal attack," Clarence tells himself. "The obstacle will have to be stormed, and then we can go straight ahead, to the South. The wall will not be overcome unless we attack it with bill-hooks."

"If only I had the strength . . ." Clarence said aloud.

"Well, what would you do?" asks Nagoa, who is holding his hand.

"I haven't the strength," replies Clarence.

"Nonsense!" exclaims Nagoa. "If you weren't falling fast asleep all the time, you would be as strong as a lion: you could give the beggar a good hiding!"

"The South . . ." Clarence mutters.

"I'm not talking about the South," says Nagoa, shaking his arm. "I'm talking about the beggar!"

"But the South—and I'm only on the outermost fringes, I've not really reached the South yet—the South has already taken all my strength," thinks Clarence. "Before . . . Yes, before . . . then I was strong. Before I set foot on these shores, I was as strong as a lion . . . Or at least I *thought* I was as strong as a lion. Oh, well! . . . To-day . . . Am I responsible for this numbness, this passiveness? Is it up to me to shake it off? But perhaps it all comes from *him*. Perhaps . . ."

"What's the use?" he says.

"It's easy to see *you're* not the one who gets his ears boxed," says Nagoa.

"What do you want?" asks Clarence.

"I want to box the beggar's ears."

"But how can we hit an old man?" says Clarence. "If we didn't have him with us now, we wouldn't know what to do."

"You shouldn't let yourself be taken in by all that crap!" says Nagoa.

"Would I be any better off listening to *your* advice? . . . Don't you remember all the tales you spun me on the esplanade?"

"Don't talk of that here!" says Nagoa urgently. "Not in the forest!"

Clarence sees him cast a frightened glance at the walls of
the tunnel.

"What's the matter with you?" he asks. "I don't see why
I shouldn't talk about it here."

"Can't you drop off to sleep again?" says the boy. "Oh!
you would have to pick this moment to stay awake, just when
I was beginning to think you were being sensible for once.
Oh, dear! Oh, dear! Go to sleep again, for the love of the
king! I promise I won't ask you about anything again . . .
you make a mess of everything! If we were to be over-
heard . . ."

And again he looked at the tunnel walls with an expression
of terror on his face.

"What are you looking for like that?" asks Clarence. "The
forest is absolutely still; it sounds completely empty; it is
lying steeped in its own peculiar odour, steeped in its own
odour as if in the blood of a crime, and it is as solitary as a
criminal.

"No one can hear us," he adds.

"Do you really believe that?" asks the boy. "Then lay a
finger on the forest and see what happens."

"If only I had a machete . . ." Clarence begins.

"Well, you haven't got one," says Nagoa, "and you'll be
well advised never to use one. You'd do better to sleep! One
day, when I've eaten enough, and when I have big strong
arms like yours, I'll give the old man a good hiding myself.
Don't imagine I eat just for fun."

"Sleep! Sleep!" Clarence tells himself. "Have I ever done
anything else since I came here? . . . It's the sort of advice
I could easily do without."

"Don't you think I sleep enough as it is?" he says aloud.

"Oh, yes, of course! . . . In fact, I've never seen anyone

sleep as much as you do. But I prefer to see you sleeping rather than talking about what should be kept quiet . . . Do all white men sleep as much as you?"

"It's just this odour," says Clarence. "How do you expect me to resist such an odour?"

"Do you sometimes try to resist it?"

"Haven't you noticed all the efforts I've been making to resist it to-day?"

"To-day, yes . . . Couldn't you make any effort at all on the preceding days?"

"I wanted to see the wall to-day."

"The wall? There's no wall here."

"I'm not talking about a real wall; I mean the wall of thorns: the wall we come up against each day."

"Well, well, well!" says Nagoa. "I can see you've had a hard day. And it's true that since the day we started walking down this path . . . But don't worry: this is the last day I'll be leading you by the hand."

"Will your companion be leading me then?" asks Clarence.

He would have liked to say "Nagoa" or "Noaga," but even after spending so many days and nights together, he still cannot distinguish the one from the other. And what does it matter! Are they not interchangeable?

"No," replies Nagoa, "neither of us will be leading you by the hand. This evening, we shall be home at last."

"Home?" cries Clarence.

He stops all of a sudden. "What's that you're telling me?"

"Haven't we been travelling long enough?" says the boy.

"Goodness me, yes, long enough indeed! Too long!"

"Then why are you so surprised?" Nagoa asks.

"Have we really been travelling towards the South?" says Clarence to himself . . . Well, they were walking in that direction: the beggar had said so often enough. But they

wouldn't get there straight away of course, not straight away
. . . They would walk and walk and keep travelling in circles;
they would always be coming up against the wall of thorns,
and then they would keep retracing their steps; they would
go on groping through the forest making their way in a dim,
subaqueous light, and at night, they would find themselves
back in the village, the same old village . . .

"Are you quite sure you will have reached your home by
this evening?" he asks.

"Before nightfall," Nagoa answers. "Have you not heard
the drums talking?"

"The drums, yes . . ." Clarence says.

And suddenly he hears the drums.

"But . . ." he goes on.

"Are we the sort of boys who would make up tales?" says
Nagoa.

"You are two rascals, and a pair of chatterboxes," says the
beggar.

"But we don't tell lies," says Nagoa.

"You're a pair of rascals, all the same," says the beggar.

"Well, we were taught by a master," reply the two boys.

And they take to their heels: but this time the beggar is
not even threatening them.

"Well, there has quite definitely been some sort of
change!" Clarence tells himself.

5

THE EXCHANGE

For several days now, in Aziana, the talking drums had been announcing the little band's approach—first the arrival of the two boys who were natives of the village and whose return was impatiently awaited; then the arrival of Clarence and the beggar were eagerly looked forward to: but it was principally Clarence's visit that was responsible for the feverish excitement which impelled almost the whole population of the village to come to meet the travellers even before they had reached the first fields.

As soon as they were seen coming out of the forest, the whole of this great crowd began to clap their hands and utter loud cries—the same cries and the same hand-claps as Clar-

ence had heard on the esplanade—and then they broke into
a dance. But their dancing was not like that of the pages:
they danced in the more rustic manner of country people,
and leaped vigorously up and down in complete confusion.

"Be careful to walk close behind me," the beggar told
Clarence. "You two, walk along behind us," he added, addressing the boys.

Then he solemnly made his salutation to the crowd, and
their little procession proceeded in good order towards the
village. The beggar affected a slowness of pace which seemed
here to pass for nobility of demeanour, but which Clarence
at once perceived to be an imposture, and a woeful one at
that; in fact it was more like an impious parody of the royal
progress. The crowd, which had quietly made way for them,
followed closely on their heels. This suddenly developed into
a rather impressive procession that went winding ceremoni-
ously through the fields of rice and millet; they were mainly
rice fields, as the ground seemed a little too dry for millet.

A little later, Clarence came to the first huts in Aziana.
They differed hardly at all from those which he had seen
beforehand; that is, the huts in that one village where they
had passed night after night following day after day of useless
wandering in the forest. Only now Clarence is no longer quite
so sure that the village was the only one; and he begins to
wonder if the resemblances that exist between all these huts
have not led him into error; in any case, he could no longer
be quite sure that the beggar had just been leading him up
the garden path.

Seen from a distance, seen from where Clarence first
caught sight of them, these huts made one think of enormous
pots surmounted by rather large and over-hanging lids. It
was difficult to estimate their real size. As one got nearer, one
still thought of them as pots, but then one was surprised by

their unusual dimensions: one wondered what mad potter had created them, and where he had found a kiln large enough to fire them in. On the contrary, the lids lost a great deal by being looked at closely: they were made of thatch, a material which seemed out of keeping with the rest.

But the rest, the main thing—what magnificent pottery it was! The walls were smooth and sonorous as drums or deep bells, delicately, delightfully varnished and patinated, with the good smell of warm brick, and what a red! . . . It was an almost unbearable red . . . Windows like portholes had been let into the walls, just big enough to frame a face, yet not so big that any passing stranger could cast more than a swift glance into the interior of the hut. This last detail has its importance: it was obviously intended to discourage inquisitive outsiders. Everything was perfectly clean: the roofs were newly thatched, the pottery shone as if it had been freshly polished. Moreover the whole village was scrupulously clean; the walls were without lizards, the ditches were weeded and the ground between the huts had been thoroughly swept. So much orderliness, after the wildness of the forest, was a refreshment to the eye and the spirit. Clarence felt it put new heart into him.

"They've swept the ground," he said to the boy behind him.

"They always sweep the ground in the towns," the boy answered. "They have a Street-Cleaning Department."

"Don't pay any attention to that little braggart," the beggar remarked without turning round. "His town—as you can see for yourself—is nothing but a very undistinguished village, a miserable little village like a thousand others. There's no more a Street-Cleaning Department in Aziana than there is cheese in the moon. Every inhabitant sweeps the ground in front of his door with a palm branch, and he's not forced to do that; it's only the desire for cleanliness that makes him do it—a desire which, believe me, is not peculiar to the South, and is far from being widespread in the South . . . If I wasn't so busy, I'd twist the ears off that cheeky little monkey."

At the same time as he was delivering himself of this speech, he was continuing to greet the rather pretty girls whose attractive little faces were framed in the portholes, as they watched the procession winding its way through the streets of Aziana.

But were these really pretty girls? Clarence wondered. The beggar kept greeting them—greeting each one in turn, of course—as if she were the eighth wonder of the world . . . It made Clarence wonder how he was able to tell whether they were pretty or not. It would be extremely rash to judge by the faces alone, though in the present case it would be quite easy to obtain certain hints from the facial features. This was hardly the case for the women who had joined the procession. Perhaps they, too, had pretty faces—surely they must have pretty faces—only it was impossible to find out, because in the formation of their breasts—and if it was not in their breasts it was in their hips—there were something so utterly provocative that—for Clarence at least—all opportunity, or all desire to raise one's eyes to their faces was completely lost.

"Well, thank goodness there are the portholes!" said Clarence.

"Yes," agreed the beggar, "there are all these portholes." And he raised his arms as if he expected to be acclaimed.

"Could it be by any chance that the portholes are used only to set off the faces?" Clarence wondered.

"Do you think . . ." he began.

"Now behave yourself," the beggar said. "We've reached the palace of the naba."

Clarence could see, behind a wall—and, more exactly, above a wall, for the wall was very low and could scarcely hide what lay behind—a hut that was considerably larger than the others and covered by a double-thatched roof. In front, there was a row of arm-chairs upholstered in velvet, and sitting in them were a number of old men with long beards. If it had not been for these very grand chairs, one would not have thought twice about these ossified creatures; not even about the person in the centre, whose rather more pointed and much longer beard nevertheless had something rather imposing about it. As soon as the beggar entered the courtyard he bowed to the ground several times in front of the arm-chairs. "Masters of the town!" he cried. "The dust of your feet salute you!"

"Do you hear that?" said one of the boys. "In the forest, and even on the road into the town, he could hardly ever bring himself to call this place a 'town.' Now you'll find he can't say anything else!"

"Shut up!" said Clarence. "You'll turn them all against us."

"Don't be silly!" the other boy said. "The naba is our grandfather . . . Hallo, grandfather!" he cried, addressing the one in the centre of the group.

But the ancestral beard only quivered a little, and the boy was given a terrific crack over the head with a stick. At first sight this blow seemed to have descended from the heavens.

"Little boys are not heard in the presence of the masters," said someone behind Clarence.

Clarence turned and saw a tall man dressed in a sky-blue *boubou* and holding an enormous stick. The fellow was smiling all over his face, but it did not seem to be the short smile one could trust: the teeth had been sharpened by a file, and seemed ready to tear to pieces the toughest flesh. "This must certainly be a place where silence is golden," said Clarence to himself.

The boy beside him was rubbing his head vigorously. When he thought he had massaged it enough he lowered his hands, revealing a lump like a pigeon's egg.

"Wait till my arms are as strong as yours," the boy whispered in Clarence's ear.

"Yes, but be quiet," said the other boy, "or else the master of ceremonies will lose no time in using his big stick to bring up another egg beside the first."

"Very amusing!" remarked Clarence.

"Really?" asked the boy.

And he shot a furious look at Clarence.

"Look here, now," said Clarence, "don't you run away with the wrong idea. I haven't done anything to you. It was the master of ceremonies who hit you with his stick."

"It was the master of ceremonies who laid the egg on your head," said Nagoa. "Have you forgotten already?"

"From now on I shall be able to tell you apart," said Clarence.

"Do you think we're so very different now?" asked the boys.

"Whether you are or not," replied Clarence, "I'm fed up with not being able to tell you one from the other—it makes my head swim."

"You've got a thick head," said Noaga.

"Thicker than yours, apparently," said Clarence, eyeing Noaga's bump.

"I was talking about what you've got inside," said Noaga.

"Wait till I've spoken to grandpa," said Noaga. "There won't be any more funny business. I have an account to settle with the beggar."

He went up to the master of ceremonies. "I wish to speak to grandpa," he said.

"You may not speak to him with an egg on your head," said the master of ceremonies. "It would not be proper."

"Well, then, Nagoa will speak to him."

"I shall conduct your brother to him, as soon as the beggar has finished his salaams. Your grandfather is too busy at the moment."

Clarence noticed that the naba was in conversation with the beggar. But the setting was different: the arm-chairs and their occupants had disappeared as if by enchantment. The naba was now seated under an arcade at the rear of the courtyard; bending over his shoulder, the beggar was talking with great volubility. The naba was looking fixedly at Clarence; occasionally he wagged his beard as if in agreement.

"They are talking about you," said Noaga.

"Yes, they are apparently talking about me," thought Clarence. "The salaams have long been over, and now they are talking about me." He felt vaguely uneasy; he could not understand why he should feel uneasy, but it was something beyond his control: he just felt uneasy. "What can they be saying about me?" he said.

The two boys turned their heads away from him at the same time, and Clarence felt his uneasiness suddenly increase.

"I don't like put-up jobs," he said.

"Leave them alone," Noaga said. "Nagoa will be having a word with grandpa soon."

"But perhaps then it will be too late," said Clarence.

Just then the naba wagged his beard. "The naba is asking for you," the master of ceremonies told Clarence. "Follow me."

He walked in front of Clarence and stopped a couple of

steps in front of the arcade; he bowed his forehead till it touched the dust. The naba signed to Clarence to draw near.

"Does this town please you?" he asked. He spoke slowly, very slowly, and as if regretfully; as if every word he spoke were beyond price, or as if he had lost the habit of speaking through relying all the time on his beard to express what he meant.

"It is very clean," said Clarence.

"No town has a better-organised Street-Cleaning Department," said the beggar.

"But I thought . . ." began Clarence.

"Never take things at their face value," the beggar said sharply.

"I shall certainly never take your words at their face value again," replied Clarence.

"Children! . . . Children! . . ." said the naba, in his slow, soft voice.

"How would you like to wait here, for the king's arrival?" asked the beggar.

"I don't mind where I wait for him, as long as it's not in the forest," said Clarence.

The naba gazed at him for a long while, looking him over from head to foot. Then he wagged his beard again.

"Come," the master of ceremonies said to Clarence. "The audience is concluded."

Clarence turned and walked back to the wall of the court-yard. When he got to the wall, a great noise of tom-toms was heard. The people who had been in the procession had assembled on the square in front of the naba's palace, and they were getting ready to dance. In the middle of the square there was a great heap of dry branches and straw, and some-one set light to it. Night fell as soon as the first flames leaped up. And at once a pair of dancers opened the ball.

Two shadows jumped up, one on the right, one on the left of Clarence, and ran out into the square: it was the two boys who were running to join the dancers. Clarence shouted to them, but they did not hear him, or pretended not to hear him. They were in the centre of the ring; it looked almost as if they were leaping about, making great leaps in the air without any consideration for the rest of the dancers. Clarence shouted to them again, but the boys could obviously not be expected to hear him now: the drums and trumpets were making a terrifying din.

"Why do they run away just when I need them most?" Clarence wondered. "If they don't speak to the naba at once . . ." And he wrung his hands. He couldn't possibly imagine what the two boys would have to say to the naba; he simply felt that by speaking to him, just by speaking to the naba, the boys would save him from a terrible misfortune . . . He looked carefully at the low wall that separated the square from the palace, and prepared to jump over it as the two boys had done; but he quickly realised that he would not be able to jump over. The wall was certainly a low one; for a good jumper, it would not present a very difficult obstacle. But Clarence was not a good jumper; and a bad jumper or even a moderately good jumper would run the risk of being caught on the sharpened bamboos which, perhaps in place of broken glass, adorned the top of the wall.

Until then Clarence had paid no attention to these bamboos which were embedded in the hard mud coping of the wall; and he even had a suspicion that when he arrived at the naba's palace a little while ago there had not been any bamboos embedded in the wall. Or was it that in daylight, under the violent light of the sun, they could not be seen? Now, on the contrary, they could be clearly seen; they stood out against the flames of the brazier like little thin, sharp shadows.

"Nagoa! . . . Noaga! . . ." shouted Clarence, cupping his hands round his mouth.

But the names were both lost in the uproar. No, just calling their names while all these drums were rolling and all these trumpets were bellowing would not bring them back to Clarence.

"But I simply *have* to get back to them!" he said to himself, looking up at the wall again. And he was just going to jump up and run the risk of tearing himself to pieces on the sharply-pointed bamboos, when he suddenly remembered the gate. "How stupid I am!" he told himself, and ran towards the gate. "I only hope they don't shut it at night!" Fortunately the gate was wide open.

As soon as he was out on the square, he looked everywhere for the two boys, but could not see them. He was now in the thick of the crowd, and his view was blocked. When he reached the bonfire, he called out again, shouting at the top of his voice, but received no answer. The boys seemed to have vanished into the night, or, if they were among the dancers, they must be making such tremendous leaps that they had become invisible and intangible. Clarence went from one group to another, calling to them all the time; but a wilderness could hardly have been less indifferent to his cries than this distracted throng. Suddenly he came across the beggar. The old man was seated in the middle of a ring of drinkers and was solemnly tippling.

"Come and sit down!" the beggar cried. "The wine's good here."

And he smacked his lips.

"I'm looking for the boys," said Clarence.

"They won't be long," said the beggar. "They have gone to see the naba."

"But I saw them joining in with the dancers!" said Clarence.

"Well, you know what they're like: always butting in where they're not wanted! . . . I'll twist the ears off them as soon as they get back . . . Meanwhile, have a drink. We mustn't be discourteous to our hosts. Such excellent wine is very rare."

And he held out a calabash.

"Be careful," he said, "it's full to the brim."

Clarence had no desire to drink. Nevertheless he took the calabash; he had already got through so many of them since starting out on this journey that habit now overcame his lack of desire. When he saw the beggar throwing back his head to drink, he put up no further resistance, but glued his lips to the opening in the calabash. And as always his eyes, while he was drinking, were fixed on the old man's Adam's apple; but this time they did not remain there: it might be said that they were called to higher things, to the eyes of the beggar himself. Then Clarence realised that the old man was watching him slyly. "What's the matter with him?" he wondered. "It's not like him to watch people while he's drinking: he's generally completely absorbed in the pleasure of the wine." There was something in the beggar's eyes which mightily displeased Clarence, though he was unable to say what it was. His uneasiness suddenly took hold of him again.

"Why are you looking at me like that?" he asked. "Your eyes . . ."

He was able to see the old man's eyes better now; and he thought he saw in them a dishonest look, a kind of irony, too, and perhaps both of these.

"Your eyes . . ." he began.

But the beggar changed the subject: "Did you not say that this village would suit you very well?" he asked.

"Suit me very well? . . ." echoed Clarence. "No, I didn't say that. I merely said that I should prefer this village to the forest, to our endless peregrinations in the forest."

"But isn't that the same thing?" inquired the beggar.

No, it wasn't at all the same thing. In Clarence's view, it was a choice between two things that were not equally disagreeable, but as disagreeable the one as the other. They were the sort of things between which one would not have willingly made a choice, things which were the result of a choice that was merely a last resource.

"All the same, you must know what you want," went on the beggar. "You say that you prefer to remain here rather than to go wandering about the forest. Well, to express a preference *is* to make a choice."

"But shall I be able to stay here?" asked Clarence.

"Why shouldn't you stay here?"

"They won't keep me for nothing."

"Perhaps you could offer some small services. And in return, you would be kept . . ."

"Are there really any services I can perform?"

"You should know best yourself," the beggar replied. "Men are hardly ever quite so lacking in ability that they cannot, on occasion, perform some small task or other. I am completely in the dark about the sort of services you might be called upon to perform, but I can find out. I could even, if it so came about, propose that you should be taken on for a probationary period."

"It wasn't exactly in those terms that you transmitted my request to the king," said Clarence bitterly.

"No. And it was wrong of me," said the beggar. "I have already admitted it: that time, I was wrong. My great experi-

ence in these matters played me false. But I have learnt my
lesson . . . Would you care for me to speak to the naba?"

"I should like that very much," said Clarence.

But at once he began to wonder whether he really *would*
like it. No, a preference was necessarily a choice. Resignation
is not a choice . . . And besides, the old man's gaze—he found
it disturbing. It was . . . But what *was* it really? . . . Something
sly, insidious? . . . Something faintly mocking? How could
one tell? . . . Perhaps here, too, it was necessary to make a
choice; and to make it under the same wretched condi-
tions . . .

"Look: I'll go and find out," said the beggar. "Our pact,
of course, made no provision for this sort of thing. But I'm
not forgetting that I owe it to you to make some amends. I'll
go and see the naba."

"In the event of my request being granted, shall I see the
king?" asked Clarence.

"Of course you will see him. Your stay here will make no
difference. You shall see the king when he makes his visitation to the naba, who is one of the great vassals of the South.
The king will come to this very spot: he will sit under the
arcade where the naba was sitting. As far as you are concerned, it would not do you any good to continue your
journey farther South."

"If that's the case, go and find out what I can do," urged
Clarence. Wouldn't anything be better than wandering
round and round in the forest?

"Success to our venture!" said the beggar, raising his calabash.

His eyes were burning again; perhaps they were burning
even brighter than before. "But why do his eyes blaze like
that?" Clarence wondered once again. "There's no reason
why they should blaze so strangely. Or is it because he has

drunk too much? It's easy to drink too much in these village
festivals! . . ." But the explanation did not really satisfy him.
It was not the weak, wavering flame of drunkenness that
Clarence could see, nor yet the fire which betokened the
unmentionable . . . It was a . . . He took some time to find
the words . . . "a formidable blaze," he said all at once. But
the word still did not express all he felt: there was, in the
beggar's gaze, a kind of anticipation, a sly anticipation, an
anticipation mingled with duplicity . . . yes, it was like an
open trap. Open for whom? . . . No, Clarence's uneasiness
could not be expected to abate just yet.

"I am going to the naba's this minute," said the beggar.
"You were able to see on what excellent terms I am with
him."

"Only too well," remarked Clarence dryly. The beggar did
not hear this, or pretended not to; he was perfectly able to
hide his feelings.

"Wait for me here," he said. "I shan't be long. If I see
those two young scamps, I'll send them to you."

He walked quickly away. He held himself very erect; he
did not look as if he had drunk too much. "But . . . Then why
do his eyes blaze like that, if he hasn't drunk too much?"
Clarence wondered once more. He realised that he had said
these last words aloud, and he got to his feet. He was shaking
with dread . . . There was something going on: he was sure
there was something going on! . . . A trap was being laid
somewhere, and Clarence was walking straight into it, or was
on the point of doing so . . . He dashed away into the crowd
to look for the boys. He still did not know exactly what it
was he was expecting of them, but he looked upon them as
a last refuge in a storm; or rather, as a shield. He suddenly
realised that he was trying to put this shield between himself
and the beggar. But why this dread? . . . He was still as unable

as ever to find any explanation for his dread; all he could be
sure of was the necessity, the urgent necessity for a shield.

"Noaga! . . . Nagoa! . . ." he cried.

"Noaga! . . . Nagoa! . . ." several voices took up the refrain.

The people's attitude towards Clarence had suddenly
changed; supposing it to have been black before, it had now
changed without warning to white. A moment ago, no one
was taking any notice of him, no one paid any attention to
his shouts, and now here was everybody repeating what he
was shouting. And not only were they repeating what he said,
they were asking after his health, and each group greeted him
like a long-lost friend and asked him to have a drink. Politeness forced Clarence to stop and reply to the questions he
was asked, and to the toasts which were being drunk in his
honour. But he was on hot bricks all the time, and as soon
as he had talked a little and drunk a little, he began to worry
about the boys.

"Why do you worry yourself about them?" he was asked.
"You'll soon find them again. They'll turn up like a bad
penny, you'll see . . . Drink another calabash of wine with us.
Don't you like it here? . . . There's no hurry: it's a long time
till dawn."

What had the dawn to do with it? Clarence thought it was
a silly remark; but after he had heard it a few times, his
uneasiness increased.

"It *is* the dawn you're talking about, isn't it?" he asked.

"Yes, the dawn," the reply would come.

"Then, tell me, when does dawn break?"

The people of whom he asked this did nothing but laugh
by way of reply, as if he had made a particularly witty
observation.

"Whenever it breaks, it will be too soon," said a woman
who was reclining under a canopy of leaves.

"Everybody talks to me about the dawn," said Clarence.

"Come and dance," said the woman, rising to her feet. She pulled a handful of leaves from the canopy and made herself a sort of diminutive apron with them. "Am I decent?" she inquired.

"I don't know how to dance," said Clarence. "Or rather, I *do* know how to dance, but they are other dances I do, not like the ones you do in the South. I don't think I shall ever be able to dance your dances."

"I shall teach you," said the woman. "It's not difficult."

"It must be very exhausting," said Clarence.

"But that's because anything worth-while requires hard work," she said, looking at him rather severely. "Come on, let's dance."

And she pressed him to her.

"And don't you worry about the dawn," she went on. "We talk about the dawn as we talk about the weather—it is of no importance whatsoever."

"But I don't want to dance," said Clarence, who was being drawn away by the woman.

"Oh, just look at them!" said a voice close to Clarence.

"Believe me," said another voice, "I just can't take my eyes off them."

"Nagoa! . . . Noaga! . . ." Clarence gave a cry of relief.

"Don't you want to dance?" the boys said.

"I do not want to dance at all," replied Clarence.

"Then why are you? . . . Shoo! Shoo!" the two boys cried, hustling the woman away. She ran off thumbing her nose at them.

"I am not afraid of you," she screamed, when she thought she was out of reach.

"You might have chosen something rather more . . ." hinted Nagoa, looking at the woman.

"I didn't choose her," said Clarence. "It was she who chose me . . . Have you ever known me to choose anything of my own free will? I hardly even know whether I am capable of displaying any kind of preference any more."

"All the same," said Noaga, "I should have thought you'd have better taste."

"Where have you been?" asked Clarence. "The beggar swore he would twist the ears off you."

"We're in for a hot time, then!" said the boys. "Dawn will be breaking by then."

"The dawn! the dawn!" said Clarence. "Why are you all talking about the dawn? . . . Have you seen the naba?"

"Yes," replied the boys.

"Well, what did he say?"

At this they both lowered their eyes.

"Have you lost your tongues?" cried Clarence.

"Well, it's like this: it had all been arranged beforehand," said the boys. They wore a hangdog look, which contrasted strangely with their usual effrontery.

"What do you mean?" said Clarence. "The beggar himself has gone to beg an audience with the naba in order to persuade him to allow me to stay here until the king comes."

"Is that what you wanted?" asked Nagoa.

"I don't want to go wandering round and round in the forest again."

"We weren't wandering round and round," countered Noaga.

"Well, anyhow, I don't want to see the forest again."

"That's not the same thing," cried the boys.

"You're a couple of arrant rogues!" cried Clarence.

After this, he couldn't think of anything else to say. He would have liked to tell them about the uneasiness the beg-

gar's eyes had awakened in him, but at the moment he could
hardly see what cause for uneasiness he could possibly have
had. Whoever would get worked up about such a silly thing?
Nevertheless the fact is that Clarence *had* got worked up
about it, and that he still felt uneasy; he would have given
a great deal to know what the naba had said to the beggar
and the beggar to the naba. But—how was he to word his
question? The two boys were rascals; they would turn it all
into a farce. "But it was not the sort of thing, not at all the
sort of thing, that could be turned into a farce," thought
Clarence.

He had lowered his head in order to think better. When
he raised it again, he could see no one in front of him. A
moment later, he saw the woman in between the two boys.
They were each holding one of her arms and making her
jump up and down; and at every jump a kind of squall
breezed through her leafy pinafore, lifting it in the air. The
woman was screaming as if she were being flogged; yet all
they were doing was to lift her by the arms and they were
following scrupulously the rhythm of the drums. "You never
know what those two will be doing next," thought Clarence.
And he started off again to cross the square.

Was it the beggar he was looking for this time? Perhaps.
Perhaps he was looking for nothing and no one, perhaps he
was just roaming around, and perhaps after all that was the
one thing he *could* do . . . All the same, it must be understood
that no sign of all this perturbation appeared on his face.
Everywhere he was joyfully greeted and invited to drink with
all the cordiality which is extended to any happy companion.
In fact, it was a night given over entirely to drinking and
dancing. "I'm going to drink," said Clarence to himself.
"When I've drunk a bit, I shall feel less alone." He began to

drink with that grave deliberation which is accorded to weighty matters. He thought it would not be long before he slipped into oblivion.

But what exactly was he trying to forget?

At present the forest was far away; at least it seemed far away. It was only a few hundred yards away at most, but it seemed to Clarence that it was very much farther. And Adramé, and the white men who had taken so much pleasure in witnessing their countryman's downfall, and the inn-keeper, and the cook and the gruesome puppet-show in the palace of justice were still farther away, were so far away beyond the forest that they had become inexistent. Could it be that luck was at last on Clarence's side? He was now at Aziana; he was going to enjoy a long rest in Aziana, in ex-change for doing a few small services—every kind of small service which a man like himself could perform for village people. For example, he could scare away the birds from the millet-fields at seed-time and harvest; or catch field mice when the corn was reaped; or kill caterpillars; smoke wasps out of their nests . . . And then the king would come . . . The king! . . . Clarence seemed to see him already, so frail, and yet so strong, supported by his pages, proceeding with ex-quisite slowness towards the arcade at the rear of the court-yard. Then the king would be seated, and then the king would allow his eye to fall upon Clarence. His eye! If only he could catch his eye, everything would be made plain. Everything! . . .

Sometimes, in the unavoidable interval between one cala-bash and the next, the people would ask Clarence if he had finally discovered where the two boys were. Oh, yes, he had found them again. And then? . . . He could do without them, he could do without everybody, he felt. He was waiting, quite simply, for the king . . . Then he would direct his steps towards another group and resume his interrupted reverie, with his lips to the mouth of a fresh calabash.

In the end he happened on the beggar again. The latter had taken up a position a little to one side, and was accompanied by someone enormous; a sort of gigantic human round-tower, topped with a face like a full moon.

"Come and let me introduce you to Samba Baloum," the beggar said.

The round-tower at the beggar's side got up with a groan and sketched a very vague bow.

"Enchanted," said Clarence.

The colossus, by way of reply, sighed deeply and began to feel Clarence as one would feel a chicken.

"He's very skinny," he said.

He pulled a face.

"He *is* a little on the thin side," said the beggar. "Our walk through the forest got his weight down. But he's fit: he's a real fighting-cock!"

"A fighting-cock! . . . A fighting-cock! . . ." Samba Baloum muttered. The face he was pulling showed that he would only trust the evidence of his hands, which were the only reliable things in a problem of this nature.

"A good fighting-cock shouldn't be too plump," the beggar suggested.

"Plump?" said the colossus. "No, it's not absolutely necessary for him to be plump; but it wouldn't come altogether amiss if he had a little flesh on his bones."

Whereupon he sighed, and then suddenly dropped Clarence's arm which he had been feeling. "Well, we'll see how he turns out," he said.

He groaned as he sat down again and pulled a more disagreeable face than ever. But as soon as he was seated, his great full face split open in an extensive smile.

"I find everything such an effort," he confided to Clarence. "You wouldn't believe what an effort I find everything."

Again he pulled a face, as if the mere thought of any kind of effort vexed his spirit in the most odious way.

"Would you be so kind, and pass me a calabash, young man?" he went on. "They are lying beside where you're standing."

Clarence picked up a calabash out of the many which lay on the ground, and held it out to him without a word. He was displeased at having been addressed so familiarly as "young man," and he was even more displeased at being felt all over like a chicken on market-day. "Who is this great lump?" he wondered. "It's not right for anyone to be as fat as that." It was frightful. It was disgusting, and frightful.

"Samba Baloum enjoys rude health," the beggar told Clarence.

"I'm not blind," said Clarence.

"Take a calabash," Samba Baloum told Clarence. "It can't do you any harm."

"It will do him a great deal of good," said the beggar. "He'll soon begin spitting fire, you'll see."

"I hope so," said Samba Baloum.

Now that he was sitting down, he seemed disposed to look on everything with a favourable eye. He was fat, far too fat and much too familiar, but he did not seem to be a bad sort; he was certainly too fat to be an ill-natured person. When he had drained his calabash, he flung it far away from him.

"Pass me another, will you?" he asked Clarence. "When you are as corpulent as I am, you very soon get thirsty."

He raised the fresh calabash and looked at it for a moment as if it were transparent.

"Here one moment, gone the next," he sighed, raising it to his lips.

"Enjoy yourself while you can," said the beggar.

Samba Baloum solemnly dandled his head. After a moment or two he fell asleep, with open mouth.

"The whole thing's in the bag," the beggar said gleefully, when he saw Samba Baloum fall asleep. "Are you satisfied?"

"Satisfied? ... Am I satisfied? ..." Clarence asked himself. "If only there wasn't that nasty little flame in the old man's eyes perhaps I should really be content. But as long as that flame burns, I really think I shall be more uneasy than satisfied."

"What about you?" he asked suddenly.

"Me?" answered the beggar.

He made a few small gestures with his hand, as if to brush carelessly away some remains of food that had fallen into the folds of his *boubou;* but they were neither millet seeds nor fruit pips which he was brushing away in this airy fashion; they were all kinds of little vanities and personal indulgences, as if he had finally risen above all carnal passions and as if nothing on earth could ever tempt him again. Was it a kind of new-found wisdom, or his great age, or simply the nature of his profession, which had apparently turned him away for ever from such things?

"Yes, I see all that means nothing to you now," Clarence said.

"Well, put yourself in my place," the beggar said.

"I don't like to be pinched all over as if I were a chicken."

"But he was interested in your form—not as a chicken, but as a cock bird!" the beggar declared. And the flame in his eyes grew brighter.

"What are you thinking of doing?" Clarence asked. "You're up to something or other."

"I'm simply going to proceed on my journey."

"Didn't you tell me the soles of your feet were raw with walking?"

"I cannot give up my job," replied the beggar. "No one willingly gives up his chosen profession." He gazed for a moment at his feet.

"There's no other kind of work I can do," he said. "So my feet will just have to lump it!"

He closed his eyes. He seemed to be plunged in deep meditation. Was he thinking about his work? Was he thinking about the soles of his feet? . . . Now that his eyes were shut and one could no longer see the little flame flickering in his eyes, his face had resumed its former happy expression. He suddenly opened his eyes and asked:

"Did you twist those boys' ears?"

"I've left that to you," said Clarence. "I don't want to get into any more trouble: the naba is their grandfather."

"I know the naba is their grandfather. But where are they?"

"Dancing, I expect," replied Clarence.

"Or making free with the dancing girls!"

"They were going dancing when they left me."

"And why haven't *you* gone dancing?"

"Yes, why do you refuse to dance?" a woman's voice inquired.

The woman wearing the little pinafore of leaves was standing before Clarence.

"Not you again!" cried Clarence.

"I ran away from the two boys to come back to you. Do you object?"

She was "fluffing up" her leafy tutu, as if trying to show her thighs off to better advantage.

"There she is! . . . There she is! . . ." cried Nagoa and Noaga.

They came dashing up. The woman ran away.

"Wait a minute, you two!" the beggar cried. "Stop a minute. I've something to say to you."

"And something to do to you," thought Clarence.

"You can pull their ears if you like," said the beggar. "But remember the naba is their grandfather."

"You're just about the most dishonest person! . . ." Clarence began.

"Did our pact say anything about honesty?" the beggar inquired. "Calm down. We're going to drink Samba Baloum's health."

"Hey, Baloum! We're going to drink your health!" the boys shouted.

Samba Baloum pulled a nasty face and woke up. "Drink!" he said, holding out his hand.

The two boys set out a row of calabashes on his right hand and on his left, so that he could reach them without having to bend down.

"Whose health are we drinking?" asked Samba Baloum.

"Why, yours, you great lump," the boys replied.

"My good health, then!" said Samba Baloum, raising his calabash . . . "But perhaps it would have been better if we had drunk to the health of this young man," he added, nodding vaguely in Clarence's direction. "He's as skinny as a day-old chick!"

They began emptying their calabashes. Clarence never took his eyes off the beggar. This time his gaze did not rest only on the old man's Adam's apple; he had fixed it straightaway on the beggar's eyes, on the little flame that had never stopped flickering in them.

"It won't be long before dawn breaks now," said Samba Baloum, yawning . . . "Help me to get up, you two," he said to the boys.

He held out his hands to them. Again he pulled a face.

"You really are a great lump," said Noaga.

"A great big lump if ever there was one," said Nagoa.

"You ought to be in bed by now, boys," said Samba Baloum. He turned to Clarence:

"Follow me, young man!"

"Well, wait till we've said so-long," the beggar complained. "The king only knows when we'll meet again!"

"Good-bye, then," said Clarence.

He wondered if he shouldn't thank the beggar for all he had done. The bald "good-bye" was perhaps rather abrupt! But the little flame was still flickering in the old man's eyes, and it did not seem to be something you could trust. It didn't seem like anything you could trust at all.

"Well, you've got lodgings, or lodgings of a sort," the beggar solemnly declared. "You have food and drink. You're starting on a new pact. Clarence, I count on your observing its terms with the greatest respect and honesty and I trust that you will show yourself worthy of, and able to carry out the small services you will be asked to perform. As for myself, I think I may claim to have carried out the terms of our pact both honourably and to the best of my ability."

"You certainly have—you've outdone us in effrontery," said Noaga.

"In cunning!" cried Nagoa.

"Quiet!" said the beggar. "We can't start quarrelling just when we're saying good-bye. It isn't done."

He got up and gave them a royal salutation. Then he went off with his loping nomad's stride.

"Come on," Samba Baloum told Clarence.

He shoved Clarence along in front of him, pushing him with his paunch, all the time pinching him and sighing.

"Like an old hen! You can feel the bones all over."

"I don't like to be called an old hen," said Clarence.

"But I can't very well call you a cock, can I?" asked Samba Baloum.

"How do you know?" the boys said.

"How do I know? . . ." pondered Samba Baloum. He stopped a while to think it over.

"Well, how should I know?" he said . . . "If you ask me, the naba hasn't bought a cock, but a pig-in-a-poke."

"I wasn't for sale," protested Clarence.

"No, no, of course not," said Samba Baloum, "of course not . . ."

He heaved a gusty sigh.

"Did I ever say you were for sale?" he asked.

"Then stop feeling me all over," replied Clarence.

"Oh, that's nothing at all," said Samba Baloum.

"It's really nothing at all," said the boys.

And they began to shriek with laughter.

"What they mean is, it's of no consequence," smiled Samba Baloum.

Then he sighed again, and it was a longer sigh than any of the others. But was it possible for something to be of no consequence? . . . No. It was not possible. "The smallest gesture, even an involuntary gesture, was of consequence," thought Clarence. And as for the others . . .

"As for the others?" asked Nagoa, encouragingly, eyeing the lump on Noaga's pate.

"Yes," said Clarence. "The others, the . . ."

He was staring fixedly at the bump. It really *was* like a pigeon's egg, it had the same shape, the same pointed end, as a pigeon's egg.

"Are you afraid it will disappear?" asked Noaga.

"No," said Clarence, "I'm quite easy about that. In fact I'm quite sure it won't. It won't disappear quite so quickly."

"A present from the master of ceremonies?" inquired Samba Baloum.

"There doesn't seem to me to be much ceremony about him," Clarence answered.

"Beware that man and his 'ceremonies'!" said Samba Baloum.

As they reached the low wall of the palace, the sun was rising. And the square was suddenly, with an almost violent suddenness, deserted . . . The dancers were going home.

"It is too late, too late, or too soon, to build you a hut," said Samba Baloum. "Now that it is day, everyone's dropping with fatigue. But don't you worry: to-night, you'll be sleeping under your own roof. The naba has given orders to his potters to make you a hut this afternoon. Until then, you can easily sleep under the arcade; it is very comfortable there, and I'm sure the boys would want to keep you company . . . Sleep well, then. Have a good rest," he concluded, giving Clarence's behind a light smack. "There will be work for you to-night!"

He bowed, probably lower than he had intended, for he made a face again. But as soon as he had raised his head, his face was wreathed in smiles again, and was as broad and shining as the moon at its full. He went off, taking very tiny steps and swaying his hips.

"We'll sleep here," said Noaga. He had begun to sweep a corner of the gallery.

"No, there," said Nagoa. He pointed to a heap of bed-clothes.

"You see, with his bump, it would be more comfortable for him there," he told Clarence.

"Hey, there!" said Noaga impatiently. "That's enough about my bump."

"I didn't mean to be nasty," said Nagoa. "I'm going to make you a cosy little nest."

"A nest?" asked Noaga. "So it's a nest, now? Look here, Nagoa . . ."

"There's the beggar!" said Clarence.

He was looking over the low wall of the palace and suddenly saw the beggar approaching. The old man was perched on a donkey and a woman was leading the beast by its bridle. The donkey seemed to be a sickly, puny beast. Or was it the beggar who was too big for it? The woman, on the contrary, was well upholstered; she had luxuriant buttocks and breasts.

"I'm thinking he no longer runs any risks of making the soles of his feet sore," said Nagoa. "If he makes anything sore, it certainly won't be the soles of his feet."

The two boys burst out laughing.

"The old rogue!" said Noaga. "He must have been thinking that up since we were on the esplanade."

"Since we were on the esplanade?" queried Clarence.

He tried to remember since when the little flame, the flame of the "unmentionable" had been burning in the beggar's eyes. He had not seen it really burning brightly until the night before; but perhaps it had been burning on the esplanade too. If only he had spent a little less time watching the beggar's Adam's apple . . .

"When did you first see it glittering in his eyes?" he asked.

"Don't you worry," said Noaga. "All that glitters is not gold."

"There's many a slip . . ." said Nagoa. "He'll have no luck at all with that outfit."

"What do you mean?" asked Noaga. "Have you something up your sleeve?"

"I'm as innocent as a new-born lamb," Nagoa answered.

"You be careful," said Noaga. "Grandpa would not allow anything like the business with the coat."

"Don't talk so loud," warned Clarence. "The beggar will hear if you do."

"He won't hear a thing," said Noaga. "They aren't the sort of things he'd like to hear."

"What I mean is, quite simply," went on Nagoa, "that he won't be able to carry out his professional duties with a donkey that arouses pity and a woman who arouses desire. He'll be giving away with one hand what he takes with the other."

"I thought he'd renounced the world of sensual pleasures," said Clarence.

"What? Someone who knocks it back the way he does?" said Noaga.

Well, Clarence had to admit that the beggar did not drink like a man who was tired of the world and all its pleasures. The old man might say he had renounced all earthly satisfactions, but his Adam's apple . . . At least, all he did then was drink. But now . . .

"No," said Clarence. "I should not have thought that at his age he would have set out in such company."

"No matter! He hasn't made as good an exchange as he seems to think," said Nagoa. "The old rascal might have got something better out of grandpa than a wind-broken donkey and a woman who, though desirable, is no longer in her first youth. He could easily have got three or four times as much. But he doesn't know how to barter. All he can do is beg favours."

"What has the beggar bartered?" asked Clarence. "Did he have something to sell?"

"Haven't we all got something to sell?" said Nagoa, eyeing Clarence rather narrowly.

"After all, he's just a little twister," said Noaga. "An apprentice."

"He doesn't really know what's what," said Nagoa.

They suddenly roared with laughter.

"You laugh like a couple of lunatics," said Clarence.

"But why aren't *you* laughing too?" asked the boys.

And they started laughing even louder.

PART TWO

AZIANA

1

||||||||||||||||||||||||||||||||||||||||||||||||||||||||||||||||||||||||||||||||||||||||||||||||||||||||

AKISSI

Clarence walked painfully to the threshold of his hut. It
was hardly more than six steps—his hut measured
barely more than six feet across—but it felt as if it were a
hundred. He was filled with an inexplicable heaviness. He was
heavy with sleep; he was as it were drunk with sleep. His head
and his limbs felt inexpressibly heavy.

He leaned against the wall; he wanted to try to understand
why he felt so heavy. But then he realised that he could not
think even the simplest thoughts; it seemed almost too much
to follow a single thought to its logical conclusion.

The heaviness was now all concentrated in his head; it was
partly of course the heaviness inside the hut: the heat, or the

smoke, or the fog of breath or Lord knows what other sultry heaviness. And he just couldn't get his thoughts together; perhaps they were holding out their hands to one another—that is, if they *had* hands—but these hands encountered nothing but the void. Yet as the dewy freshness of the dawn began to bathe his forehead, Clarence began to see that the hands would meet in the end. The heaviness inside him was gradually dwindling away.

At that very moment the sun rose on Aziana. A great rosy flame leapt up the sky and chased away the remains of fog and mist, and everything became of the same rosy colour as the flame: the mists, the public square under the bombax trees, the huts, the low wall of the palace, and the arcade at the back. Then the mists evaporated; and the huts, the wall, the gallery and the earth in the public square turned red; the red earth regained its supremacy; the huts and the gallery took on once again their blood-red tint; the earth was red again, a darker and more velvety red. And the sky turned blue and bluer, and still more blue—gradually turning to that sheerest blue that would soon be unbearable in its azure brilliance.

Then Clarence returned to those thoughts which only a short while before had been holding out their hands to each other in the misted heaviness of his being. The first to meet him told him something about a light, soft object which he had kicked with his foot on rising, and which had almost made him measure his length on the floor. He went back into the hut. At the bedside, he stumbled against a pile of leaves or grasses. But . . . No, they were neither leaves nor grasses! Now he knew what it was: there was no need to look, no need for any more light than that which feebly lit the interior of the hut, in order to find out what it was; there was no need for him to have gone to the bedside, and to have tripped over

something light and soft: all he had to do was to breathe the
air as he came back into the hut.

When he went outside again, he found he was holding a
great sheaf of flowers. He looked at it for a moment with
disgust, then threw it angrily far away from him. It was not
the first time he had found these sheaves of flowers in his hut.
He had expressly forbidden Akissi to bring any more, but
Akissi took no notice of him; she liked the flowers' insidious
fragrance.

"Akissi!" he shouted.

A woman came timidly out of the hut.

"Did I not forbid you to put flowers at the bedside?"

The woman made no reply; she stood with her head hanging low, as if she were trying to hide her face.

"Go and throw this rubbish on the square," said Clarence,
pointing to the flowers. "It stinks the place out."

The woman picked up the sheaf of flowers and went
through the gate of the courtyard. Now she was standing on
the square looking from left to right, as if uncertain where
she should throw the flowers. Clarence was watching her
from behind the low palace wall.

"Throw it down where you are," he shouted. "That's quite
far enough."

He took a deep breath of fresh air. He felt as if he were
breathing for the first time since he had got up. That heavy
odour of flowers and leaf-mould was the odour of the forest—
an abominable, unmentionable odour! The woman came
back to the courtyard and started walking at once towards
the neighbouring huts.

"Where are you going?" shouted Clarence.

"I'm going for water," she replied.

He watched her walking away. "Queer woman!" he
thought to himself. "Never the same for two days on end."

And he began to ponder over that continual change. Was it not strange? It was incomprehensible. He closed his eyes, the better to ponder over it. In Aziana, as in Adramé, everyone closed their eyes when they were thinking. When he opened them again, Akissi was coming back from the fountain; she was bearing a tall earthenware jar on her head.

"Here is water," she said, putting the great jar down on the ground. The jar had the same red colour as the hut, the same light glaze as the hut's.

"You should not expose your body to the morning air," she went on. "The morning air is sharper than the air of night. You will catch cold!"

It was quite true. He was running the risk of catching a bad cold, after the heavy warmth of the hut. In the mornings, the air was particularly keen.

"Put on your *boubou*," said Akissi.

He donned his *boubou*.

"Where did you get that jar?" he asked.

"I went to get water," she said.

"That's not what I asked you. You left this hut without a jar and now you come back with a jar on your head."

"The jar was at the fountain."

"But I don't like using other people's jars. You don't know where it might have been."

"This one was very clean."

Yes, the jar was probably clean. The people of Aziana were very clean. All the same, one shouldn't go borrowing other people's jars. It might cause unpleasantness. What would the woman say when she came to the fountain and found her jar had disappeared?

"But when you left here you didn't have a jar," he said.

"Naturally I did not have one; this one I borrowed."

"You do not understand what I mean. I was wondering

how, when you had no jar, you could have gone to get water."

Akissi hesitated a moment, then said: "I knew that I should find some jar or other at the fountain."

Lord! what a queer way of thinking Akissi sometimes had! It was impossible to follow her, thought Clarence. She made your head spin! . . . But perhaps she had just as much difficulty in following Clarence, too.

"There are moments when I just don't understand you," he said. "No more than I understand the way you change each day. Just now I was watching you going to the fountain and you were a different woman. I sometimes wonder if you are always the same woman."

"Is a woman ever the same?" she said.

No, a woman isn't always the same; she could not always be the same. He himself . . . But the whole thing was too vexatious to be funny.

"Next time, don't put flowers in the hut," said Clarence.

He squatted down by the door and began gazing at the sky. "Another killing day!" he thought. Ah, yes, he had killed a good deal of time already! If his days had left their bones behind them, he could have filled many huts with their remains. But the days left nothing behind. All those days, when one came to think of it, were just a great emptiness; and to-day would be the same as every day. Yet if Nagoa and Noaga were to come and have a chat, and if Samba Baloum were to come and join them, the day would pass fairly well. It's terrible to have nothing to do!

At first, when he had left the forest behind, it had seemed rather pleasant to be able to sit on one's behind and receive board and lodging in return. But then he had begun to be terribly bored. The beggar had hinted at the small services Clarence might be asked to perform, but there had never

been any services to perform, either great or small. Everyone
seemed to consider Clarence incapable of doing any work.
But he was quite able to work and had proved it. When they
had begun to pick cotton, he had watched the women working—for it was women's work—and when they had beaten
this felt-like wadding and when the women had spun it, he
had still gone on watching, for it was still women's work. But
when the cotton had finally been transformed into great
hanks of coarse thread, he had begun to work for at that
moment it had become men's work: he had woven the cotton,
and had even become expert at it. But could one really go
on weaving all day long?

Why was he not given any work? He was becoming fright-
fully lazy hanging round like this. His woman, Akissi, whom
Samba Baloum had brought him on the first day, when he
had been showing Clarence the hut which the naba's masons
had just finished for him, Akissi relieved him of all material
worries. Well, perhaps others could get used to that way of
life; perhaps others could allow themselves to depend on
their women for everything; but not Clarence. And he
yawned at great length. This day did not look like being any
less tedious than the others.

Akissi came out of the hut with her mortar and pestle. She
sat down on a little stool and began to pound millet. As
always, she was the first to beat out the rhythm of the mortar
and pestle in Aziana, and this must certainly have disturbed
those who were hoping for a long lie-in. She lifted her arms
very high, and the pestle fell with a heavy thud into the
mortar; a fine floury dust began to rise.

"I wonder if I should get washed?" Clarence thought. "If
I don't wash now, when the air is still cool, I shan't have the
strength to do so later on."

"Akissi, where is the jar?" he asked.

He knew perfectly well in which corner of the hut Akissi put it; in fact, the sole aim of the question was to have the jar brought to him, and Akissi took the hint. She came out of the hut with the jar firmly planted on her head. "I get lazier every day," thought Clarence. And he slipped off his *boubou.*

"Are you sure the jar was clean?" he asked.

"It could not have been any cleaner than it was," replied Akissi.

Clarence looked suspiciously at the water. He poured out a little, examined it in the palm of his hand, sniffed it, and then, reassured, dashed his face with water and rubbed his fingers with it. "I wash myself like a cat," he said to himself. "I shan't get rid of the odour like this."

"Bring the stool," he told Akissi.

He thought that the only way to rid himself of this odour that seemed to be sticking to his skin, sticking to it like a second skin, would be to have a shower. Akissi brought the stool and stepped on to it. She put the jar on her head again and tipped it towards Clarence.

"Right!" said Clarence.

The water poured over him like a real shower. It was very pleasant. Clarence had invented the system and now many people in Aziana washed themselves in this way. Clarence rubbed himself down very energetically.

"I don't like you to take jars that don't belong to us," he said. "You'd better put this one back where you found it, as soon as you've finished with it."

Yes, this invention of his wasn't bad at all, though of course it didn't need a genius to discover it! The water poured over one with delicious coolness, and one could get a thorough wash. Moreover, the water seemed to replenish the body with delightful stores of energy which one could not use in any way; or at least, Clarence could not use them in any way: they were gratuitous stores of energy, free to all, and yet they were energy all the same—real energy!

Aziana was now waking up. Clarence could see, beyond the low wall, people coming and going on the square. They would shout "Good morning" to one another from opposite sides of the square. People kept asking Clarence how he was or if he had slept well; a few came and leaned on the wall and had a little chat with him—small talk that did not commit any-one. Or they would congratulate Clarence on looking so well. Yes, that shower taken on his own doorstep and punctuated by friendly greetings had been a splendid thing; it had been a real pleasure.

"Here comes Samba Baloum," said Akissi.

Clarence saw Samba Baloum coming his way. The big lump, as the two boys called him, was walking as always, with tiny steps and swaying hips. There was no hurry: he was never in a hurry about anything.

"Slept well?" Samba Baloum inquired.

"Badly," replied Clarence. "The odour of the forest stank out the whole hut."

"It's not an unpleasing odour," said Samba Baloum.

"It's the sort of odour that drives men mad," said Clarence.

"Heh! . . . Heh! . . ." said Samba Baloum.

His mouth had split wide open, but it only brought forth a faint, dry cackle. Yet this was supposed to be laughter; but laughter was already too much—it was too fatiguing for words. That is why Samba Baloum's enormous hilarity expressed itself in a little cackle.

"Wash my back, Baloum," said Clarence. "I can't reach my back properly. And Akissi cannot pour water and rub my back at one and the same time."

Samba Baloum washed his back.

"How's that?" he asked.

"That's fine," said Clarence.

How soft Baloum's hands were! They were soft as sponges. No—as soft as chamois leather. Hands like that ought not really to be used for cleaning things—they were too plump, too soft. One couldn't imagine what Baloum had inside him—lots of fat, certainly, and then lots of flesh probably; and yet—there was still something else: something vaguely spongy; or perhaps it was wind; perhaps he was like those bagpipes made of animal skins that the musicians played on the nights when there was dancing in the square. Akissi, now, had a rather rough hand, a real hand.

"You're looking better than you did when you came," said Samba Baloum.

"Does that surprise you?" Clarence cried. "Do you realise that I am doing nothing at all? Abso-lute-ly nothing!"

"It's all right, you're doing quite enough," said Samba Baloum. "The naba is pleased with you."

"The naba! . . . The naba! . . ." cried Clarence.

He couldn't bear the sight of the naba's beard any more. Everything hung on that beard—favour and disfavour, grace and disgrace. Who did the naba think he was? He thought he was God Almighty! That old mummy thought he was God Almighty!

"You're getting quite chubby," said Samba Baloum. "When the beggar first brought you here, you were like an old hen."

"Why did Nagoa and Noaga call him an old rogue?" asked Clarence.

"Now if you're going to listen to those two scamps! . . ." protested Samba Baloum.

But the beggar was really a bit of an old rogue. A bit of

a rogue and a bit of a knave. He was a lot of rather unpleasant things. "And yet," thought Clarence, "in suggesting that
I should take my ease in Aziana, he had the right idea
. . . He had an eye for comfort . . ." Was it the same eye in
which the suspicious little flame would blaze?

"One can't really call him an old rogue," he said.

"No, one can't," said Samba Baloum. He cackled weakly.

"But what *are* you doing, Samba Baloum?" demanded
Clarence. "I can quite well soap my thighs myself."

"Oh, well, then, I've finished," said Samba Baloum. And
he gave Clarence a hopeful smack on the backside.

"I don't like to be slapped like that," said Clarence.

"You are a real fighting-cock," said Samba Baloum. "The
beggar knew what he was talking about."

Akissi began to dry Clarence. She used a kind of spongy
towel. Before Clarence came to Aziana and learnt to weave,
this kind of material was quite unknown; people dried themselves with horribly rough cloth which nearly skinned them
alive. But Clarence had learnt to weave with yarn which had
been deliberately made very soft; now people used these
towels all the time.

"Noaga! Nagoa!" Clarence joyfully shouted.

The two boys had just jumped over the wall. Their company would bring a little life into the dullness of the morning.

"Up already?" said Clarence.

"Yes, we are!" cried the boys.

"If they're up early," remarked Baloum, "they're up to no
good."

"Clarence, will you tell us if it's altogether unpleasant to
be dried like that by Akissi?" said Nagoa.

"What do you know about it?" asked Clarence.

"He has a good idea," said Noaga. "Now then, Akissi,
don't blush like that."

"If you're looking for children, you won't find them here,"
said Samba Baloum. And he gave Noaga's backside a playful
slap.

"I don't know why you go round smacking people's backsides," said Noaga. "If you're not smacking Clarence's,
you're smacking Nagoa's, or mine. You shouldn't do it."

"If you do it again," said Clarence, "I'll boot your bottom
so hard you won't be able to sit on it."

"May I remind you that, as far as I am concerned, such
things have not the slightest importance," said Baloum.

"You are a queer man," said Clarence.

"A man, did you say? . . ." said Samba Baloum. And he
sighed.

"The king only knows! . . ." he said.

Clarence put his *boubou* on.

"Akissi, don't forget to take the jar back to where you
found it," he said.

"Isn't it yours?" asked Baloum. "I'd have sworn it was
yours."

"It's a jar I borrowed," said Akissi. And she gave Samba
Baloum a little wink.

"Yes, this jar is not as beautiful as your own," said Baloum. "The material is not so fine."

"It's not that it is any less beautiful," said Clarence. "It's
simply that I don't like using other people's jars."

And now what should he do? He had washed, he had
chatted, but the day had hardly begun, and it would be a long
one.

"What shall we do?" he asked. It was not one of those days
when he would have liked to weave.

"We'll go and see Fatou's presents," said Noaga.

"Fatou? . . . Who's Fatou?" said Clarence.

"The girl who's just got engaged," said Nagoa.

"First we'll sit in the shade and smoke a pipe," said Samba Baloum. "We'll smoke a pipe and treat ourselves to a calabash of wine . . . Here, you two," he said, addressing the boys. "Go and get some calabashes from the naba's."

"And what if the master of ceremonies finds out?" said Nagoa.

"Will *you* take the beating?" asked Noaga.

"If the master of ceremonies shows his face," said Samba Baloum, "you can take to your heels."

And he walked over to the arcade with Clarence.

"Let us sit here," said Samba Baloum.

They squatted down, and Baloum pulled his usual face; a nasty grimace it was, but which, like everything else to do with him, was not of the slightest importance.

"I shouldn't like the master of ceremonies to find us out," said Clarence.

"Pah!"

"Don't you know, he's always on the look-out!"

"Don't worry," said Samba Baloum, "I'll look after him!"

He took his pipe out of his *boubou*. Akissi had gone back to her pestle and mortar, and the rhythm of the pestle pounding the mortar could be heard. Several other women had joined her, and their pestles were all falling in time.

"Why! here they are back already!" said Samba Baloum. "The master of ceremonies can't have been so very terrifying."

The two boys had slung the calabashes on a stick and each bore an end of the stick on his shoulder. They lined up the calabashes in front of Clarence and Baloum, and sat down facing them.

"I drink to the health of the master of ceremonies," said Samba Baloum.

"That's a bright idea," said Clarence.

"Here's to him. And the devil take him, if he hasn't done so already!" cried the two boys.

"It's never too late to mend, remember," said Samba Baloum.

All the time he was drinking, Clarence was watching the sky. The sun was still not very high in the heavens.

"The days are very long," he remarked, putting down his calabash.

"As long as they're fine . . ." said Samba Baloum.

"They're *too* fine!" thought Clarence. "Too uniformly fine for my liking. The days follow one another, and they're all alike—deceptively alike; there's not one you could pick out and say it was different from the rest."

"On the other hand, the nights are short," said Samba Baloum.

"The nights?" said Clarence. "I wasn't talking about the nights."

"Heh, heh! I know what I'm talking about," cackled Samba Baloum. "The nights are always too short."

"But I *don't* know what you're talking about," Clarence protested. "What do you mean? Not all nights are short."

The night he had just passed, its air rank and foul with the odour of the forest, was not a short night. That heat, that furious exacerbation of the senses, that dark state in which one ceased to be oneself and was transformed into a sort of beast—all that clashed with the idea of a short night.

"There are nights that are so thick, you can cut them with a knife," he said.

"*You* needn't grumble!" said Samba Baloum.

"If we were in your place, *we* wouldn't grumble," said the boys.

They were eyeing Akissi. Clarence followed their gaze. "How stupid they are!" he thought. None the less he went on watching Akissi, watching her raising the pestle high in the air and pounding it in the mortar . . . the thrusting movement of the pestle . . . "I've got a dirty mind," he told himself. And he blushed violently. Yet . . . Yes, Akissi *did* have her good points. No, he did not mean that in the sense in which Samba Baloum would have taken it; Akissi's qualities were not foreign to her nature, but Clarence did not want to think about them. He knew quite well that he had become a different man since he had come to live in Aziana. But he detested this new man, he refused to countenance this new man who at night so utterly abandoned himself because of the odour of a bunch of flowers. Akissi had qualities that had nothing to do with that kind of baseness: she was courageous, she was scrupulously clean, she had learned to cook rather less glutinous dishes than those which were customary in the South . . . She had—yes, she had very great qualities. And she also had some incredible faults; one would swear she did things on purpose sometimes—those sheaves of flowers that she left lying around the hut, or that borrowed jar which did not belong to them . . .

"I'm not grumbling," he said.

Samba Baloum and the two boys laughed heartily.

"Oh, you make me sick," said Clarence.

"You're a real fighting-cock," said Baloum.

"First I'm an old hen, then I'm a fighting-cock . . ." cried Clarence. "I've already told you often enough that I don't care for such comparisons. Besides, you ought to make up your minds: I can't be a cock and a hen at one and the same time."

"I've made up my mind," said Samba Baloum. "At first, I didn't know whether you were a tup or a ewe: you were all skin and bone, and there was no way of telling. But now you're a different person altogether."

"You have Akissi now," said the boys.

They laughed, and Samba Baloum laughed too; they were laughing as if the joke they had made were in the very best of taste . . . "Yes, I have Akissi . . ." Clarence said to himself. And he turned again to watch her pounding millet. "I have Akissi, changeable as she is; I have a different Akissi every night." He puffed fitfully at his pipe. His thoughts began to dwell on his past life. If anyone who had known him in those days could have seen him now, smoking and drinking, crouching in the manner of black men under the arcade, and dressed in a *boubou* like a black man, he would have appeared quite unrecognisable.

And who could tell just what had happened to him? Clarence himself did not know. The odour of the forest had probably had something to do with it; certainly that caressing odour which is the very odour of the South itself—provocative and cruel, lascivious and unmentionable—that had something to do with it all. But Clarence breathed this odour with great distaste, and he always thought about it with disgust. Buttocks and breasts—that's all one saw, and perhaps that's what one breathed, too—the odour of buttocks and breasts. In this respect Akissi was no different from the others; Clarence could not have distinguished her from any of the others in this respect. He could not recognise her face any more than he could recognise the faces of the other women; the only time he could be sure it was her face was when she showed it in the porthole of the hut: Akissi would put her face in the porthole's oval frame, and Clarence would be able to recognise it as hers. But as soon as he saw her whole body, it was as if he could no longer see her face: all he had eyes for were her buttocks and her breasts—the same high, firm buttocks and the same pear-shaped breasts as the other women in Aziana . . . And he found the day too long; he kept waiting for the night, but not in the way Samba Baloum meant. Good heavens, no! Not in that way! . . . He was afraid of the night; he did not look forward to it. The beast inside him was looking forward to it perhaps, but he feared it, detested it . . .

He wanted to get up and go, but he found the master of ceremonies standing before him. The man had approached in his own furtive way, appearing unexpectedly and in a manner that was intended to catch people napping. Yet he was only a master of ceremonies, he was not even the naba's right-hand man. Why did he try to give himself such airs?

"Are you drinking?" the master of ceremonies asked.

"I've got to do something to pass the time," said Samba Baloum. The master of ceremonies looked at each of them in turn.

"I can't help wondering where you got this great pile of calabashes," he said, when he had finished inspecting them.

"Don't worry your head about that, and have a drink with us," said Samba Baloum.

"We are inviting you to join us," said Clarence.

"Do you hear?" said the boys. "He's inviting you to join us."

"Don't let's stand on ceremony," said Samba Baloum. "It's part of a stock of wine that Clarence keeps in his hut and which he intended us to drink."

"Your good health!" said Clarence, toasting the master of ceremonies.

"And yours!" replied the master of ceremonies.

He took a sip and kept it for a moment in his mouth.

"It's first-rate, isn't it?" said Samba Baloum.

"It tastes exactly like the naba's wine," said the master of ceremonies. He looked hard at the two boys.

"If I ever catch you pinching the naba's wine . . ." he began.

"What, us?" cried the boys. "Us, pinch grandpa's wine? . . . Baloum, you know the sort of boys we are . . . say something!"

"They're no angels," said Samba Baloum. "Everybody knows that they're no angels. They're not expected to be; it's not their job. But as for pinching the naba's wine—I can give you my word that they would never do such a thing."

"But they're no angels," remarked the master of ceremonies.

"Who wants to be an angel!" asked Samba Baloum. "Apart from myself—I can't help it . . ."

"Good for you, Samba Baloum!" said the boys.

They all laughed, even the master of ceremonies, who showed all his cruel teeth.

"*He* at any rate," said the master of ceremonies, pointing to Clarence, "*he* would find it difficult to pass himself off as an angel. Every night . . ."

"That's enough!" said Samba Baloum sharply.

"What do you mean, 'every night'?" asked Clarence.

"I know what I'm talking about," said the master of ceremonies. "You can play the startled innocent if you like, but you won't take me in. I'm no angel either. I know what *your* little game is!"

"I'm not playing any game!" protested Clarence.

"You're not going to tell me that night after night you . . ."

"Not another word!" broke in Samba Baloum. "If the naba were to hear what you've been saying, it would cost you dear, master of ceremonies or no. You might find you'd broken your stick across your own back."

"My stick?" said the master of ceremonies. "I should like to know where it has got to. I've been looking for it ever since I got up."

"We're not interested in your stick," said Clarence. "I should like to know what you are insinuating when you say . . ."

"Poppycock, that's all it is!!" said Samba Baloum.

"If you were referring to the wine . . ." Clarence went on.

"It was nothing to do with the wine!" said the master of ceremonies. "And if it were a question of the wine—no one knew that you had a private stock of wine."

"No one enters my hut without my permission, either!" cried Clarence.

"Now that's going a bit too far!" said the master of ceremonies. "And you have the face to tell me only a moment ago that you weren't up to any kind of game? You must certainly take me for a bigger fool than I thought you did . . . What woman were you with last night?"

Samba Baloum struck the master of ceremonies across the mouth. "You'll answer to the naba for that impertinent question!" he cried.

"If that's the way you want it," said the master of ceremonies, "I'm going. I, too, could if I wished strike you across the mouth, but it would ill behove me to strike a low creature like you. Do you hear me? You're a low creature, not a man. You can take that whichever way you like . . . But as for *him!* . . ." he said, pointing to Clarence. "As for him! . . ."

He rose proudly to his full height. He was going to leave them when he noticed the stick the boys had used to carry the calabashes.

"My stick!" he cried. "What's my stick doing here?"

"How were we to know it was your stick?" said the boys.

"It shall be brought to the naba's ear that you have been

drinking his wine," said the master of ceremonies, thrusting the stick under his arm.

"And it shall also be brought to the naba's ear that you drank some of it yourself," said Samba Baloum. "And the words you have uttered will be brought to his ear at the same time."

"I don't give a damn for you and your fighting-cock!" cried the master of ceremonies, striding stiffly away.

"Windbag," said Samba Baloum under his breath.

"But look here, will you tell me? . . ." began Clarence.

"Drunken drivel," said Samba Baloum, "the sheerest drunken drivel!"

"He wasn't drunk," said Clarence. "He couldn't have been drunk, when all he had was half a calabash-full of wine."

"He's never sober," said Samba Baloum.

"I was with Akissi last night," said Clarence.

"Of course you were!" said Samba Baloum. "Who else would you have gone to bed with? You see it *was* just utter drivel, drunken drivel. I can't understand why you seem to attach so much importance to it."

"Because you do so yourself," said Clarence. "Otherwise you would not have threatened to report what he said to the naba."

"I just said that to frighten him," said Samba Baloum. "I just said that to keep him quiet about the wine."

"I'm beginning to understand," said Clarence.

"Of course you're beginning to understand," said Samba Baloum. "Everything is clear now, and you understand. I had to frighten him off and I seized on the first excuse I could find. But as you could see it did not have much effect; it wasn't, I'm afraid, a terribly good excuse."

"No, it wasn't very good," Clarence agreed. "But he called me a fighting-cock all the same."

"He only said that because he's ridiculously jealous of his women. He has several women, and a few of them are really rather pretty, and so he imagines that every man is paying court to them. He must have thought that you, too, were spending nights on the tiles at his expense. He accused you falsely in order to find out the truth. He was pumping you, don't you see? That's the way he is."

"I've never looked at his women," said Clarence. "I don't even know who they are."

"But he believes everybody is running after them and going into ecstasies at the sight of them."

"Idiot!" said Clarence.

"That's the word for it," agreed Samba Baloum . . . "Come on, let's go and see Fatou's engagement presents." And he got up, pulling a frightful face. "She will certainly have received some magnificent presents," he went on. "They get engaged, and as long as the engagement lasts everything flows with milk and honey . . . Akissi!" he shouted. "Stow these calabashes in the hut, there's a good girl. One never knows; some wicked person might come along and steal them."

"Akissi," said Clarence, "where were you last night?"

"Where else would she be, if not in bed beside you?" said Samba Baloum.

"Akissi, this morning when you left the hut you were walking in a way that I had never seen before," said Clarence. "It was not the way you usually walk."

"I was tired," she said, and she stretched voluptuously. "I had a good right to be tired, hadn't I?" she said, smiling suggestively.

"Heh! heh! What a fighting-cock you are!" said Samba Baloum, giving Clarence's backside a resounding smack.

"Lay off, Baloum," said Clarence. "This is more serious than you might think."

"They're just cock and bull tales, and more cock than bull, heh! heh!" said Samba Baloum. "Nobody's asking you what you were doing last night . . . Oh, come on," he said, putting his arm round Clarence's waist and drawing him away. "Oh, you *are* getting chubby, aren't you, and all over, too! Isn't he getting chubby, boys?"

"Chub, chub, chubby!" chanted the boys, and they felt him all over with their lively hands.

"Oh, *you're* not going to start now, are you?" groaned Clarence.

"Oh, they're just a couple of jokers," said Samba Baloum.

"I suppose you call yourself a joker, too," said Clarence, trying to avoid the boys' playful hands. "You all of you keep feeling me all over as if I were a bird ready for market."

He thought for a moment.

"No, not like a bird," he went on. "You keep going over my points, feeling me as if I were a prize stallion!"

"A stallion?" cried Samba Baloum. "Oh, that's a good one! I've got to laugh. Excuse me, but I've got to laugh."

He cackled much more loudly than before. As for the boys, they were doubled up with laughter.

"A stallion, a stud-horse, a travelling sire, that's what you take me for!" cried Clarence.

He looked from one to the other and found it rather strange that they should turn their eyes away. Had he said something incongruous? If he had, it wasn't anything more laboured or coarser than what they had said themselves. But it was not at all incongruous: he really *was* a stallion. There were nights, those nights when the odour of the forest filled the hut, when he was simply a foul, filthy stallion . . . One day, the king would come and sit under the arcade, he would come and sit in the very place where they were sitting now, fragile and pure, and strong with a strength that was drawn from that purity, so indescribably pure, so rare! . . . Clarence heaved a sigh . . . Could a stallion approach the king? . . . He sighed again . . . Oh, how long these days of waiting seemed, waiting for the king's coming! And how heavy! These days were a great void, and a terrible burden; they were . . . One couldn't say what they were . . . They were messy and glutinously filthy . . . Would the king be able to see anything else but this filth? He would see nothing but the filth, the foulness, and he would draw away in disgust, he . . .

"Are you coming?" the boys were saying.

"I'm coming," said Clarence.

2

‖‖

THE MASTER
OF CEREMONIES

"One moment, Akissi," said Clarence.

He was half out of bed and he was calling back
Akissi who was about to go to the fountain with her jar.

"Stand by the window," he went on, getting out of bed.
He went outside and stood beside the porthole.

"Where are you?" he said.

"I'm here," she said. "I was just putting my jar down."

Her pretty little mug appeared, framed in the oval of the
porthole. Yes, it was Akissi all right. It was she, beyond all
shadow of a doubt. Of course it was not always easy for
Clarence to tell one black face from another; but this was
definitely, incontestably Akissi's face which was framed in

the oval of the porthole window. Two very large eyes, perhaps no larger than anyone else's but appearing even larger
than they really were because of the violent contrast between
the white of the eye and the ebony blackness of its setting;
a pretty little nose, with a rather roguish tilt; and then a pair
of well-defined, almost too well-defined, lips . . .

Clarence suddenly thought of Akissi's body. He could only
see her face, but in his imagination he suddenly saw Akissi's
naked body, and he thought of the way in which their two
naked bodies, his own and Akissi's, would lock together. He
felt a dark fire smouldering through his legs, a fire as dark as
Akissi's naked flesh. And he was ashamed . . . But did he
always feel ashamed? . . . "Sometimes I do not feel ashamed,"
he admitted to himself. "There are nights when I am without
shame, when I seem to go mad, when I really seem to go
mad." He sighed . . . How was it that such a fire, such a dark
and burning fire, could shoot through all his being? How was
it that he could at one and the same time abominate, and yet
so frantically lust after such a thing? . . . He felt his legs
trembling with desire.

"Go and get water," he whispered.

He slid down to the ground beside the wall and found the
sun was rising. His legs were no longer trembling now; they
were just shivering slightly, and for quite another reason:
they were welcoming the sun's first rays. This faint touch of
sunlight in the cool air of morning was extraordinarily soothing; it drove away the night and the horrors of the night, the
odours of the night: it drove the South far away. It was a
promise, and for the moment it did not matter that it was
a baseless promise. Clarence did not even realise that he was
stark naked. At night, he was conscious of his nakedness; but
in the mornings, sitting in the early sunlight, he was no longer
aware that he was naked. The air was so new, so fresh, so

innocent! No, he never realised he was naked in the early
sunlight, that cool, sweet air; nor did it enter his head to
cover his nudity. The people in Aziana did not veil their
nakedness any more than he did: they never thought about
it; they just enjoyed life. Clarence was at that moment enjoying life too.

If on getting up he was often assailed by gloomy thoughts,
and if all kinds of worries, whether real or imaginary came
to haunt him, such things lasted only as long as the mists of
night, the odours of night still hung about him. Later, when
they had disappeared, Clarence enjoyed life—his life in the
sun, and, of course, in the shadow as soon as the sun became
too strong; that African shade which still has something of
the sun in it, which holds the scarcely-attenuated passion of
the sun, and is scarcely less gay and bright than the great sun
itself.

"I enjoy life . . ." thought Clarence. "If I filed my teeth
like the people of Aziana, no one could see any difference
between me and them." There was, of course, the difference
in pigmentation in the skin. But what difference did that
make? "It's the soul that matters," he kept telling himself.
"And in that respect I am exactly as they are." And was it
not better that way? Was it not far better than being Clarence? And that was why he was pursuing the downward path,
the one the people of Aziana preferred, though it was not his
own. But what exactly was "his" path?

"I have no particular path," he said.

He watched Akissi going to the fountain with her great
earthenware jar balanced on her head. It was Akissi all
right—that was the way she walked. No, Akissi simply
couldn't have a different way of walking every morning; it was
only at night that she changed character, when she would
come and place a sheaf of forest flowers beside their bed.

Then she had quite a different way of walking, she became another Akissi altogether. But as soon as she had moved round a little in the air of morning and breathed a little of the air of morning, as soon as she went to the fountain, she became once again the Akissi he had always known. "Do I myself walk in my accustomed fashion when I leave the hut after these terrible nights? I don't seem to walk in my usual way; I feel heavy, and as if I were drunk: I *am* drunk! I don't walk in my usual way, no more than Akissi does: I drag my feet, I drag myself along. It is only the air of morning that brings me to myself again."

"Here is water," said Akissi.

"I shall wash myself straight away," he said. "Get the stool."

He suddenly began to laugh.

"Would you believe it," he said, "I ran away from Adramé because some idiot or other wanted to take my underpants from me?"

"Why should you allow someone to steal what belongs to you?" she asked.

"You don't understand. I didn't give a fig for losing my underpants. But I didn't want to go stark naked."

"Well, you've certainly changed your tune!"

"I should never have thought it possible. I should never have come here if I had."

"It is better to wear a *boubou*," she said.

"Of course it's better. But *boubou* or no *boubou*, I find it no longer matters."

"If you weren't a white man . . ." she began.

"You mean I'm even blacker than the blacks? Go on, say it; I don't care."

"Why don't you care?"

"How should I know?" he said.

He was suddenly deep in thought. But one could not very well wash oneself and think properly at the same time. It was like rubbing one's forehead vertically with one hand and rubbing one's stomach horizontally with the other; the two movements were completely at variance.

"There's a time for everything," he went on. "A time to meditate and a time to wash oneself. A time to . . ."

Oh, there was time in plenty—there was plenty of that all right! The problem was what to do with it all. The whole of the morning would be wasted thinking up ways of passing the time, until, generally around noon, it became clear that none of these plans were workable.

"Have you got the calabashes put away in the hut?" he asked.

"They are right at the back."

"Then bring them out into the courtyard as soon as Baloum arrives," he said. "But you must not wait until I give the order; you must bring them without being told: Baloum must be made to feel that we appreciate his company. Do you think he'll be coming soon?"

"Doesn't he come every morning?"

"He's a real friend. If he were here, he'd wash my back for me. Not that I care much for his hands: they are too soft, too tender and too caressing, but you have to give him his due . . . Don't forget to bring the calabashes as soon as he arrives."

"I shall not forget."

Yes, Baloum was a trusty friend. And utterly devoted, too. As faithful as a pet dog and more utterly devoted to him than anyone he had ever known. If Clarence needed something— and one was always needing something or other—he had only to ask him for it, and he brought it along; or rather he had it brought along: he didn't like exerting himself. Oh, what a great fat lump he was!

"He never does a stroke of work," said Clarence.

"Who's that?" she asked. "Baloum? . . . You forget that his many appointments include the management of the harem."

"Oh, well, he doesn't lose much sleep over that!"

"I could do a job like that," he thought. "I could look after a dozen harems! Why shouldn't I be manager of the harem?"

"I could do his job for him," he said.

"You could not possibly do it."

"What do you mean, I couldn't do it? I don't see anything difficult about that sort of job."

"That's not the point. What is needed is . . . is the kind of man . . . But you must understand that when I say 'man,' it's just a manner of speaking, for in actual fact, what is needed is a man who is *not* a man; it must be someone in whom the naba can naturally have confidence . . . 'Naturally,' do you understand?"

"Is it the . . . the *you know what* you're talking about?"

"Yes," she said. "I mean the sort of man who would do no more than smack the backsides of the naba's wives."

She was drying him all over. Suddenly she laughed at the top of her voice.

"You are certainly not the sort of man who would be satisfied with smacking their backsides!" she said. "Here's your *boubou.*"

"No, give me my Sunday one," he said. "I'm hoping to obtain an audience with the naba."

"You can't do that. The master of ceremonies is in prison, and therefore there is no one to present your request."

"Oh? Did Baloum succeed in getting him locked up?"

"He is going to be tried shortly," she replied.

Well, wasn't that a way of passing the time? At least he wouldn't have to spend his time wondering how to get through the day as pleasantly as possible.

"Get my Sunday *boubou,*" he said. "I shall go and act as a witness at the trial."

"Baloum is the witness," she said.

"I, too, shall be a witness. The master of ceremonies didn't say anything very serious; a few irresponsible remarks, that was all."

"Baloum will do."

"But Baloum is the plaintiff."

"Exactly!"

"Oh! I'll bet it's going to be a real farce!"

"Isn't it always a farce?" she said.

Clarence seemed to see again the courtroom at Adramé and the old rogue of a judge crouching over his table and telling his beads. What a lot of balderdash he had talked!

"Give me my Sunday *boubou,*" he said. "I can't miss this."

"It is not a public trial," she said. "That would lower the tone. Of course everything is done as if the public were present; but in fact the public is not admitted. Only the naba and the highest dignitaries are present."

"The ones with the wagging beards?" he asked.

"All the ones with the wagging beards."

"Couldn't I wear a false beard?" he asked.

She burst out laughing again.

"I shouldn't like you with a beard," she said. She was still laughing her head off when Nagoa and Noaga arrived.

"Do you know what he said?" she asked the boys. "He said couldn't he wear a false beard!"

"I want to go to the trial," said Clarence.

"*You* can't go," said the boys.

"I've been trying to make him understand that for the last half-hour," said Akissi, "but he can't get it into his head."

"Go and get my Sunday *boubou,*" said Clarence. "If I can't go to the trial—which is still to be proved—there is nothing to stop me putting on my Sunday *boubou*. I suppose I may wear whatever I please?"

Akissi went to fetch the *boubou* from the hut.

"You'll be bored to death," said the boys.

"I'll be bored to death, will I?" thought Clarence. "But has there been a single day since I arrived in Aziana when I have *not* been bored to death?" Had there been a single day when he had not sat vainly waiting for the king to come and take his seat under the arcade? If he was going to be bored to death again today, it wouldn't make much difference.

"Why should I be bored to death?" he asked.

"Even if you are not bored to death, you will be worried about spoiling your best *boubou,*" said the boys.

"There are things more important than *boubous,*" said Clarence.

And he put on the *boubou* which Akissi had been holding above his head. It was a saffron-coloured *boubou* with a pattern of red roses, a real Sunday garment, garish and unpractical.

"Don't you go sitting down just anywhere in that *boubou!*" Akissi warned him.

And she unrolled a mat.

"Sit on this mat."

"I shall wait for Baloum," said Clarence, sitting down.

"Is he coming?" asked the boys.

"He always comes," said Akissi.

And then she gave them a broad wink. Then she went back into the hut to get her pestle and mortar.

"Bring out the calabashes," said Clarence. "Baloum won't
be long now."

"It's not absolutely necessary to wait for him before we
begin," said the boys. "Let us drink to his health."

"Do you think Baloum will get the better of the master of
ceremonies?" asked Clarence.

"He'll have his life," said Noaga.

"Indeed he will," said Nagoa. "The master of ceremonies
is a crafty man."

"But Baloum has grandpa's ear," said Noaga.

"Why may I not attend this trial?" asked Clarence.

"You know quite well why—you haven't got a beard,"
said Nagoa.

A beard? . . . Why should he have to have a beard, for
goodness' sake? As if it wasn't all a childish game anyhow,
the gruesome farce that was about to take place! Or as if
there were so many frivolous pleasures at Aziana that one
didn't know where to turn next! But nothing ever happened
here! Aziana was a forsaken hole, it was a desert! And now,
just when something was about to happen, the children were
forbidden to attend the performance!

"There is surely some way of getting in without being
seen," he said. "Now you two must surely know some way
of getting in without being seen. Two little scamps like
you!"

"We are two little scamps, as you say!" the boys laughed.

"Then why don't you take me?" went on Clarence.

"We cannot," said Nagoa. "If ever it were found out . . ."

"No one need ever know," said Clarence.

"But *you* will know," said Noaga.

"Of course!"

"And you will let it out," said Nagoa. "The first thing you
do will be to let it out."

"It's quite obvious that you simply don't know how to hold your tongue," said Noaga.

"I shall be as silent as the grave," said Clarence.

"You must not speak so lightly about the dead," the boys objected. "It is most imprudent."

"How shall I get them to take me?" Clarence wondered. "I shall give you my *boubou,*" he declared at last.

"Your Sunday *boubou?*" the two boys cried.

"Upon my word of honour, I'll give it to you. It's big enough for both of you to make a garment out of it."

The two boys thought hard for a moment. The *boubou* was hideous, but obviously they thought differently. They looked at it and then they looked at each other, looked at it again, then looked at each other, looked at it again, then looked at each other again. It was a real conflict of wills. Something like Virtue at war with Honour—the honour of wearing a fine *boubou,* of course.

"Come on, then," they said.

"Akissi, we're going across the square," cried Clarence. "Don't forget to put the calabashes away."

The two boys turned to the left of the naba's palace. Between the outer wall and the wall of the palace there was another wall, a wall whose presence it was difficult to detect unless one was right on top of it. The passage thus formed was of the narrowest conceivable; and it did not give them any cover, for both walls were ridiculously low. But a few yards farther on a flight of steps appeared which seemed to indicate that the stairs went far down, much lower than one would have expected in a land where architectural methods were not very far advanced. At the bottom of only a few steps, however, Clarence and the boys found themselves in an obscure tunnel which would have been pitch-dark if the numerous doors which here and there were let into the walls had not been set with frosted glass. This glass allowed an almost submarine light to filter through—the light from the lamps that were burning in the numerous cells whose presence was indicated by all these doors. The corridor recalled more or less the one in the palace of justice at Adramé.

"Haven't I been here before?" asked Clarence.

"Shush!" said the boys.

They were walking along quietly, with not a glance at the numerous doors they were passing. At the end, the corridor bifurcated. The two boys stopped. Obviously they were hesitating about which direction to take.

"Isn't one corridor just as good as another?" whispered Clarence.

He kept thinking of his flight through the palace of justice at Adramé, that endless flight which in the end had brought him back to the courtroom.

"Of course not!" exclaimed the boys. "Can't you hear something?"

Clarence listened. He seemed to hear, far away, voices raised in argument. But how could one tell whether these voices came from the left or from the right? They were so far away, so vague . . .

"I can't make out anything," said Clarence. "I can't catch what it is."

"There *is* another way," said the boys.

Whereupon one of them began to revolve so fast that his face was soon just a vague blur. Suddenly he dropped to the ground. His head pointed ever so slightly towards the right. It was not a very clear indication. Nevertheless it was the corridor on the right which they took. And apparently the indication was more exact than they had hoped, for suddenly the voices rang out loudly. Clarence discovered a tiny window in the left-hand wall: the voices were coming from there.

The window gave on to a courtroom similar in every way to the one at Adramé, and just as bare and ugly, just as dilapidated and pretentious. The master of ceremonies was speaking in a thunderous voice.

"I have revealed nothing that the white man did not already know!" he was shouting.

He was kneeling in front of the very same ceremonial chairs that Clarence had seen on the day of his arrival in Aziana. The same ossified old men with beards were occupying the chairs, sitting so motionlessly that one might easily have taken them for wax-works, had it not been for a certain brilliance of the eyes. The naba was enthroned in the centre, and his beard seemed to wag more despotically than ever. Baloum was seated behind the master of ceremonies.

"I can testify that the white man had no suspicion at all," cried Samba Baloum. "But I shouldn't like to say what he really thinks now."

"The white man is no fool," went on the master of ceremonies in a loud voice. "He is perfectly well aware of the difference between Akissi and the women of the harem who visit him during the night. Moreover, one has only to notice his embarrassment in public after these visits."

"I claim that the white man was never aware of anything," cried Samba Baloum.

"Liar!" the master of ceremonies howled.

"Liar yourself!" shouted Samba Baloum, kicking the master of ceremonies in the back of the neck. "I repeat that the white man was never aware of anything, and that he could not be aware of anything, for each woman, on entering his hut, placed a sheaf of forest flowers beside his bed; their odour filled the hut at once and rendered the white man unconscious."

"What on earth is he talking about?" Clarence asked the

boys. "He's telling a pack of lies! He won't have the master
of ceremonies' life if he goes on like that."

"Don't talk so loud," said Nagoa.

"I can't help myself," said Clarence. "It's really too stupid!"

"You'll be heard," said Noaga.

"I don't know why I have not been called as a witness,"
mumbled Clarence. "I could have warned Baloum not to go
about things in this stupid way."

He put his eye to the aperture again and heard the master
of ceremonies shouting at the top of his voice:

"What does it matter anyhow whether the white man
knows or does not know, now that all the women in the
harem have paid him a visit!"

"Wrong again!" shouted Baloum, pressing hard on the
master of ceremonies' neck with his foot. "There are several
women who still have to pay a visit to the white man; besides,
not all of those who have been to his bed are hoping for
a happy event yet. There is still a great deal to be done.
Now that the white man's suspicions are aroused, there's
no saying when the work will be brought to a satisfactory
conclusion."

"What a lot of silly lies!" Clarence told the boys. "I should
have thought Baloum had more sense than that. Why doesn't
he speak about the wine, instead of arguing about the nonsense the master of ceremonies talks? . . . And why are they
shouting their heads off like that? The naba isn't deaf, is he?
. . . Doesn't Baloum understand that he's playing into the
hands of the master of ceremonies?"

"Why can't you speak more softly?" the boys whispered.
"We'll be discovered if you go on like this."

They had no sooner said this than Clarence found he
couldn't hear another word of what was going on in the

courtroom. He could see Baloum gesticulating in his ponder-
ous fashion and the master of ceremonies raising his arms,
but he could not make out one word, not a single word. One
might have thought he was at least a thousand yards away
from the plaintiffs, and could only see them so close because
he was looking at them through a telescope, or because the
window was fitted with magnifying lenses. But perhaps the
window really was fitted with magnifying lenses? In any case,
it was glazed now, which it certainly had not been when
Clarence had first looked through it.

"What's happened?" he asked the boys.

"Can't you see they've shut the window?" the boys exclaimed. "They must have seen us. Quick! This way, quickly!
. . . They may fall upon us any moment now . . . Come on,
or we won't be responsible for what happens! . . ."

They made off; Clarence followed them. At the end of the
corridor there was a door which the boys, to save time,
opened by using their heads as battering-rams. Clarence had
a fleeting glimpse of a room no less encumbered with debris
and rubbish of all kinds than those at Adramé. The next door
opened on a room neither less derelict nor less wretched; and
those that followed were exactly the same. "Have I come
back to Adramé?" Clarence wondered. He had obviously
returned to Adramé, for the same heaps of dirt were scattered over the rooms he was passing through. "Or could it
be that the sordid justice of mankind can only be meted out
in foulness and filth?"

"Stop!" he cried suddenly. "I can't go on!"

And he collapsed on the ground.

"Get up!" the boys cried. "Get up, or you'll have us all in
court. We shall both be sorry for it, but you'll be sorry too
for what you've done. Can't you try to go a little farther?
We're not far from the way out."

Clarence got up and struggled on. If it had not been for the boys, he would have given up, for he did not believe they were any nearer to finding a way out, and he imagined from one moment to the next that he was going to find himself back where he started, in front of the tiny window. But they really were getting closer to the way out, for soon a less humid breath of air indicated the proximity of the outer world. Clarence hastened his steps. And suddenly he was out in the open air! The fugitives found themselves on a small terrace from which one could look out over a certain district in Aziana. Clarence recognised the district at once.

"You can get your breath now," said the boys. "We are out of reach of our pursuers."

They flopped down on the ground, and Clarence too flopped down beside them.

"Well!" said Clarence, when he had got his breath again, "I have never, no, never known anything quite so extraordinary! Yet the Lord knows the session in which I was cross-examined was extraordinary enough. But this surpasses anything I've ever known. They all seemed to have gone quite crazy . . ."

"The master of ceremonies is done for, all the same," said Noaga.

"Done for?" said Clarence. "You don't mean . . ."

"If you have the patience to wait, you'll hear him screaming soon."

"He was screaming quite hard enough, wasn't he?"

"Yes, but now he'll be screaming harder than ever."

"It's sheer spite that makes you talk like that," said Clarence. "If, on your return to Aziana, the master of ceremonies' stick hadn't raised a bump the size of a pigeon's egg on your head, you would not be speaking like that. You've got that egg on your mind too much."

"Noaga is right all the same," said Nagoa. "The master of ceremonies is done for."

"Done to a turn, you might say," said Samba Baloum, whose full-moon face was seen to rise over the edge of the terrace.

"Baloum!" cried Clarence.

He wanted to get up, but both boys gave him a dig with their elbows and knocked him back.

"Baloum," said Clarence, rather more calmly now, "what a pleasant surprise!"

"What are you doing here?" asked Samba Baloum.

"We came up here to get a breath of fresh air," said Clarence.

"On the terrace?" asked Samba Baloum.

"Yes," replied Clarence. "I thought that the higher we climbed the fresher the air would be. But it doesn't seem to have turned out that way."

"It's lucky for you that the terraces in Aziana are no higher than this," said Samba Baloum.

"Perhaps I am lucky that way," said Clarence.

"You're going to catch the sun here good and strong," said Samba Baloum. "Come and sit under the arcade."

They followed Samba Baloum from the terrace and from granary to granary until they reached the edge of a deep yard, a sort of bear-pit such as one might see in zoological gardens, only much larger. Of course, it could not be a bear-pit, but nevertheless that is what it made one think of, because whatever creatures, beasts or men, were put in it, would not have been able to devour the visitors or to escape.

"What yard is this?" said Clarence. "I've never seen this yard before."

"You're not supposed to see it either," said Samba Baloum. "It is the harem."

"The harem? Really?" said Clarence.

"Yes, the harem. But you must go very quickly. The naba doesn't like people to look into his harem."

"But aren't you looking into it?"

"I have special permission to do so."

"Don't you know that for Samba Baloum such an act is of no consequence at all?" cried the boys, bursting with laughter.

"You scamps!" said Samba Baloum.

"We're only repeating what you said yourself."

"But this is hardly the time and place to do so," said Samba Baloum reprovingly.

"Let me look in—just once," said Clarence.

"You may look for a second if you like," said Samba Baloum. "But only for a second. I don't want a quarrel with the naba."

Clarence looked down into the pit. At first it seemed empty, but now . . . was it because he was leaning right over, or because his eyes were no longer dazzled by the sun?—it seemed to him quite miraculously full of movement all of a sudden. In the shadow of the wall, there were a number of women, each one surrounded by a swarm of children; nearly all of them held in their arms or carried on their backs or in swaddling clothes much smaller children, whose café-au-lait complexions proclaimed them to be mulattos.

"Where do they come from, the little half-castes?" asked Clarence.

"They are not half-castes," said Samba Baloum.

"Then why have they got such light skins?"

"Many are born with that colour skin," said Samba Baloum. "It gets darker as they grow older."

"You mean they become as black as you?"

"Exactly! Come on, now, you've been looking at them for longer than a second."

"I'm only looking at the little half-castes," said Clarence.

"But I've told you they are *not* half-castes! Come on, let's go. Don't just stand there."

"How long does it take for them to turn black?"

"The sun turns them black. But come along now. I can't leave you here any longer."

"I'm coming," said Clarence. "I could have sworn that they were half-castes."

They went past several other courtyards, or several bear-pits, all of them serving such incomprehensible purposes that one might have imagined that they had been built for the pure pleasure of digging and constructing them. Then they entered a corridor whose walls were no less low and no less close together than the one which Clarence and the boys had entered at the beginning of their expedition. This corridor led them straight to the gallery. The naba was seated there with his dignitaries. As soon as he caught sight of Clarence he made a little sign with his beard as if in greeting.

"The show is about to begin," said Samba Baloum. "The naba wishes you to know that the spectacle is about to commence," he added unctuously.

"He just made a little sign with his beard," said Clarence.

"Precisely," said Samba Baloum. "For what he had to tell you could not be conveyed by any more expansive sign. But take a look to the right."

Clarence looked straight at the master of ceremonies. This unpleasant personage was stretched out with his face to the ground, and his hands and feet were tied to pegs. Now that he had been stripped of his *boubou*, he seemed longer and more angular than ever.

"What's happened to him?"

"Nothing—*yet,*" said Samba Baloum. "But he's done for, as you can see."

"He's going to be roasted," said the boys.

"You don't mean to say he's going to be roasted alive?" asked Clarence.

"Do you take us for cannibals?" said Samba Baloum. "No, only his skin will be cooked. The skin, and of course, a little more: an inch or two of the flesh underneath the skin."

On the square, a kind of uproar was suddenly heard. A great wave of heads came swarming over to the low palace wall and at every opening in the bamboo railings eyes shining with greed peered in.

"Let us be seated," said Samba Baloum. "We shall be able to see everything from here. We can see better from here than if we were under the arcade."

The naba wagged his beard. One of the dignitaries who was holding a stick left the group and walked over towards the master of ceremonies.

"Have you any calabashes left?" Samba Baloum asked.

"I told Akissi to bring them as soon as you arrived," said Clarence.

"Akissi!" cried Samba Baloum.

Akissi appeared with the calabashes.

"I was waiting until you had sat down," she said. "Drink as much as you like. The naba has had a fresh lot sent."

Samba Baloum raised his calabash in the direction of the master of ceremonies.

"Your good health!" he cried.

The master of ceremonies replied with a glance full of fury.

"Don't take it to heart," said Samba Baloum. "Your health is more precious to me than you might think. It is a guarantee of your powers of endurance."

The naba at that moment wagged his beard more energeti-

cally than he had done so until now. And the dignitary who
had crouched beside the master of ceremonies, as if in order
to see him better, rolled his eyes with cruel glee. At once the
stick came into play; it came whistling down on the master
of ceremonies' backside.

"It stings like mad," said Noaga. "It's the very stick that
belonged to the master of ceremonies."

"You ought to know all about that," said Nagoa.

"But I'm not going to be the only one to know all about
it!" replied Noaga. "Get that into your head, and get it firmly
imprinted, just as the master of ceremonies is getting it firmly
imprinted on his backside."

"It's not nice to take pleasure in another's misfortune,"
said Clarence.

"I don't seem to remember you sparing my feelings when
you joked about my bump!" said Noaga.

"The pigeon's egg," said Nagoa.

"You'd do better to watch what's going on, instead of
bringing up all that again," said Noaga.

The stick was coming down with such force and precision
that the master of ceremonies could not help groaning. All
along the outer wall, the people were getting noisier and
noisier. They had greeted the first sharp strokes with the
same indifference as the master of ceremonies. But now they
were roused, though one could hardly tell whether it was
intense pleasure or extreme pity that prompted their shouts.
But soon it became apparent that they were prompted by
pleasure alone, for short bursts of laughter kept breaking out.

"They're enjoying themselves too," said Noaga.

"There aren't many distractions in Aziana," said Samba
Baloum, shrugging his shoulders slightly.

"But that does not necessarily mean the master of ceremonies agrees with you," said Clarence.

He did not feel that the pitiful spectacle, given at the expense of the master of ceremonies, and of his backside, was a fit subject for laughter, and he felt the master of ceremonies could hardly be taking much pleasure in it.

"Well, now that's where you're wrong," said Samba Baloum. "The master of ceremonies is of exactly the same mind as myself. Is it not his job to organise the public spectacles?"

"You're joking," said Clarence.

"I can assure you that that stick is no joke," replied Baloum.

"That's what I was telling you."

"Well, then, we're in agreement," said Samba Baloum. He cackled faintly and raised his calabash to his lips.

"*Tan!*" exclaimed the dignitary who was wielding the stick.

"What did he say?" asked Clarence.

"He said '*ten.*' But don't worry, it's just the beginning: he can do wonders with that rod. You can look on all this as a mere hors-d'oeuvre; when the feast begins . . ."

He stopped to spit on the master of ceremonies' backside.

"What are you doing?" asked Clarence.

"It will cool him down," said Samba Baloum. "The stick warms his behind, and I cool it down."

He began cackling gently again. Behind the wall, other mouths were opened to spit at the master of ceremonies' well-basted buttocks.

"They shouldn't do that," said Clarence.

"But it cools him down, after all!" said Noaga.

And he spat in his turn.

"Well, I don't like that sort of thing," said Clarence.

Every time the rod landed on his behind, the master of ceremonies rose in the air like a fish jumping; but that was all he could do, because the four pegs prevented him from jumping any higher.

"That man is suffering," said Clarence.

"Well, you couldn't very well say he was dancing for joy," said Noaga.

"Noaga, I should never have thought it of you," said Clarence. "I tell you that this man is suffering, and that you ought to have pity on him. And you laugh, you have the nerve to laugh!"

"Was the master of ceremonies weeping his eyes out when he laid the egg?" asked Noaga bitterly.

The fact is, he was laughing, or at any rate smiling broadly. Clarence remembered quite clearly his cruelly sharpened teeth. But perhaps it was just the teeth, perhaps . . .

"Mouan!" exclaimed the dignitary who was laying on the rod.

"Twenty!" translated Samba Baloum. "Just a trifle!"

"When does it become something more than a trifle?" asked Clarence.

"I don't know," said Samba Baloum. "At thirty, at forty perhaps . . . The master of ceremonies is a hard nut to crack."

"You don't mean to say that he will get twice as much as he has already?" cried Clarence. "He would never stand it."

"He can stand a great deal," said Samba Baloum. "You have no idea just how much a man *can* stand. The master of ceremonies is in excellent health. Just now, remember, we drank to his health. He is very thin, but . . ."

"But his backside's beginning to swell already," said Noaga.

"His backside has taken a lot of punishment and has swollen considerably," said Nagoa.

Under the gallery, a second dignitary got up and came over to the one who was manipulating the rod in such a sprightly fashion.

"What is he saying?" asked Clarence.

"He's telling him to lay it on a little harder over the left buttock," said Samba Baloum. "The naba is of the opinion that the left must not be cheated in favour of the right."

"Tell the naba that this man's had enough."

"I cannot," said Samba Baloum. "The naba is a just man."

"All the more reason then for speaking to him. The naba cannot be such a cruel man."

"But he is not cruel at all. He is just! He does not wish the right buttock to suffer at the expense of the left."

"It's downright cruelty," said Clarence.

"Maybe it *is* cruelty, but it is justice too."

"You call that justice?"

"I am no judge," said Samba Baloum. "I am the manager of the harem. But just men call this justice. Is it my fault if just men have so much inventiveness?"

"Tan saba!" exclaimed the dignitary with the stick.

"Thirty!" said Samba Baloum. "Thirty already!"

"This is going to be good," said Noaga.

He spat on the backside of the master of ceremonies.

"I'm not staying here," said Clarence.

"Wait a little longer," said Samba Baloum. "The best part's still to come."

"No," said Clarence, "I'm going."

He looked at the inflamed and swollen backside of the master of ceremonies; the skin would soon be starting to split. And then . . .

"It's disgraceful!" he said. "And it's you, Baloum, you and no one else, who are the cause of it!"

"Me?" said Samba Baloum.

"Yes, you!" cried Clarence. "You and your idiotic accusations!"

But the boys were digging him in the ribs with their elbows. "Must I really hold my tongue?" Clarence wondered.

"I can't stand it any longer." He could hear the shrieks
uttered by the master of ceremonies, shrieks which were
becoming shriller and shriller. It would certainly not be long
before blood was drawn. Perhaps they stopped then? No,
nothing would stop them—they were nothing but savages
. . . Clarence got up.

"You're not going away just when the nicest part is about
to begin?" protested Samba Baloum.

"I'm going."

"*Do* stay! I'll request an audience with the naba for you."

"You're a good sort, Baloum," said Clarence. "You're a bit
slow, but you're a good sort. Tell the naba this man's had
enough."

He sat down again.

"Don't stir from here. I'm going to speak to the naba
straight away."

He pulled a face and struggled to his feet; then he spat
copiously on the backside of the master of ceremonies.

"They have swollen to enormous proportions," he said
meditatively.

"Hurry!" urged Clarence.

"Don't move from here," said Samba Baloum. "I'm
going."

Taking small, tripping steps, he walked over towards the
arcade and prostrated himself in front of the naba who, with
a wag of his beard, signalled to him to draw near. Samba
Baloum sat down beside him. But the rod kept whistling
down, each stroke ending in an agonised scream from the
master of ceremonies.

"Do you think they'll take a long time to decide?" said
Noaga.

"They won't do it in five minutes," said Nagoa. "You have

to allow plenty of time for an exchange of flowery compliments."

"But do you think they'll take a *very* long time?" asked Noaga.

"If it lasts any longer," said Clarence, "that backside is going to split open and start bleeding. It's tight as a drum already and . . ."

"But of course it's going to bleed!" said Noaga.

"So you're just waiting for that?" Clarence cried. "In that case . . ."

Again he rose to his feet. Samba Baloum made a soothing gesture towards him with his hands, as if to say that all was going as well as could be expected and that the best thing for Clarence to do was to sit still. Then the great fat lump began whispering urgently in the naba's ear again. Clarence sat down again. What could he do? "Savages!" he muttered to himself. But he would just have to wait; there wasn't anything else he could do. Even if Clarence went away now, the rod would go on whistling down with undiminished ferocity on those grossly swollen buttocks; on the contrary, if he remained where he was perhaps the naba would decide to put an end to the torture.

"A little wine?" Noaga suggested.

"No," said Clarence. "I don't feel like drinking."

"Don't forget, you promised us your *boubou*," said Nagoa.

"I won't forget."

"Have some wine," said Noaga. "Then you can spit a mouthful over the backside of the master of ceremonies."

"What do you take me for?" cried Clarence.

"Have you no pity?" replied Noaga. "A good mouthful of palm wine would help to cool off the master of ceremonies' burning cheeks."

Clarence took a mouthful of wine, but swallowed it almost at once.

"No, I couldn't do it," he said.

"You are completely without pity," said Noaga. "You take a mouthful and swallow it; you swallow it, when the master of ceremonies' cheeks are burning and inflamed and swollen to bursting point. And you have the nerve to call me heartless! Just look how enormous that behind has grown! . . . It's easily twice its original size."

Fortunately Samba Baloum was coming back, and Clarence did not have to look again at the frightful backside of the master of ceremonies. Samba Baloum bent over the dignitary who was wielding the stick and the strokes stopped.

"The naba, at your request, has decided to interrupt the display," Samba Baloum told Clarence. "But believe me the people of Aziana won't like it. You've offended their sense of justice."

"Hah!" Clarence scornfully replied.

They had untied the master of ceremonies and had raised him to his feet. Perhaps it would have been better if they had left him lying on the ground. The unfortunate man could hardly put one foot in front of the other and it was only with the greatest difficulty that he managed to stand upright. The dignitary had to hold him up.

"He must have received at least fifty strokes," said Noaga.

"He's more dead than alive," said Clarence indignantly.

"Nonsense!" said Nagoa. "He'll find it rather painful to sit down, at the very worst."

"Let him stand up!" said Noaga. "A master of ceremonies doesn't need to be sitting down all the time."

"What he *does* need," said Samba Baloum, "is a good cold compress on his backside."

The master of ceremonies and the dignitary had at last

reached the arcade. One by one, as if regretfully, the heads had disappeared from above the outer wall.

"They're certainly far from being pleased," said Nagoa, eyeing the crowd on the square.

"They are just men," said Samba Baloum.

"That is why they are looking so ugly," said Noaga.

"Let them!" cried Clarence. "I don't care how ugly they look!"

"But they cared very much about what happened to the master of ceremonies' backside," said Samba Baloum.

"Well, you can take it from me, Samba Baloum, these 'just' men's faces and the backside of the master of ceremonies look exactly alike to me. I wasn't able to bring myself to spit on the backside of the master of ceremonies, but I could certainly bring myself to spit on the faces of these 'just' men!"

"Don't get worked up," said Samba Baloum. "It's not worth getting worked up about a pair of buttocks, or about any number of buttocks for that matter, even if, as in every crowd that is roused by a sense of justice, there's more than a baker's dozen. It's just not worth it!"

"Anyhow, don't forget about your *boubou!*" the boys said. Clarence pulled his *boubou* over his head.

"What are you doing?" asked Samba Baloum.

"I promised them my best Sunday *boubou*," said Clarence.

"But you can't let the naba see you naked! It's not done!"

"Then he'll have to give me another *boubou*," said Clarence. "I can't bear the sight of this one any longer. These red roses on their saffron background turn my stomach."

"You've certainly had me on the hop to-day!" exclaimed Samba Baloum. "You can believe me or you can believe me not—I'm done up!"

He walked nonchalantly over to the gallery and began

whispering in the naba's ear again. He spoke to him for quite a long time; it seemed that the naba was reluctant to grant his request. Finally the beard gave an affirmative wag. Samba Baloum signed to Clarence to draw near.

"The naba wishes to know whether a green *boubou* with a pattern of pink flowers would meet your requirements," he said.

"With pink flowers?" said Clarence. "What does he take me for—a parakeet?"

"You know quite well he takes you for a fighting-cock," said Samba Baloum reprovingly. "There was no need to take all your clothes off in order to remind him of that."

"I want a green *boubou* with a pattern of white flowers," said Clarence.

"With a pattern of white flowers?" said Baloum. He seemed to be thinking it over. "I don't think that would really suit you," he said. "I don't think it would look nice."

"Who's going to wear it—you or me?" cried Clarence.

"Well, *I* shall have to look at it," said Samba Baloum in a pained voice. And he heaved a protracted sigh. "The white man desires a pattern of white flowers," he announced to the naba.

The naba wagged his beard, and the dignitaries arose. At a fresh sign from the naba, they went to the main building and returned a little later with a lot of chests. They were of all ages and sizes, from the humble tin trunk of a colonial officer exiled in the bush to metal-bound teak chests, the sort that are usually full of pirate gold. The naba handed his bunch of keys to Samba Baloum.

"Let them be opened!" he announced with great solemnity.

The first chests that Samba Baloum opened were full of rats.

"Fine lot of treasure you have there!" said Clarence.

"Don't be so sharp!" said Samba Baloum, flapping a hand at Clarence.

"You know quite well I can't go on standing naked in front of the naba," said Clarence.

"Well, I'm glad you've realized it at last," said Samba Baloum.

He opened a chest which was full to overflowing, and there were no rats inside.

"Look right at the bottom," said one of the dignitaries. Samba Baloum plunged his hands right down to the bottom of the chest and pulled out, with a double grimace—one for the effort he was making, and another for what his hands had brought up—a green *boubou* patterned with white flowers.

"Is that what you want?" he asked Clarence, haughtily.

"That's the very thing," replied Clarence.

Whereupon the naba rose to his feet and departed, followed by the dignitaries carrying the chests.

"What awful taste you have!" said Samba Baloum, going to join the boys.

"I'm not as vulgar as a parakeet in my choice of colours, anyhow," retorted Clarence.

"Stop talking about parakeets," cried Samba Baloum pettishly. "I can't abide those birds!"

"Didn't you know he only likes cocks?" cried the boys.

They were rapturously cutting up the saffron *boubou*, following the outline of the red roses. When they had finished cutting it up, each one draped himself in a piece.

"You look frightful," said Clarence. "I just can't tell you how frightful you look! . . . Akissi!" he shouted, "come and sew up their *boubous* for these two little scamps!"

Akissi came and plied her needle.

"What did the naba say?" she asked.

"He can only talk with his beard," said Clarence. "I should very much like to know what all those chin-wags mean."

"He expresses himself with perfect clarity," said Samba Baloum. "You could see that by the way he stopped the beating. No, it's not all make-believe, as you imagine. I wish I were half so good at it: because it's not at all tiring."

"What a great fat lazy lump you are!" said Clarence.

"Haven't I been running around after you all day long?"

"But you only did so in order to do the master of ceremonies a bad turn."

"A bad turn, you call it? . . . You wait, he'll be strutting around, proud as a peacock with a compress on his behind!"

"He won't be able to strut very far."

"If you hadn't interrupted the display, he wouldn't be able to walk at all," said Samba Baloum.

"People weren't at all pleased," said Akissi.

"I don't care about people!" said Clarence.

"That was no reason for taking off your *boubou* and exhibiting your nakedness to everybody."

"That's right," said Samba Baloum. "It was the master of ceremonies' backside people wanted to see, not your . . ."

And he began to cackle.

"Here are your *boubous*," Akissi told the boys. "They are rather skimpy, but that's the way you cut them."

Nagoa and Noaga took off their loin-cloths.

"What a pair of chickens!" said Samba Baloum.

"Just you wait, Samba Baloum," said the boys. "One day, the chickens will be cocks and will give you more than you bargained for."

"If I catch you hanging round the harem . . ." said Samba Baloum threateningly.

The two boys slipped on their *boubous*, then looked at one

another as if they had been looking at themselves in a mirror; then they put out their tongues and burst out laughing.

"We're off to see Fatou," they cried.

"Very well, but look out, I'm warning you!" said Samba Baloum, giving their backsides a couple of possessive smacks.

And the two boys strutted proudly away.

3

THE FISH-WOMEN

"Akissi!" Clarence shouted. "Akissi, get up!"

He was at the doorway of the hut. His head felt horribly heavy and his body odiously sticky; his whole body—nose, mouth, eyes—the eyes particularly—and also, inside his body, his lungs, belly and everything the odour found no difficulty in reaching as well as everything it could reach only by devious means—his heart, muscles, veins, the very blood in his veins—all this was heavy and sticky, glutinous and turgid, and as if made of lead. It all seemed pasted together by the odour, and his brain felt tackier than all the rest.

"Akissi, come to the window."

He had managed to totter to the door. Still tottering, he made his way outside and round to the porthole-window. The air of dawn was making him shiver. He had a vague idea that the cool air was scraping patches of odour from his contaminated skin; but the patches were as small and tenacious as flakes of dandruff. He was so slimed over with the odour— had it ever been as bad as this?—that the morning air was unable to wash him clean.

"Akissi, I told you to come and stand at the window!"

But there was no answering voice from within.

"Have I to come and fetch you?" he cried.

He had shouted this as if he were not already angry with her, as if, since nightfall, he had ceased to be angry with her. It was those flowers, always those flowers, those flowers beside the bed! Had he not expressly forbidden her to put any more flowers in his hut! Well, Akissi did not take the slightest notice of him. But what pleasure could she have in smelling those flowers, breathing in their poisonous miasma? Oh! those flowers! And that habit she had of putting them right beside the bed! One day . . . One day they would neither of them wake up. They would be found asphyxiated in their beds.

And then there was the master of ceremonies who kept on coming in, under cover of darkness; who took advantage of the deep sleep brought on by the odour of the flowers to creep into the hut and spy on him. "Akissi? . . . Is Akissi here again?" the master of ceremonies would cry. "But look here, this is at least the twentieth time she has visited your bed to-night! . . . You're not going to try to make out that she's unfaithful to you now, are you?" And his lips would be bared on his cruel teeth; his lips would twist into a cruel and mocking smile; his lips were always a denial of the integrity by which he set such store. "Hold your Akissi tightly in your arms, Clarence. Hold her tightly, or she will slip away from you again. Oh, not for long, of course. Just long enough to go and then to come back." And then, probably because Clarence would tell him to leave the hut, because Clarence would curse him and want to know what right the master of ceremonies had to enter his hut, he would cry: "But Clarence, take a good look at her, take a good look at your Akissi . . . Lord! what a changeable woman you have there! Never the same, is she? . . . Oh, you're a lucky man!" And his smile would grow wider and turn into a really wicked grin, a wicked and insulting leer. You would think his sharpened teeth were tearing the laughter to pieces as it left his throat.

Finally it had been too much for him: Clarence had not been able to bear that cruel, mocking laugh any longer. He had picked up a stick that was lying near at hand, perhaps the very stick used by the master of ceremonies, and he had turned on the odious fellow. He hadn't bargained for this, and had left the hut in great haste. That should have been enough, one might think. But Clarence was too annoyed to let it rest there; his patience was at an end—it was extraordinary how he had kept it so long—and he had run under the arcade after the master of ceremonies, had chased him and hounded him down, had rained terrible blows, most of which unfortunately had missed their mark. And in this way he had rushed through several courtyards before his fury had abated. Then suddenly the master of ceremonies had vanished.

But Clarence had not given up the chase. He had crossed still more courtyards, all curiously lighted, with one bright light at the centre, leaving the edges in darkness, as if the light—but where did the light come from?—had suddenly grown weaker and unable to reveal anything of what lay in the shadows. After having dashed through several courtyards

like this, without encountering a living soul—at least, in the
lighted part of them, because one could not tell whether the
master of ceremonies was in hiding at the side of the courtyards or not—Clarence found he was lost.

In fact, he must already have been lost for quite a while
in this labyrinth of deserted, or supposedly deserted courtyards. But it was some time before he suddenly realised this.
And as he was looking for someone to show him the way, he
had suddenly seen a great crowd of women, who had hitherto
been hidden by the shadows, rushing towards him, crying:
"Clarence! . . . Clarence!" Then each one had presented him
with a little half-caste child. "Say hallo to your son!" they
kept crying. There was such an uproar and so much confusion that in the end Clarence had been completely swamped,
for all round him there was nothing but waving arms and
brawling brats.

Then he had woken up and smelt the abominable odour
of the forest flowers. It had been a silly dream! . . . But he
had not looked upon it in that light at first; and even now,
even in the cool air of dawn, there were still moments when
he wondered whether he had really dreamed it or whether
the master of ceremonies had really come to pester him in his
hut. And certainly as soon as he had wakened up he had only
thought at first of settling his account with the master of
ceremonies, as if this malevolent being had deliberately in-
cited that crowd of women and half-caste children. It was
only when he had reached the door of the hut and had taken
a breath of fresh air that Clarence had realised that it had
all been a dream. But almost immediately afterwards everything had once more become confused and muddled in his
brain; the odour of the flowers had made everything confused
and muddled again: it was all topsy-turvy—the innumerable
visits he had received, or was supposed to have received, the

insinuations of the master of ceremonies, the half-caste brats, the women's insulting shouts, and Akissi's comings and goings. Was it not extraordinary the way Akissi kept coming and going? Wasn't it rather suspicious?

"Akissi!" he shouted again.

Seeing that she persisted in her obstinate refusal to speak or come to the door, he decided to go and drag her from the bed. He did not accuse her of anything—at least not yet—but he suspected her; his dream was still too fresh in his mind and his eyes still too full of sleep for him not to suspect her. He wished she would come and show her face at the window; then he would know for sure if the woman who had shared his bed was really Akissi or . . . He felt his face grow red with rage.

"No, don't you get the idea you can make fun of me!" he growled.

He went back to the door of the hut. He was not staggering now; if his mind was still rather fogged and full of shadows, his legs at any rate had become steadier. But as soon as he got inside the hut the odour overpowered him again, and he toppled over the bed.

"Well, you see what happens when you don't answer me and don't get up when I tell you," he said. "Have I hurt you?"

But he received no better answer than before. At last he began to wonder about the silence. He groped around for a while—rather a long while, for his fingers encountered nothing but the rough material of the bedclothes. He finally grasped the fact that the bed was empty.

"Akissi!" he cried in a strangled voice.

The silence suddenly became very oppressive; its weight lay upon him like a dense mass . . . Clarence still did not quite realise what was happening to him; but this dense mass that weighed now upon his heart was more persuasive than any argument . . . Akissi was not in the bed and she was not in the hut either.

Clarence wanted to get up but he was lying full length across the bed and his head was practically lying in the flowers, getting the full force of their peculiar odour . . . For a moment he wondered if it were not the odour that had taken Akissi away from him . . . He made another effort, and this time succeeded in sitting up. At the same time, he felt as if he were in the presence of a stranger. Could it be Akissi, playing hide and seek?

"Akissi, don't play around like this," Clarence said. "It's gone beyond a joke. Don't you understand—this is no joking matter?"

He tried to peer through the darkness inside the hut; it was not Akissi he saw: what he saw, or imagined he saw, was the smile of the master of ceremonies—a smile that was curiously, incomprehensibly detached from the rest of his face: that cruel smile, perhaps more mocking than cruel; the tightly-stretched lips, rather drawn back, or drawn back too much from the pointed, too-pointed teeth. Just those lips, just those teeth could be seen, as if the darkness or the semi-darkness of the hut—for the sun was now rising—had devoured the rest of the face.

Then, very distinctly, Clarence heard words coming from those strange lips. "What's your little game?" they were saying. And because Clarence was silent, probably because the terror that froze his heart prevented him from uttering a word, the voice went on: "You're not silly, Clarence. You know quite well the difference between Akissi and the women of the harem who visit you during the night . . . Come on, admit it! Stop putting on this act which deceives no one! . . . What else can you do now but confess? . . . All those little

half-caste brats in the courtyard of the harem didn't just
drop from the clouds!"

Then Clarence was again convulsed with fury. Terror had
made him freeze, but now anger made him jump into action.
He gave the mouth a punch with his fist; he punched it with
all the strength he could summon. He would have liked to
pound those lips and smash those teeth. But his fist met
nothing, nothing but air. Carried away by the force of his
projected blow, Clarence lost his balance and fell down by
the side of his bed.

His anger left him as soon as he touched the ground, and
fear suddenly got the upper hand again. He got up quickly,
and, pressing his hands against the walls, moved towards the
doorway. He would have liked to run; he wished he could
have got to the door in one big leap. But he went forward
as if he were crawling through a bog. He was crawling
through the odour, and it was as if his feet were being trapped
in its terrible glue—his feet were stumbling against roots and
catching in grasses. For a moment he wondered whether he
would ever reach the door . . . When at last he reached it,
he slithered down the jamb of the door; he was at the end
of his tether. He felt drained and weak, and he was shaking.

He lay there shaking a long time. The air was cool, chill
enough to make him shiver—never had the morning air appeared so chill—but it was something else that was making
him tremble: it was all this double-dealing he had been let in
for. And he was in it up to his neck. No, up to the eyebrows.

Suddenly he caught sight of Akissi. She was running. At
first he did not know whether to be happy or sad at seeing
her; he felt he ought to be sad, but perhaps all the time he
was hoping against hope.

"Here I am," she said.

"Where have you been?" he asked. "Didn't you hear me when I told you to come and stand at the window?"

"I went out for a moment," she replied. "I went to see the naba's manager."

"There was no need for you to go out so early," he said. "I called you I don't know how many times."

"I heard you quite well," she said, "but we had no millet."

"Then why did you not answer me? I shouted loud enough for you to hear me." He saw she was panting. "You've been running," he said.

"I hurried over," she replied.

"How did you manage to hear me, if you were in the manager's office?"

"Well, you were shouting so loud I couldn't help hearing." She was still panting.

"Why did you have to run so far?" he asked. "There is a millet granary next to the palace."

"I did not go far," she answered. "But I thought you might be getting impatient, and so I ran hard."

He knew that she was lying and he thought it would not be very difficult to catch her out. She had her answers all ready, but they were not convincing. When had she started lying to him? Lord knows how long she had been telling lies! She seemed to think that as long as you are taken by surprise you can cover up a lie; but everything she said gave her away. If he had pressed her . . . But what was the use? Would he have discovered anything more, and would her discomfiture have been any greater? . . . He pretended not to have noticed anything and sat down in front of his hut.

"I shall fetch you your *boubou* and then go for water," she said.

He did not reply; he could not have replied. When he had

left the hut for the second time, the sun had been aiming its first bright shaft at the departing night, but now its rays illuminated everything clearly. In Clarence's mind, too, and in his own dark night there had been a first shaft of light—it had wounded him. But then everything had become clear, everything had become violently and cruelly clear. Clarence was now perfectly aware that he had been dreaming; but he could also see now that his dream was true, and that the master of ceremonies had spoken the truth. All the things which until now had never made any impression on him, which had left him as cold as marble, now forced themselves upon his consciousness, and fell like an avalanche about his head. He was literally annihilated.

"Here is your *boubou*," Akissi said. "I am going for water."

"Throw the flowers out on the square as you go," he said.

"What flowers?" she asked. "I have not seen any flowers."

"Can't you smell the odour?"

"I can assure you, there are no flowers here," she said. "Come and see for yourself."

He got up, but sat down again straight away; if there were no flowers, it was because they had been taken away, and so it was useless to go and see if they were there. Clarence had made quite a big enough fool of himself already.

"Go and get water," he said.

She went to the fountain. When she came back, Clarence was leaving the hut. He had not found any flowers there, but the odour still lingered by the side of the bed. He would have liked to know at what moment the flowers had been taken away. When he had come back into the hut to drag Akissi from her bed, it had seemed to him that the flowers were still there. Or was it that the odour had not had time to clear away? . . . No. Someone must at that moment have slipped

into the hut and taken the flowers away. Oh! they spared no
pains in trying to hoodwink him! They were all in league,
they were all plotting against him . . .

"Will you get washed now?" she asked.

"I shall wash at the fountain," he replied.

"It would be more convenient for you here."

"Do you think so?" he asked. "Do you think fewer people
go by here than at the fountain?"

He had to restrain himself from telling her that as many
people could be seen round the hut at night as by day.

"I shall put the jar in a cool place," she said. "When you
have made your mind up, come and tell me."

She went to get the pestle and mortar; and the rhythm of
the pestle was heard again, like a ceaseless chant. "A chant!"
thought Clarence bitterly. He sneered. "That dull, monoto-
nous sound—is that what they call a chant, that stupid
thumping?" He got up and went over to the fountain. He
very rarely went there; he preferred to wash in front of his
hut. But a feeling which he could not quite fathom had
prevented him from washing himself in front of Akissi; and
now the sound of the pestle pounding the mortar had made
his mind up. It was really too silly, to sit there and listen to
the noise of the pounding pestle!

At this early hour, there were few people on the streets of
Aziana. There were people yawning on their door-steps, and
from time to time a woman would go by with a large earthenware jar on her head. But there was already a crowd round
the fountain. A joyfully talkative crowd composed of women
who were waiting their turn to draw water and who were
passing the time gossiping. A little to one side of the fountain
there were men standing in the stream who were washing
themselves and playfully splashing each other, giving each

other resounding smacks on the backside and suddenly stopping to shout absurd and witty remarks to the women higher
up.

Clarence began to take off his *boubou* before joining the
bathers; but all of a sudden something stopped him. At first
it was just an imperceptible hesitation, but which turned to
a definite reluctance to take his *boubou* off. No, he could not
possibly strip himself naked in front of all these people; not,
at any rate, in front of all these women who were waiting
their turn at the fountain. Of course, he had done it before—
on previous occasions he had displayed his nakedness to all
and sundry without the slightest feeling of embarrassment.
But now? . . . No, things were different now; perhaps they
had never been any different: but Clarence had loyally held
to the belief that they were. And in return . . . he had been
laughed at for his artless simplicity. "I shall begin by getting
rid of Akissi," he told himself. "I won't have a lying slut like
that in my house . . . I shall request her to take her pestle
and mortar elsewhere. I've had enough of this lark!"

This decision gave him some relief, but he felt he would
leave it until later; he did not feel in the humour for going
back to the hut just now and having to listen to a fresh lot
of lies or the inevitable lamentations that always followed.
"Inevitable?" The word seemed almost too inadequate to
express what he felt about those lamentations. He began to
roam the streets in an aimless fashion. "This day," he
thought, "is going to be worse than any other day I've ever
known." He would have liked never to see another living
soul, to go away into the desert where no one could bother
him—especially Akissi, Baloum and the two boys who were
all hand in glove with one another, telling him lies and trying
to hoodwink him; they were all so kind, but now he had got
the measure of that kindness.

Only instead of finding himself a retreat, in the end he
went to see Diallo, the blacksmith; either because he just
happened to walk that way, or because he felt a vague longing to unburden himself and have someone commiserate with
him. He went there as if he had never declared, only a few
moments ago, that he did not want to see another living soul.
He found Diallo lighting his forge.

"Fine day," remarked Diallo.

"It's going to be very fine," said Clarence.

"Smoke's rising straight in the air," said Diallo.

He pointed to the smoke which in fact was rising into the
deep-blue air without a single twist or turn. The apprentices
were crouching beside the forge ready to blow through the
tue-irons.

"You're up early," said Diallo.

"I always rise at dawn," replied Clarence.

"Oh!" said Diallo, casting a swift glance at his visitor.

"Does that surprise you?" asked Clarence.

"No," said Diallo.

"Oh," said Clarence, "I thought you looked surprised.
Getting up at dawn can cause trouble; you find out things
you aren't supposed to know . . . Is that what you meant?"

"I didn't say anything like that. All I meant was that the
early hours of the morning are always the best."

"Sometimes," said Clarence. "Sometimes not. Don't you
agree?"

But Diallo did not seem to have been listening. He had
placed a piece of iron in the furnace and was watching it
intently. The fire round the iron flared up, the flames turned
blue and finally flickered all over the metal, which became
red and then white—the incandescent whiteness of the sun.
Then Diallo leapt into activity; he seized the iron tongs and
threw it on the anvil. Then he set to work on it with tremen-

dous hammer-blows. So even if he had heard Clarence's question, he had also avoided giving a reply—an escapade like the one in which the master of ceremonies had been involved had demonstrated to all the virtue of discretion.

"What are you making?" Clarence asked.

"An axe," Diallo replied.

Sparks were flying under the hammer. There was a smell of flint and iron.

"That 'do' didn't last very long yesterday," said Diallo.

"It lasted quite long enough," retorted Clarence. "If I had had any say in the matter, it would never have taken place."

"Was it you who asked for it to be stopped?"

"I couldn't bear the sight of it any longer."

"Why?" said Diallo. "Everybody was having a good time, weren't they?"

"It was sheer cruelty! I don't think I have ever seen anything quite so cruel."

"Would you say it was cruel of me to beat this piece of iron?" Diallo asked scornfully.

And he put the piece of iron, which had begun to cool, back into the forge. The apprentices started to blow through the tue-irons again.

"You shouldn't have stopped the display," said Diallo.

"But can't you see that the master of ceremonies' backside is not a piece of red-hot iron?"

"Well, everyone can see that. But the master of ceremonies well deserved the spanking he got. He was having some sense knocked into him, and they were dealing with his backside as I deal with iron on the anvil."

"And what if he had only been speaking the truth?" Clarence demanded.

"It's not always nice to tell the truth."

"But the truth is always worth hearing."

"It's neither worth speaking nor hearing," said Diallo.

He had pulled the iron out of the fire and now was hammering it with sharp little blows.

"Surely you haven't reached your present age," he went on, "without knowing that certain things are better left unsaid?"

"He's right," thought Clarence. "In a way he's right. If I had not heard the home-truths which the master of ceremonies dinned into my ears, I should not have lost my temper. But now, unfortunately, it is too late to go back."

"Truth," Diallo continued, "is something which must be handled with even greater precautions than a piece of white-hot iron. However careful you are, you get scorched, and you burn much more than the tips of your fingers. So I . . ."

But he did not finish his sentence, either because he felt that the tales he could have told on this subject were quite insignificant, or because they would have taken too long to tell.

"Your request," he added, "cannot have pleased the naba very much."

"What do you know about it? As soon as I'd made the request, the naba decreed that I should have a new *boubou*."

"Exactly! A green *boubou* with white flowers!"

"That is the kind I asked for."

"Not really?" said Diallo.

He looked at Clarence and forgot to go on hammering, he was so startled.

"I could have had a *boubou* with a pattern of red flowers on it," said Clarence, "but I didn't want to go round looking like a parakeet."

"A parakeet!" Diallo cried. "What *are* you talking about? Where would you ever see a parakeet that would dress itself up in a *boubou* patterned with red flowers, not to mention *white* flowers, which would be even worse? Everything you tell me convinces me that the naba was not pleased with you. He does not give things away lightly—remember that. He would no sooner give away a *boubou* with white flowers, which he detests, than a *boubou* with red flowers, which he hates just as much. If he decided to give you a *boubou*, it's because he entertains certain thoughts about you which weighed more strongly with him than his own avarice."

"For a man who is tight-fisted," said Clarence, "he was extremely generous in the number of strokes he gave the master of ceremonies."

"He is a man of principle," said Diallo. "He's famous not for his open-handedness, but for his firmness."

"Yes, a man of principle, a man who has his ministers beaten within an inch of their lives, and, as Baloum would say, a just man . . . Well, Diallo, that's the sort of rogue I abominate more than any other!"

"You wouldn't talk like that if you had a beard," said Diallo, putting the iron back in the forge.

"But you haven't got a beard either, Diallo!"

"I am not a man of principle, either. I was pleased with the display yesterday, but it only pleased me in so far as it illustrated the uses of cruelty. That is, I'm no different from the rest of my fellow-men; but the bearded ones took pleasure in it only in so far as it satisfied their sense of justice."

"You needn't expect me to make such fine distinctions," said Clarence. "However you look at it, the result is the same."

"Exactly the same. But that is simply because different causes can have the same effect."

"You mean to say there is no difference between the just and the unjust?"

"I don't know if that's really what I meant; I'm not the

sort of man to split hairs: I'm a blacksmith. In fact, it couldn't have been that I wanted to say; and yet, it comes to the same thing in the end."

"But it shouldn't be like that!" said Clarence.

"Well," said Diallo, "I suppose just men would be much less just if their justice pandered less to their love of cruelty."

He took the iron out of the fire; it had become white-hot again, and he started to hammer it once more.

"This axe will cut like a razor," he said. "Even the mightiest trees will fall like straws before it."

"Trees?" Clarence asked.

"Yes, trees. And heads, too. The mightiest trees, and the heads most proudly set on their shoulders . . . It has to be a very fine axe, the finest ever made in fact; the strongest and the sharpest I shall ever fashion, for the naba intends to present it to the king."

"Will the king be coming soon?"

"He alone knows. He will not come without any kind of warning at all, but it will be very sudden. He'll take us by surprise, just as if he had not been expected."

"How is that?" asked Clarence.

"It's like this: we are waiting for him. Every day and every hour we wait for him. But we also get weary of the waiting. And it is when we are most weary that he comes to us. Or we call to him—every moment we are calling him; but however hard we try, we do not call to him all the time—we keep forgetting to call to him; we are distracted for a fraction of a second—and suddenly he appears, he chooses that very fraction of a second in which to make his appearance. Or even when we are waiting and calling to him constantly, even when our vigilance is perfect and unremitting, his arrival nevertheless finds us in great confusion, because it is of such a nature that it inevitably throws us into confusion. Even if we were without reproach—and the king knows how far from being irreproachable we are—his arrival, his sudden coming would make us tremble all the same."

"Will your axe be ready by the time he comes?" asked Clarence.

"Probably," Diallo replied. "Anyhow, I hope it will be. But what is an axe. I have forged thousands of them, and this one will undoubtedly be the finest of them all; the others will have been no more than experiments I made in order to forge this one perfect axe. So that this will be the sum of everything I have ever learnt; it will be like my life, and all the effort I have made to live it well. But what does the king want with an axe? . . . He will accept it; at least I hope he will accept it, and perhaps he will even deign to admire it: but he will accept it and admire it only in order to give me pleasure. After all, what sort of pleasure could he take in it? There will always be axes that are finer and more deadly, more murderously sharp than any I can fashion . . . Yet I go on forging it . . . Perhaps I can do nothing else, perhaps I am like a tree which can bear only one kind of fruit. Yes, I am like that tree . . . And perhaps, in spite of having so many faults, perhaps because I am like that tree and lack the means to do anything but this; in spite of everything, the king will give me credit for my good will . . . But as far as the axe itself . . ."

He shrugged his shoulders and placed the roughly-shaped iron on the fire again.

"No," he went on, "you shouldn't always tell the whole truth, or listen to it either. Sometimes . . ."

He did not finish: he was watching the roughed-out shape of the axe that was slowly turning to red again on the fire. And he sighed. He did not finish what he had to say, any more that he had finished the anecdote which he had been going to tell Clarence a little while before; but this time it was evident that he had wanted to allude only to his axe and to his craft and that he considered it tedious to mull over certain truths which would have discouraged him in his work.

Clarence too was watching the fire; he was watching the little blue flames licking round the iron of the blade. The lump of iron had begun to take shape under Diallo's hammer; at the heart of the fire it formed a red crescent that was growing ever whiter and was already dazzlingly bright.

Suddenly Clarence seemed to see himself hundreds of miles away from the place he was in at the moment. He was in that mountain village that he had been wont to visit every year for the summer holidays, and where, with a crowd of other boys, he used to watch the shoe-smith's blazing forge. That fire which shone with such a lively flame, and in which the metal finally took on such an unendurable brightness, fascinated him more than he could say. How many were the hours he had spent there! Careless hours, hours that were the essence of childhood! But now . . . Oh! those childhood hours! Where were they now? . . . "Oh, to be a child again! To be a child, a little child again!" he whispered to himself. And he blushed violently; he was all at once the child who would blush at the sight of the man he had become; he felt himself burn all over with shame, burn as the incandescent iron was burning. For the man he had become no longer existed; that so-called man was now a beast—a cock!

"Clarence! . . . What are you doing here?"

He raised his eyes and saw the two boys.

"It's not the first time you've seen me here, is it?" he growled.

"We've been looking for you everywhere," the boys declared. "We've been looking for you for hours; Baloum is waiting for you outside the hut."

"Let him wait!" cried Clarence. "He's not pressed for time. He does not know what to do with his time. I came here to talk to Diallo."

"But you weren't speaking," the boys said. "You were sleeping."

"Sleeping?" said Clarence. "I wasn't sleeping at all. Ask Diallo here."

"You hadn't spoken a word for quite a while," said Diallo. "I thought perhaps you were dozing."

"I was thinking of the past," said Clarence. "I imagined I was a child again, paying a visit to a shoe-smith who was a friend of mine."

"Did he ever forge axes?" Diallo asked.

"He forged shoes for the horses."

"For the horses?" said Diallo. "But horses don't need shoes."

"He used to nail horse-shoes to the horses' hooves," said Clarence.

"How horrible! Couldn't he find anything better to do with his time?"

"Don't misunderstand me," said Clarence. "He didn't do it out of cruelty; he did it to protect their hooves. He did it to help the horses."

"I couldn't bring myself to do a thing like that," said Diallo. "I wouldn't have the heart."

"Well, it was quite a different song when you were watching the backside of the master of ceremonies!" said Clarence.

"Is that any reason why you should accuse me of being lacking in sensitivity?" asked Diallo. He gazed thoughtfully at Clarence. "They told me," he went on, "that you refused to spit upon the master of ceremonies' bottom."

"But how could I do such a thing?" cried Clarence.

"I don't think you understand what I mean."

"I understand you perfectly. Noaga explained it to me."

"Well, then?"

"I just couldn't. I'm too sensitive."

"You *are* a complicated fellow!" cried Diallo. "Horses, horse-shoes . . . And, on the other hand, the master of cere-monies' backside, the display which *you* put a stop to . . ." He fetched a sigh. "You are too complicated for me," he continued. "You're too much of a white man for my liking. Yet you must realise that no one has ever wished you any harm. People were disappointed when they saw that the display was being cut short, but they did not really hold it against you; not even the master of ceremonies."

"I should hope not!" cried Clarence.

"But you couldn't have foreseen the outcome," said Diallo. "The master of ceremonies will enjoy no respite now, and all through you. If the display had been allowed to pursue its rightful course, he would have been able really to enjoy the respite, the sense of relief that the conclusion of a well-regulated torture always affords. Whereas now he has to drag himself around as if he had never received a single stroke. Yet he did receive a certain number of strokes, though not the full number; and he did not receive the severest ones. But he received enough to have something to show for it all."

"He certainly *has* something to show, with that great swol-len bottom," said Noaga.

"His backside is like a balloon," said Diallo.

"It certainly is!" said Nagoa. "He's wearing an enormous cold compress on it. If his backside had not really become so terribly distended, would he have needed a cold compress of such voluminous proportions?"

"Didn't you tell me yesterday that his behind was twice its natural size?" said Clarence.

"Noaga said that," said Nagoa. "You mustn't always believe what Noaga tells you . . . But the backside has had time
to subside a little since then."

"I hope it has!" declared Clarence.

"You ought not to express such a hope," said Diallo. "The
master of ceremonies certainly would not wish you to do so;
the poor fellow's bottom wasn't swollen nearly enough as it
was . . . Don't you understand that now everyone will look
upon his backside with the greatest suspicion? It is only like
feeling half the pain, to receive strokes the marks of which
one can display to the public; but to have received them, felt
them bite into one's flesh, and to have felt the flesh smart like
fire, and then not be able to display one's weals is to suffer
meaninglessly. In the end, no one will be satisfied—neither
the people, nor the master of ceremonies himself."

"You mean that, because of my intervention, people will
feel that justice has not been done?" asked Clarence.

"Exactly. Why didn't you think of that earlier? You see,
you can see things as clearly as anybody when you like."

"Didn't *you* see that I said it with my tongue in my
cheek?"

"Well, I'm surprised at you!" said Diallo. "I should never
have thought that you would take the backside of the master
of ceremonies as a butt for your jests."

He was hammering away furiously at the piece of iron. At
each stroke, the metal became a sparkling star. Diallo was
certainly hammering harder than was necessary, as if he had
been disgusted to find that anyone could use the backside of
the master of ceremonies as a butt for his jests.

"You're hammering it as if you were stone deaf," said
Clarence.

"The deaf have all the luck," said Diallo. "The others
. . . I should like to have been born deaf!"

He still looked sour, but suddenly he burst into laughter.

"The deaf cannot be reached by home-truths," he declared. "If they can't profit from them, at least they can't hear them . . . Why weren't *you* born deaf? *You* ought to be stone deaf!"

And he burst out laughing again.

"Do you not think I have turned a deaf ear long enough?" said Clarence bitterly.

"Well, apparently there are some things a man never tires of."

"If the naba were to hear you, he'd warm your backside till it was as white-hot as the iron you're working."

Noaga and Nagoa burst out laughing in their turn. Diallo turned his eyes away.

"Well, this time you must have thought that the white man isn't quite as complicated as you imagined—you understood him only too well!" the boys cried delightedly.

Diallo did not continue the conversation. He kept on hammering away at the bit of iron and did not look up; but he could easily have raised his eyes and given Clarence a piece of his tongue, for Clarence was sunk deep in thought; he was going over everything that had happened since his arrival in Aziana. Actually there was nothing he had *not* been aware of; he had been alive to everything that was going on; he had never ceased being aware of what was happening, and yet the most obvious warnings had passed him by. But now that everything had become clear, he could see it all at last, with sickening clarity—he realised now what the "small services" had been with which he had paid for the naba's hospitality. What had the beggar said? "There is no man, however humble, who cannot, on occasion, perform some small services" or something like that. The old man must have known, when he said these words, the sort of services that would be re-

quired, otherwise he would not have had that strange glint
in his eye.

"The rascal!" Clarence spat out angrily.

"Who do you mean?" the boys asked. "Baloum?"

"Baloum? . . . Yes, Baloum . . . And Akissi . . . And the
naba . . . And . . . And the beggar! . . . Oh, the beggar is the
biggest rascal, the biggest swindler of them all!"

"Didn't we tell you so?"

"But you, too, never said a word about what was going
on!"

"Well, you see, Clarence, we, too, have backsides . . ."

"Then stuff your backsides!" said Clarence. "Be sure and
keep your precious backsides safe from harm. But from now
on I never want to see you again—neither from the front, nor
from the back!"

He got up, and in spite of the heat began striding away at
a great pace.

"Clarence!" the boys were shouting. "Clarence! . . ."

"I forbid you to shout my name after me or to follow me,"
Clarence cried.

He was walking fast. He was walking along as if the sun
were not at its height. When he had got as far as the last huts
in Aziana, he had to slow down in spite of himself, for the
sweat was running into his eyes, the sweat was pouring down
his spine. From this point he started walking in a more
leisurely fashion, without leaving the shade of the banana-
trees. Where was he going? He didn't know. He only knew—
as he suddenly remembered—that he wanted to find a desert
retreat where he would never see another human being. It
already seemed as if he had reached that retreat, for the road
he was walking along was quite deserted, as were the fields
from which the labourers had been driven by the heat of the
mid-day sun. These fields soon began to grow less frequent,

then disappeared, giving place to a savannah that was covered with thick grass at first, and then dotted with trees and copses. Then Clarence noticed that he was going in the direction of the river, as if the coolness of the water had been calling to him.

Now he could smell the odour of the forest. The odour was not very strong as yet, but it was slyly and insidiously creeping around him. Soon it would grow denser and rise in front of him like a wall, for the horizon was for the most part shut in by the green and ashen cliffs of high jungle vegetation. In the shadow of the wall, Clarence found himself bathed in the penetrating odour. He breathed in great lungfuls of it, as if all he wanted was to poison his whole being and sink into oblivion. Fifty yards farther on, the river appeared through the branches. It was flowing slowly, with a dull slackness, yellowish, drugged, between its mud-caked banks.

Clarence sat on a rock and began staring fixedly at the water. Whole trees went gliding by, dragged along by the slumbrous current. The biggest ones sometimes remained stranded on the little islets which were scattered over the broad surface of the river; then they would display their roots, which made him think of forest boughs ravaged by the winds of autumn. This memory of autumn, in the hot-house heat that rose from the river, had something incongruous about it. Yet the heat was diminishing in intensity. Or was it merely the odour of the forest that was gradually numbing Clarence's senses? It was more likely to be the effect of this sickening odour; for the heat would not relent until the approach of night. But to Clarence it seemed already as if the heat had lost some of its intensity; a kind of well-being began imperceptibly to flow through his limbs—the deceptive and fallacious well-being of a senseless stupor.

Clarence wanted to get up; but the odour was working on

him, and as always he felt his will-power draining away. He remained seated. Again he felt for a moment in possession of his faculties, his body. He was determined not to let himself be led astray by this body which kept behaving like a filthy beast. But what could he do against this odour, against the South?

"Is the king never going to come?" he said aloud.

And he closed his eyes, he covered his face with his hands. The king . . . What would the king say when he came? . . . Diallo said that the king would not even look at his axe, the finest axe he had ever forged, or that he might glance at it merely out of pity . . . Would it be merely out of pity that he would cast his eye upon Clarence? But could one cast one's eye upon a beast, even if merely out of pity? The king would turn away from this unclean beast, he would turn away in horror and disgust . . . One day, the king would come; but it would be as if he had not come at all.

"If only death might deliver me . . ." Clarence thought. But did death bring freedom? Did it not rather place fresh fetters upon you? It would release some, but it would enslave others. And what indication was there that it would release him, rather than lay its chains upon him? . . . Perhaps there was nothing now that could set him free from himself, from Clarence.

When he opened his eyes again, the sun was about to disappear beneath the horizon. The odour had grown much denser and stronger; it seemed to be both dripping from the trees and oozing up out of the earth, and there was a place where the two currents met and at intervals flowed towards Clarence and completely submerged him.

"This odour lies upon me like a winding-sheet," Clarence whispered to himself.

Suddenly he felt himself tremble all over. In the middle of

the river, close to an islet that was in the middle of the river, a vague female form was slowly emerging. It was only vaguely female, for if the breasts were obviously women's breasts, the head was very much more like the head of a fish than the head of a woman. Unfortunately the light had grown too dusky to be able to make out the shape clearly.

The form moved briskly towards the islet and there hoisted itself upon a bed of grasses. What a strange creature! . . . Now that the body could be seen, it looked as if it ended in a fish-tail. If the head had displayed any human features, however plain, if there had been the slightest wisp of hair upon it, and even if that hair had only been tangled weeds, one would have recognised a siren; but that inhuman head, or that only-too-human head, that bald pate clashed with the conventional idea of a siren, even though such an idea might only be tolerable because of legends one had heard, because of the literature that casts a more seductive veil over unpalatable fact. The form was now moving forward in an undulating manner among the reeds and grasses, and appeared to be grazing on them. Each time it turned over, the breasts, opulent and dead white, were gruesomely revealed, and it looked as if they must be impeding the creature's progress rather than assisting it. But this was not certain because, deprived of their support, perhaps the creature would have been quite unable to move.

"I'm dreaming," said Clarence to himself. But a second form, and soon a third, emerged from the river and hoisted themselves up beside the first. He wanted to turn his eyes away from such an abnormal conjunction of improbable shapes: such a revolting conglomeration of forms would have stupefied the liveliest mind; and his own, fogged and clouded-over by the odour, was far from being still alert. In any case he could not turn his eyes away; he felt himself at once revolted and attracted, more violently attracted, and more violently revolted than he had ever been by the odour of the forest. He rubbed his eyes, thinking that this figment of his disordered fancy would vanish, but the three forms went on peacefully undulating and grazing. "I'm going mad," Clarence said to himself. He got up, equally divided between the desire to flee from the disturbing herd and the desire to know them.

The moon at that moment bent upon the waters of the river a languid and silvery regard, and Clarence knew then quite certainly that he was not dreaming. The three fish-women continued to drag themselves over the grass where their scaly robes now glimmered spectrally like robes of dying moonlight. As long as one saw them from behind, one could easily mistake them for large-sized fish; but as soon as these ambiguous creatures turned over, as soon as their dead white breasts flashed their gleaming scales beneath the moon's sepulchral light, one thought at once of women, one could not help thinking at once of women.

All at once, the desire to swim across to the islet overcame all of Clarence's other repulsions. It appears that the odour of the forest was not without some bearing on this decision; it was the same odour nevertheless, and the same intoxication which the forest-odour caused, that prevented Clarence from putting his plan into action. His head was heavy and he could not stand up straight; as he drew near the river's edge his feet became entangled in creepers—or was it the suddenly stronger gusts of the odour that were incapacitating him?—and he fell with brutal suddenness among the undergrowth.

His fall stunned him less than the stench which rose from the earth. At this spot dead leaves formed a bed in which the fermentation was even more active than in the most impene-

trable parts of the forest. Clarence had fallen with his face
flat in this fetid mess, and he breathed in the poison through
his mouth as well as his nostrils. He tried to rise, but the
efforts he made seemed to suck him even further down into
the hotbed of putrefying leaves. A kind of dry rattling groan
came from his throat.

This groan sounded very loud in the stillness of the night;
it became louder and seemed to be rising to a shriek as if it
were tearing him apart—like the death-rattle of a dying
invalid in a closed room. Clarence would have liked to stop
it, but he did not succeed in doing so; and perhaps he was
not trying very hard either: perhaps he did not really want
to stop it, for this awful sound, which both terrified and
exhausted him, was at least the one living thing he had left,
and he did not want to let it go, lest he have nothing . . . At
one moment, he thought he heard his name being called, but
he must almost certainly have been mistaken; who would
have been calling his name? Only his own agonised scream
rent the night, and seemed to occupy the whole of it . . .
Clarence was no longer even trying to restrain it. Even if this
screaming was wearing him out, perhaps it was also prevent-
ing him from suffocating, perhaps such a scream alone was
strong enough to cut through the miasmal exhalations of the
rotting earth, perhaps even . . . Again he had the impression
that someone was calling his name. Would the fish-women?
. . . No, what was he thinking about! . . . But just then he
felt all over him the touch of what seemed to be hands. Could
it be that the fish-women had hands? . . . He could not
remember having seen them with hands. They just had
breasts; he could distinctly remember those breasts, but not
the hands. Yet they were really hands that were fumbling
him all over. A feeling of immense disgust swept over him,
and he tried to utter a few words of protest, but found he

could not—only that dry, screaming groan kept coming from his throat. At a loss for words, he tried to struggle out of their clutches; then he let himself go limp, limp and heavy; he lay as heavily as he could with his body face-downwards to the earth, the better to keep those hands away from . . . But obviously the hands were stronger than . . . he felt himself sliding, sliding helplessly sliding down and over, and suddenly the weight of his body seemed to melt away. He was sliding into the river!

It was some time before Clarence realised exactly what had happened. He had thought he was sliding "into" the river; in fact, he was "on" the river; he was sliding along the river.

The water which during the hours of daylight had already seemed very muddy and thick with earth, appeared to have taken on an even thicker consistency, and now it seemed to have, if not the absolute firmness, at least some of the resistance of solid ground; and Clarence was sliding along its surface, borne away by the current. The water, as well as being of a thicker consistency, had also lost its disagreeable yellowish tinge; it was now silvery-white and scattered with shadows of a fine metallic blue. It did not appear that this change of tone could be attributed to the effect of moonlight, for the moon had disappeared; even the sky had disappeared; at the very most there was just a hint of distant moonlight in the chalky radiance on the crests of the highest trees, whose foliage covered the sky completely. They rose up very straight and tall on either side of the river, then, curving inwards, met over the middle of the waters that flowed beneath their leafy vaultings.

Clarence had reached the middle of the river and he had completely forgotten what had brought him there. He let

himself be borne along by the current, being careful only to
avoid, by using swift side-strokes, the islets which strewed his
path. He must have passed almost at once the islet on which
the three fish-women were so peacefully grazing.

He was rather worried by a kind of buzzing that followed
him. This buzzing or humming was probably nothing important; perhaps it was simply due to the water flowing and
lapping against the banks; but perhaps it was also a warning
of far-off cataracts, in which case the water might become of
a more watery consistency again, for Clarence was certain
that it could not possibly retain its present quasi-speed, and
this did not seem to be an altogether favourable omen. Even
if the cataracts were purely imaginary, the current was real
enough; and its continual acceleration was becoming rather
disturbing because of the many islets which kept breaking
through the surface of the river. Now these inlets were
becoming more numerous; if the current went on gathering
strength and speed like this, Clarence would finally and inevitably be dashed against one of them, with fatal results.

Suddenly he noticed that these islets were all populated by
fish-women. Was this something new, or had he only just
become aware of it? He couldn't say. All he could say was
that the spectacle afforded him very little pleasure, and his
unhappiness increased as the islets grew more numerous.

If Clarence had at first been attracted and at the same
time revolted by these ambiguous creatures, it was now only
revulsion he felt for them, all the more so since the fish-
women had interrupted their peaceful grazing and were staring fixedly at him as he went gliding by. He felt a kind of
awful anguish at the thought that some unconsidered movement might cause him to brush, in passing, against the glittering opulence of those dead white breasts. Such a fear was

by no means groundless, for the banks of the river had come considerably closer together, and the foliage above was thickly interlocked. In fact it had become so dense that there was soon little more than a narrow corridor left between the banks. The fish-women were all lined up in little groups on both sides of the corridor. They were raised up, like sirens, on their tails, and they kept thrusting out their great, voluptuous tits, they kept pushing their dead-white, ungovernable tits out over the water!

Clarence tried to fight against the current. But was it any use now? The water no longer had the same density; it was now a sort of mud that sucked in the feet—a gluey clarts from which it became easier and easier to lift the feet; a sort of pitch or bituminous substance that was as heavy as lead. Clarence made renewed efforts to rid himself of this claggy stuff, but without success. And surely the fish-women must have noticed the futility of his struggle, for they were smiling broadly now. And they were even calling out, crying "C-larence! . . . C-larence! . . ." Yes, they were calling out and crying like real women now.

Clarence kept his arms pressed tightly against his sides. In this way perhaps he would be able to glide past without brushing against them. But almost immediately he had to abandon this rather feeble hope: the corridor had become so ridiculously narrow, and the fish-women were obtruding their great pointed tits with such a shameless lack of decorum that he could not help brushing against them.

He began to fight against the mud and the current again; but this time the fish-women took his despairing efforts very badly. Their calling voices became more imperious and they seemed barely able to keep a note of irritated impatience out of their cries; moreover, they were thrusting out their breasts

at him with an even greater lack of decorum than before.
Clarence could see that the moment would come when he
would not just brush against them, but actually bump into
them, bump right into those pallid mounds of urgent flesh,
bump into them with his face and his hands, with his whole
body; and feel on his hands and on his head and on his cheeks
their glutinous softness and their overpowering warmth. He
uttered a loud cry, he made a supreme effort, and disengaged
his feet so forcibly from the mud and the current that he felt
a great shock, a curious feeling, as if, in falling, he had struck
the very bottom of the river, the pebbly bed of the stream
itself.

"Well, couldn't you really hold on to him any better than
that?" asked a voice.

"We *were* holding on to him! . . . We were holding him very
tightly. But the last great kick he let us have . . ."

"You are a couple of scamps!" the voice went on.

"Baloum!" cried Clarence. "Chase them away, Baloum!"

"What's that you say?" said Samba Baloum.

"Chase them away, I tell you!" cried Clarence.

"Well, they certainly deserve to be chased," said Samba
Baloum. "But how could I carry you all on my own? You are
heavy!"

"Don't you understand?" cried Clarence. "I'm telling you
to chase the fish-women away!"

"*What* fish-women?" said Samba Baloum. "There's only us
chickens here—Nagoa and Noaga . . . What's all this about
fish-women? Such things don't exist!"

"Chase them away!" shouted Clarence. "Their tits! . . .
Oh, those terrible tits!"

He began to struggle wildly.

"Listen," said Samba Baloum, "don't start kicking and

screaming again; you've already given us trouble as it is
. . . And stop babbling about fish-women. It's dark now, and
you might frighten the boys if you go on like this."

"Oh, Baloum!" Clarence groaned, "can't you see their
breasts?"

"Shut up," said Samba Baloum. "Shut up, will you?"

"For goodness' sake, shut up!" cried the boys.

"Shut up and stop wriggling," said Samba Baloum. "We're
nearly back in town, but stop flinging yourself about, or we'll
never get there; the sweat's pouring off me."

Clarence was suddenly very surprised to see the sky over-
head. The sky was packed with stars, and nothing impeded
his view of them—there was no leafy vault, no vault of any
kind . . . So he was no longer gliding along the river? No
longer hemmed in by a double row of fish-women's tits?

"Where have they gone—the fish-women?" he asked.

"There have never been any fish-women," said Samba
Baloum. "Get that into your head, once and for all, and stop
wearing us out with your impossible tales! That's not the sort
of thing one should talk about when it's dark."

"But . . ." Clarence began to protest.

"But me no buts!" laughed Samba Baloum. "You can tell
us all about it when it's daylight . . . Come on, you two," he
told the boys, "you take him by the legs."

"Where are you taking me?" asked Clarence.

"To your hut, of course. Where else would we be taking
you?"

"I don't want to go back to my hut!"

"Rubbish!" snorted Samba Baloum. "Akissi will mull some
wine for you. You have obviously caught a nasty cold."

"I never want to see Akissi again!"

"Are you out of your mind? You'd go a long way before
finding a woman as devoted as she is."

"Or such a liar!"

"Rubbish again! Just a lot of rubbish, like your tale about
the fish-women! When we have got you back to your
hut . . ."

"But I don't want to go back!" Clarence shouted. "Let me
go!" He had begun to fling his arms and legs about again. But
this time the two boys held on to him.

"Don't start kicking your legs about again," said Samba
Baloum. "You've got such strength! . . . Not a bit like what
you were when you first came to Aziana. You've grown as
strong as a lion!"

"Oh, all right, do as you like," said Clarence. "Just go
ahead and do as you like. But I warn you I won't stay in my
hut!"

"When you've had a drink of mulled palm wine, you'll feel
differently," said Samba Baloum.

"Never!" shouted Clarence. "I'll never feel any differently! Do you hear, Baloum. I'll never change my mind!"

"All right, all right!" said Baloum. "There's no need for
you to yell like that. Meanwhile, do me a favour—don't fling
yourself about so. I've never felt so utterly exhausted."

He was breathing very hard: his breathing sounded like the
bellows of a forge.

"What a job!" he said after a while.

And he fetched a sigh.

PART THREE

THE KING

1

D I O K I

"He will sit under the arcade, where the naba sits," Clarence whispered to himself.

He was looking at the arcade. He was sitting in front of his hut with the two boys, and he was looking at the arcade, where cool shadows were lying and where, nearly every day, he would come and sit a while; where the naba, too, would come and sit with his dignitaries in the afternoons.

The arcade extended very far; so far that it was not easy for the naked eye to see just how far it reached. There was a very long colonnade on each side of it, which contained so many pillars that the eye, after toying with the puzzling perspectives, soon gave up trying to sort them out. Besides, after a certain point, the pillars seemed to join together to form a continuous wall; but doubtless that was only an optical illusion. The uniformity of these arcades and pillars had something depressing about them too. It was rather like life itself: day was joined to day with the same boring repetitiveness . . .

"If he sits there, where the naba sits," Clarence went on whispering, "I shall not fail to see him. I shall be able to see him from the doorway of my hut."

But wouldn't the king sit higher up? Wouldn't he sit where the pillars seemed to meet? . . .

"How far does the arcade extend?" Clarence asked the boys.

"A long way."

"But where does it end?" he asked.

"We don't know," replied the boys. "We have never been that far."

"But I thought you went poking your noses in everywhere!" said Clarence. "Do you mean to say that you were born in the palace, and you never went right to the end of the arcade?"

"No one ever goes right to the end of the arcade," said Noaga. "Not even the naba."

"But he could if he wanted to," said Clarence.

"Why should he want to?" asked Nagoa. "There is nothing at the end of the arcade."

Nothing? That seemed really extraordinary! Could it be that the arcade served no useful purpose whatsoever? The naba would not allow that, despite his great display of wealth and all his other peculiarities. The arcade must surely lead somewhere, perhaps to the inner courtyards; perhaps it led to those deserted courtyards, to that labyrinth at the end of which lay the harem.

"It must be the harem at the very end of the arcade," he suggested.

"Nonsense!" said the boys. "You won't get to the harem simply by following the arcade. Baloum would never allow it."

"Baloum?" Clarence asked.

"Yes, Baloum," the boys replied. "Old Baloum would be out of breath by the time he got there."

"Too true!" thought Clarence. Baloum took little tripping steps, but Baloum got there all the same; Baloum . . . All at once, Clarence remembered the night, that famous night when he had pursued the master of ceremonies through the courtyards of the palace. Could he have followed the windings of the arcade on that night?

He tried to remember, but did not succeed: it was all too long ago now. He had left his hut, yes; and a little later had got lost in that labyrinth of inner courtyards which he had never seen before, and which he had never returned to. He could remember all that perfectly. But as for the path he had followed . . . No, he had paid no attention to where he was going; his one thought had been to dog the master of ceremonies' heels and to rain blows on him with his stick—unfortunately he had always missed, or nearly always . . . But that was all too long ago, and Clarence only had a very confused memory of what had happened. It had all taken place . . . But when exactly *had* it all taken place? . . . Oh, it was the night after the master of ceremonies had been flogged. Yes, that was the night, or the one after, perhaps . . . No, that was the night when the fish-women . . . Clarence shuddered when he remembered the fish-women . . .

"Sea-cows! They were quite simply sea-cows, or manatees you saw!" Samba Baloum had assured him. "I don't know why you had to be so scared of a few old sea-cows. When the naba used to send you, as a special delicacy, some of their liver, you didn't turn up your nose at it, now did you?"

"You don't mean to tell me that I have eaten women's livers?" Clarence had cried.

"But what makes you think they were women?" Baloum had replied. "They are fish! . . . Can't you tell the difference between a woman and a fish? . . . I should have given you credit for more intelligence. I don't want to be offensive, but all the same . . . Akissi used to cook them in a kind of delicious wine-sauce."

"I always cook them in wine-sauce," Akissi had said. "They are better that way than braised."

"Will you kindly shut up?" Clarence had cried. "I forbid you ever to serve up that sort of muck to me again!"

"Manatee's liver is not muck," Akissi had retorted. "It's a real tit-bit."

"Don't talk to me of tits!" Clarence had shouted. "I've had enough of their tits!"

"I always thought you were a great tit-fancier," Baloum had remarked. "Anyhow, it's because the liver is a great delicacy that the naba sent it to you."

"I never want to touch it again!" Clarence had cried. "Never! . . . Do you hear, Akissi? Never again!"

"No one's forcing you to eat it," Baloum had said. "When next the naba sends you a piece of sea-cow's liver, give it to me, and I'll make a pig of myself."

"You make me sick," Clarence had replied.

He seemed to see again the dead white breasts, the double row of dead white breasts . . .

"Have you never seen their breasts?" he had asked.

"Everybody knows what *they* are like," Baloum had answered. "What you mustn't look at is the head. As soon as a fisherman harpoons a sea-cow, he shuts his eyes and cuts off her head; he doesn't open his eyes again until he's thrown the head back in the river."

He had fallen silent for a moment. Then he had gone on, lowering his voice: "They say that a fisherman who looks on a manatee falls dead on the spot . . . I don't know much about it: I have never fished for sea-cow, and I've never met a fisherman who has looked a sea-cow in the eye . . . Perhaps they say that to stop . . ." He had left his sentence hanging in the air.

"To stop what?" Clarence had demanded to know.

"Well, you see, in days gone by . . ."

"Well, in days gone by? . . ." Clarence had echoed.

But he had not been able to finish the phrase, for it had suddenly reminded him of the legendary sirens, and he had felt sick. "Why do you tell me these horrible things, Baloum?" he had asked.

"I did not want to tell you," Baloum had replied. "But you keep on and on asking questions like a child; you spend your whole life asking questions!"

Those horrors were all a part of the South. It was not always just the South, but it *was* the South, all the same. As soon as one began to think about the South . . .

"I must go to the end of the arcade one day," Clarence said.

"If the master of ceremonies catches you . . ." said Noaga.

"I'll give him a good hiding," said Clarence. "I'll give him a good hiding, like the night . . ."

Now was it the night he had chased him through the deserted courtyards? It was probably that night . . . The memory of the fish-women had interrupted his investigations into the past.

"Did you give the master of ceremonies a good hiding?" asked Noaga.

"Of course I did," replied Clarence. "I gave him a good hiding the night he wouldn't let me sleep."

"You never mentioned it before," said Nagoa. "Are you quite sure it *was* the master of ceremonies?"

"I'd know him anywhere," said Clarence.

But had he really given him a good hiding? He had aimed numerous blows at him, he had gone on aiming blows at him, but the master of ceremonies had run like a hare . . . No, he couldn't have hit him very often. Perhaps he had not even hit him once.

"Whether I gave him a good hiding or not," he said, "is after all without the slightest importance."

"Absolutely without the slightest importance," said Nagoa. "Even if you didn't do it, the naba did."

"I *did* do it!" said Clarence.

"You forgot to mention it to us," said Noaga.

"Am I obliged to tell you everything?" Clarence asked.

He had drawn his brows together, because he wasn't really certain whether he had given the master of ceremonies a good hiding or not. And he wasn't really certain either whether he had run after him with a stick, raining blows upon him. He might quite easily have dreamt it all . . .

"But why should I make up such tales?" he asked himself. "Do I really need to make up stories like that? Isn't there enough funny business going on without making it up? Or am I turning into just as barefaced a liar as the rogues I have round me?" Why not? What difference was there between them and him?

"There's no difference," he muttered.

Certainly there had never been so little difference between them. Never had Clarence been so deeply sunk in his present position as he had been since the day he had resolved to escape from it and to go and live in the desert. He had gone

off to look for a retreat where he would never see another
human being. But the very first thing he had done had been
to go and have a chat with Diallo; and when night had fallen
on his desert and he had fallen into his absurd reverie about
the fish-women, he had been quite content to go back to the
village, quite content to sit in his hut and drink a bowl of
mulled palm wine. He had consented to see Baloum again,
and Akissi, had agreed to speak to Akissi, to speak to Baloum. Was there anything he had not agreed to? He had
given in to everything. The women who came to him at night
no longer took the trouble to hide their identity . . . And that
way everything was more open, it seemed . . . But it was the
openness of utter abjection; it was pure cynicism.

The king . . . This was a nice time to think of the king, after
all that had happened! . . . Yet, in spite of everything, it was
the king Clarence was thinking about; he was counting on
the king to give him his freedom. Yes, the king would come
and deliver him . . . It was utterly senseless, yet it was true;
this frail and foolish hope still haunted his inmost thoughts:
the king would come and sit under the arcade, and would
deliver him! And that is why, day after day, Clarence kept
looking at the arcade; that is why, as the days kept passing,
he turned his eyes more and more often towards the arcade.
The king would sit . . . But would the king really sit where
the naba sat? . . . And if he sat higher up . . . What if he sat
in a position in which, from the doorway of the hut, he could
not be seen, where the pillars . . .

"Does the king always sit where the naba has been sitting?" he asked the boys.

"In the very same place," the boys replied. "Each time he
has come, he has sat there."

"Then I cannot fail to see him," thought Clarence. "I shall
no sooner have crossed the threshold of my hut . . ." But

could he depend on the boys, could he depend at all on what they said? Did they even know what they were talking about? They were so young; how could they know what the king would do?

"Have you seen him sitting there?" he asked.

"We have never seen him. The last time he came here, we were too little to be allowed to see him; we were always kept in the harem. But everybody says it is there he sits each time he comes; next time, he will sit there too."

"Yes, 'next' time," said Clarence.

He had stressed the "Next," and he sniggered. When would there be a "next" time? . . . Perhaps there would never be a "next" time! And he had waited all this time . . .

"He will not come," he said.

"How can you dare to say such a thing?" the boys asked. "He won't be much longer!"

"And how many times have you told me that?"

"But he *will* come one day, and then . . ."

"Yes, he will come one day," said Clarence, "but that day cannot be reckoned. Diallo says that it cannot be reckoned. Meanwhile, months and years go by. In the end one no longer expects him to come: that wonderful day is so vague, so unpredictable, that in the end, one ceases to believe in it."

"But it's not altogether unforeseeable!" cried the boys. "Now Dioki almost certainly knows when the king will come."

"Dioki? That silly old woman who filled my hut with smoke and nearly asphyxiated me when I had the fever?"

"You shouldn't talk about Dioki like that."

"I don't care."

"She might be listening . . . She hears everything."

"So much the worse for her, then!"

"She'll make you catch something nasty."

"Well, I should like to know what worse things could happen to me, after all I've been through!" said Clarence.

All the misfortunes he had suffered since his arrival in Aziana came back to his mind. And all those he had suffered before coming here, too. Yes, everything. It had all started the moment he had crossed the reef; the moment he had had the bad luck to cross the reef and set his foot on the red soil of Africa.

"Nothing worse can ever happen to me," he said. "I don't need a miserable old fortune-teller to tell me that."

"She sees everything and finds everything out," said Noaga.

"If she can see everything, why don't you ask her when the king is coming?"

"She wouldn't tell me."

"That's very useful!" snarled Clarence.

"She never tells you everything," said Nagoa. "She finds out things and lets you see them happening. But you do not find them out or see them happening unless you take the trouble to watch very carefully."

"You mean she talks in riddles?" asked Clarence. "She skilfully and imperceptibly pumps the information out of you, then serves it up on a silver platter; and you don't realise, of course, that you've told her everything yourself!"

"Why don't you go and consult her?" said Noaga.

"I was wondering whether I should," said Clarence. "I was saying to myself just at that very moment . . . But never mind. Let's go and see her. We don't get much amusement here, and we might as well go there as anywhere. Come on!"

He got up.

"You can't go empty-handed," said Nagoa.

"No, of course not," said Clarence. "Perhaps I should take her some flowers?"

He burst out laughing. "Flowers for that old bag!" he cried. And he slapped his thighs.

"If you don't take her anything, she won't tell you anything," said Nagoa.

"But what *can* I take her?" cried Clarence. "At her age, what she wants is a funeral wreath."

"Shut up!" cried the boys. "She might hear you . . . And anyhow, why do you make jokes at the expense of the dead? It isn't nice."

"If two young scamps like you are to tell me what to do and what not to do . . ." said Clarence. "I'll go and give her a few calabashes. She's the sort of old woman who likes her drop."

"She *does* like a drop."

"Well, that's what I said."

"But you will have to give her something else," said the boys.

"Akissi!" Clarence shouted. Akissi left her pestle and mortar. "Akissi, I want to give Dioki a present. I want to take her some palm wine, the old soak."

"She's not an old soak," said Akissi.

"Maybe not, but she likes to pickle her nose!"

"The snakes do that for her."

"The snakes?" said Clarence. "I shouldn't like to use snakes to pickle my nose with."

"But that's how *she* likes to pickle her nose."

"Don't argue, Akissi. Once you start to argue, we'll never be done. Tell me what I should give her."

"You could give her a necklace."

"A necklace?" said Clarence. "What would that old trout want with a necklace?"

"She has some very pretty necklaces."

"Have *you* any necklaces?"

"You could ask the naba for one."

"That's what you think! And have me watching him parade his empty trunks?"

"They are not all empty."

"They are full of rats," said Clarence.

"Then take her some rats."

"Rats?" cried Clarence. "Are you quite mad?"

"Her snakes will eat them," replied Akissi calmly.

"But I want to give *her* something," said Clarence. "What do I care whether the snakes have anything to eat or not?"

"In a way, those snakes are a part of her; they *are* her. If you do not feed them, they will bite you."

"Why don't you give her some eggs?" asked the boys.

"What? To sit on?" said Clarence, and he slapped his thighs.

"For the snakes," the boys answered. "Snakes eat eggs."

"Well, then, let's have the eggs!" said Clarence. "Do you understand, Akissi? Fill a basket with eggs . . . no, two baskets . . . A good laugh is something worth paying for; these two scamps are right. And for the old girl herself, put in whatever you like: some crunchies, perhaps."

"Crunchies? What are they?" asked Akissi. "Something you crunch?"

"That's right."

"But she hasn't any teeth left!" said the boys. "She wouldn't take well to that."

"Pity!" said Clarence. "I thought the old thing would be able to crunch up a few roasted grasshoppers."

"Grasshoppers—that's very tasty," said Akissi.

"Some folks have queer tastes," said Clarence.

"But you yourself are very fond of snails," said Akissi.

"That's different . . . Come on now, give each of the boys a basket of eggs. What is lacking in variety will be made up for in quantity."

"But we're not going in!" said the boys. "We'll carry the baskets, but we won't go in; we'll put the baskets down by her door."

"Why?" Clarence asked.

"What about the snakes?" cried the boys.

"Am I afraid of snakes?"

"Maybe not, but we are!"

"Very well then, you can put the baskets outside her door. But you are a couple of wet hens."

Akissi went to fill the baskets with eggs, and Clarence tied half a dozen calabashes together with creeper.

"Here we go!" he said.

"What about your *boubou?*" said Akissi.

She handed him his *boubou.*

"Don't break the eggs," she warned the boys.

Dioki lived in a hole in the ground, or a ditch, or a courtyard—the boys didn't quite know where—in one of the outlying districts of Aziana. To get there, they had to pass the forge. When Diallo saw the little band approaching, he stopped hammering.

"You're well loaded," he cried.

"With wine and eggs," said Clarence. "Only we aren't coming to visit *you.* We are going to Dioki's."

"To Dioki's? . . . What do you want with Dioki?"

"I'm going to have my fortune told."

"I don't think that's a very good idea," said Diallo.

"I don't, either," said Clarence. "It wasn't my idea."

"Was it those two scamps who put it into your head?"

"Who else would it be?" said Clarence.

"If I were you, I shouldn't go," said Diallo. "It's silly."

"It won't be the first silly thing I've done since I came to Aziana."

"No, but it might be the last."

"Do you think I'm afraid of a few little tame snakes?"

"If that's the way you look at it . . ."

"I look upon it as a joke," said Clarence. "I'll come and tell you what the silly old bitch sees in my hand. Good-bye!"

"Perhaps for good!" said Diallo. He shook his head. "If I were you," he said, "I shouldn't go."

"It's too late now!" said Clarence, and went walking on.

"Don't swing the baskets about like that!" he told the boys. "If Dioki wants to make an omelet, let her break her eggs herself . . . Well, what's the matter?"

The boys had stopped short in front of a palisade made of bamboo; it was quite high, and rather impressive, but curiously dilapidated, curiously tumble-down and rickety. They put the baskets at the foot of the palisade, without bothering at all about whether a piece of bamboo might not unexpectedly fall on them, or the whole palisade tumble down.

"This is Dioki's," they said.

"But all I can see is this palisade," said Clarence. "And some palisade it is! It's falling to pieces!"

"It's behind here," the boys said.

"But where is the door?" asked Clarence. "I suppose there *is* a door?"

"You go in there," said the boys.

They pointed to a narrow path that lay along the palisade and which could have led anywhere, though hardly to a respectable habitation.

"The door is at the end."

"Well, you might come as far as the door with me," said Clarence. "I can't carry both the baskets and the calabashes. And don't leave the baskets at the foot of the palisade. Can't you see the whole thing might fall on our heads at any moment? It's a real death-trap you've brought me to."

He sighed.

"Come on, then! Come as far as the door."

"All right, but we won't go any farther," said the boys, picking up the baskets again. "We're not going to throw ourselves into the snake-pit!"

Clarence went down the path. The palisade cast a sinister shadow over it and supported creepers of an unknown variety: fragments of bamboo cluttered up the path, witnessing to the decrepitude and insecurity of the palisade. At the end of the path, a back gate opened on a little courtyard surrounded by a low wall—it was a miserable little yard whose walls were hardly less secure than the palisade. At the back of this yard a flight of steps gave access to a second yard even more exiguous than the first, and which certainly looked more like an animal's den than a regular yard.

"We're not going any farther," said the boys, putting the baskets down at the foot of the steps. "We've already come much farther than we intended."

"You will wait for me here!" said Clarence, pointing to the first step.

"Oh, no we won't!" they said. "We'll watch for you over the wall. The snakes might creep up the stairs."

"What funks you are!" said Clarence.

"Call Dioki," said the boys. "Don't go down without first having called her name."

"Dioki!" cried Clarence.

"Who is calling me?" said a voice which came from the shadows.

"The white man," replied Clarence.

"What have you brought me?" the voice went on.

"Palm wine. And eggs for your snakes."

"Come down the steps," said the voice.

Clarence went down with the calabashes and put them on the bottom step, then he went up again for the baskets. When he went down the steps again, he saw Dioki drinking.

"Don't drink too much before I've asked my questions," he told her.

"Are you afraid I'll get drunk?" she said. "It'd need a lot more than what you've brought me to go to *my* head."

"Is that where you sleep?" asked Clarence, pointing to a low hut decorated with white and yellow colour-wash.

"The snakes sleep in there," she said. "What do you want to know, white man?"

"I should like you to tell me when the king will be coming."

"The king! . . ." she said.

For a moment she seemed to be lost in thought, then she raised the calabash to her lips and emptied it at one go.

"I don't think much of your palm wine," she complained.

"It comes from the naba."

"That's what I thought."

"Look, Dioki, I didn't come here to listen to you running down the naba's wine. The naba is somebody. Nobody very much, of course, and perhaps not even as much as that; but his wine isn't bad. I came to ask you when the king would be coming."

Dioki whistled, and the snakes came out of the hut. They were of all sizes and all colours. There were certainly some poisonous ones, and others who obviously did not need any venom, who only had to roll themselves tightly round their prey to suffocate and crush it to death.

"I shall consult the snakes," said Dioki.

"Could you not consult them in their hut?" asked Clarence.

"Are you afraid? They're all afraid in Aziana."

"I don't like snakes."

"There are no more faithful creatures," she said.

She held out her arm to a snake. At once the creature crept up the arm and wound itself round her neck.

"Are these your necklaces?" asked Clarence.

"These are my necklaces," she said, playing with the coils.

"Clarence!" the boys shouted.

"What?" said Clarence.

"The snakes!" cried the boys.

Clarence saw that the snakes were all round him; they were grovelling at his feet and even wriggling over his feet. And all the time they kept coming. They kept coming out of the hut, but it looked as if they were also coming from all directions; they were even coming out of the wall.

"I hope they're tame ones," said Clarence.

"They are as gentle as doves to those who treat me well," she said.

"Oh, it would never enter my head to treat you otherwise," he said. "You're past the age when men would want to ill-treat you."

"Clarence!" cried the boys.

"What is it now?" asked Clarence.

"Be careful!"

"Don't bother me!" cried Clarence.

But at that very moment he found a snake coiled round his waist. The creature was richly ocellated with green and violet. In a way, it was beautiful—one couldn't have called it *not* beautiful—only the scaly surface of its skin was extremely unpleasant. It was cold and a little slippery, like stiff watered silk, but too mobile and too cold: alive, but at the same time too much alive and not alive enough: too much alive, because it was not natural that watered silk should be endowed with life, and not alive enough because the coldness of its scales was completely opposed to the living warmth of life. The creature lifted its head towards Clarence's face, raising its head almost imperceptibly, with a very graceful undulating motion, and finally, having reached the level of his face, held itself completely rigid and looked fixedly into Clarence's eyes. There was really no animosity in the creature's expression; no particular charity, either: it was rather a sort of curiosity it displayed, with a hint of fascination behind it.

"This has gone beyond a joke," said Clarence.

"If you have no wicked intentions, you have nothing to fear," said Dioki. "All the same, don't move; and be sure not to ill-treat me, in thought or word or deed. Don't stir. The snake is going to speak, and I shall repeat to you word for word what he tells me. Ask me a question."

"When will the king sit under the naba's arcade?" Clarence asked . . . "But hurry up and reply; I haven't any confidence in your serpents."

Dioki shivered for a long time.

"The king is coming!" she said, suddenly raising her arms.

"People have been telling me that for years and years," said Clarence.

"But this time, he really *is* coming! He is leaving his palace, and he is coming. He is sitting on his steed, and his pages are all riding beside him and all his vassals are making way for him. The great red cloud is rising straight into the sky, rising high and straight as a pillar, and covering the whole sky . . . Do you follow me, you poor white man? The king is on his way. He no longer gets ready to come: he has already started! He is coming!"

A little foam came round her lips. The snake that was coiled round her neck brought its head close to her lips to sip the foam.

"Is that all you want to know?" she said.

"You haven't told me anything yet," Clarence protested.

"I told you that the king is on his way. What more could I tell you?"

"When will he sit under the arcade? You must tell me the precise moment."

"He will sit there in the afternoon."

"This afternoon?"

"It will be an afternoon like any other afternoon. But an afternoon such as you will never know again—unspeakable, more radiant than the sun at his zenith, more vast and more profound than the sky itself. An afternoon without parallel."

"That's no answer!"

"Was your question a question?" she asked.

She had closed her eyes, and it looked as if her face had become drained of all colour. It did not turn white, but grey, dirty grey, an ashen grey; and perhaps it really had turned quite white, but the dust of the years, or simply the dust, had soiled it. "How ugly you are!" thought Clarence. He could see her quite clearly. He could never see any woman's face, except in the oval frame of a hut window; but he could see Dioki's face perfectly clear. When he met other women, all he could see were their breasts and their buttocks; he could not take his eyes away from their breasts and their buttocks; but Dioki was different. Her dugs were so withered that his glance was not encouraged to linger on them; as for her buttocks, they had collapsed long ago: one would have sworn that she had no buttocks left.

"Your question wasn't a question," she said. "It's as if you were to ask the snake at what instant he will bite you. He doesn't know himself. No, one could not give an answer to your question."

"But doesn't your profession oblige you to answer all questions?"

"Am I the king?" she said.

She cast herself down on the ground and began rolling in the dust.

"I am not the king!" she cried. "I am not the king!"

She was rolling in the dust, among the serpents and these were hissing and rolling themselves round her body. They were embracing her, enfolding her: and she—she was crying out. But what sort of embrace was this? Clarence could hardly believe what he saw. These were the passionate convulsions of love itself!

Clarence would have liked to run away; but the snake that held him prisoner in its coil was watching him narrowly; at the first movement Clarence made, the creature showed its fangs. "Don't stir!" Dioki had told him. Clarence realised that he must remain completely motionless if he did not want the snake to bite him. "A weapon . . . If I had a weapon," he said to himself. But he had no weapon. And even if he had had one, what could he have done with it? The snake would have forestalled him!

"Dioki!" Clarence cried.

But Dioki did not answer. She was too busy doing something else: she was heaving up and down among the snakes and obviously that was all she could think of at the moment.

"Silly old woman!" Clarence hissed between his teeth.

Had he to watch this display to the very end, this lascivious spectacle of an old woman whose writhings were obviously related to the lustful jerkings of physical passion? . . . He closed his eyes. But then he seemed to see even more clearly the old woman and the serpents; he could see with the utmost distinctness their ignoble fumblings and penetrations; he could hear even more plainly the sighs and the groanings of the old woman's ecstasy, the hissings and slitherings of the serpents . . .

Then he opened his eyes again. He tried to fix them on something, to occupy them with something, anything to spare them the sight of the old woman and her snakes and their orgiastic writhings. For want of anything better, he decided to fix his gaze on the yard he was in. Oh! he did not succeed in turning away his eyes straight away. But when he had managed to eradicate from his sight and as it were wipe the old woman and her serpents from the face of the earth, he marvelled at the tremendous extent of the courtyard.

When he had looked down on it from the top of the steps, it had appeared to be merely a ditch, the sort of ditch where a wild beast rather than a human creature would have its abode. But now it was an endless courtyard, a courtyard that could not be compassed by the naked eye. And above, the sky was no longer there; but high, very high, as high as the heavens, was a rocky vault.

This vault was of the same red colour as the ground, the same red as the great cloud that had hung over the esplanade; like the cloud, it was radiant with light, radiant with sunlight, though the sun was absent from the cavern and the light seemed curiously to emanate from the rock roof itself.

After a moment, Clarence saw a shadow advancing towards him across the vault, as if clouds were passing over that rocky heaven. The shadow gradually grew longer and longer, and finally occupied a considerable space. Then a second shadow, smaller and shaped like a tower, rose up out of the first. So placed, the two shadows made a curious impression—they were like the royal palace in Adramé: the first represented the long wall, and the second the round-tower behind the wall. As for the lighter-coloured rectangle that lay above the two shadows, it gave a no less curious impression of the esplanade at Adramé.

And these were not just the shapes that one thinks one sees in clouds, for those shapes are too vague and too fleeting. No, the outlines of the shadows become more and more pronounced, and now Clarence could make out the crenellations of the long outer wall of the palace and the exterior stairway round the central tower. The vision rapidly grew clearer. Soon, Clarence could see the platform at the top of the central tower as clearly as he had seen it on the day when he had gone up to the esplanade. As on that day, the platform seemed to give access to the sky itself, seemed to link the palace with the sky and to make of it some strange earthly territory of the heavens.

Clarence's eyes were fixed on the central tower when the sun appeared over the edge of the platform. In that star-shaped radiance of the rising sun, a slighter radiance appeared, a frail and formidable radiance. And suddenly the king revealed himself! Pages ran to him at once and seized the king's arms, upheld them, guided their sovereign's steps; the great white mantle was floating lightly on the air of morning.

The king slowly descended the steps of the outer stairway. For a moment, the long wall hid him from sight; and during that moment the wall itself, as if illuminated by a great inner radiance, sprang to life; the colonnade stood out clearly, and the little door stood out like a brighter shadow. Then the door was opened, and the king left his palace in a flood of light. The esplanade was covered by a `dense throng of people who were hopping up and down, clapping their hands and probably uttering loud cries. Behind the king came the escort of dancing pages, and the royal palfrey; and all around were warriors mounted on prancing horses that were wearing their long kilts. When he reached the centre of the esplanade, the king was elevated into his saddle. The kilted horses pranced, and the warriors cleared a path through the crowd. Then the king began to move forward, protected from the heat by an enormous parasol . . . It seemed as if the entire scene which Clarence had witnessed on the esplanade had taken place all over again, only in reverse.

Then the palace, the central tower and the esplanade faded away, and the king began to proceed with his entourage towards the open country. It was the very countryside that Clarence had journeyed through after leaving Adramé; a countryside scattered with peaceful farmsteads and rich in cornfields; and perhaps the procession was taking the very same route, or if it was not the very same, it was a parallel one, for soon the wall of the forest appeared in its turn. The wall was no less dense and no less formidable—and one can imagine that the odour was no less heavy and no less suffocating—but the king had no sooner begun moving towards the forest than it started opening up in front of him. The king entered this breach which split the forest in two, which split it right down the middle as if it had been no more than a bit of old threadbare cloth.

Clarence could see the king distinctly. He could see him, in spite of the shadow cast by the great parasol, as clearly as if he had been within a foot of the royal personage . . . And because he could see the king so distinctly, because he felt himself so close to the royal presence, because it seemed to him that he would never again be quite so close to the royal presence, he tried to catch the king's eye.

"If only I can catch his eye now . . ." he thought. And he felt a sudden glow which had as it were borne him forward and brought him even closer to the king.

But he soon realised that the king's eye noticed nothing, and that the sovereign was moving on as if he were apart from everything around him. His eye, it seemed, might have been turned inward or might have been contemplating his own person . . . And where could such an eye have found a place of rest, if not in himself? . . . All the same, so much indifference cast a chill . . . Of course, one could understand such indifference—Clarence understood it—and one could accept it, one could resign oneself to accepting it. One knew quite well that one had no right to anything but indifference and that in fact one deserved to be treated with repugnance: but all this did not make that indifference less chill, or less cruel, or less desolating . . . Clarence suddenly felt himself chilled to the marrow . . .

Almost at the same moment, a great cry made the vault where all this had taken place vanish away. And the sky reappeared with its profound blueness, its blueness that was almost as deep as black, its unbearable brilliance. Clarence lowered his eyes. At his feet, the old woman was rising painfully from the ground, and the serpents one by one were falling from her; they left her gently, and as if regretfully, and as if they could not bring themselves to abandon her without a last intimate caress. The old woman raised tired eyes to Clarence.

"You know," she said. "You know now."

"Yes, I know . . ." said Clarence.

"Go away," she said. "Go away now . . . Leave me alone."

The snake that had been coiled round Clarence suddenly uncoiled itself and dropped loosely into the red dust.

"Go on! Go away!" cried Dioki impatiently.

She bent down to pick up one of the calabashes that Clarence had brought her and raised it to her lips. She drank so greedily that two thin trickles of wine flowed from the corners of her toothless mouth. Clarence backed away. As he moved away from her, he saw that the two baskets of eggs were empty.

"Haven't you gone yet?" said Dioki.

"I'm going," said Clarence.

She gave him a quizzical look.

"Remember there's no woman so old that she cannot be ill-treated!" she cried.

Whereupon she began to laugh at the top of her voice, and her laughter made her shake all over, and even seemed to make her bones shake; those bones which in places seemed to want to stick through the naked flesh, and that were like dead sticks in a wrinkled and rotten old bag.

Clarence went swiftly up the steps. The two boys at the top were waiting for him; their teeth were chattering with fear. No sooner had he reached them than they each seized him by an arm and ran with him towards the palisade. They ran as if the whole pack of serpents was at their heels.

"Did you see the cavern," the boys replied. "But we saw Dioki coming towards you with her serpents, and we thought you were going to die."

"I might easily have died!" said Clarence.

But he was not thinking about Dioki or the snakes; he was thinking of the king's eye . . . Now he was moving forward, and of the radiance of the king very slowly; he was feeling strangely shattered, strangely torn; his legs hurt him, as if he had been sitting too long in an uncomfortable position, or as if . . . But the comparison was so unthinkable that Clarence dismissed it at once. When he reached Diallo's forge, he paused.

"Let's rest here a moment," he said.

He crouched down in front of the fire.

"I was beginning to wonder if you were coming back," said Diallo.

"I'm done in," said Clarence.

"What did she tell you?"

"Less than nothing. She hardly told me anything. But I *saw*."

"Did you have a dream?" asked Diallo.

"I don't know . . . Yes, perhaps it *was* a dream."

That rocky vault, and the shadows on its roof—perhaps after all they were only the figments of a dream. But do dreams record events with so much detail? Do they ever record anything faithfully?

"It cannot have been a dream," he said. "But how can I tell what it was? . . . Perhaps it was a vision."

"And what about these two?" asked Diallo, pointing to the boys.

"They did not see anything," said Clarence.

"We saw the old woman coming towards you," said the boys. "She put her arms round your shoulders and pressed you against her. She . . ."

"Shut up!" Clarence said sharply. "You just make these tales up."

"But . . ." the boys began.

"No, they did not see a thing," said Clarence. "They make up things all the time; they think it makes them more interesting."

But had the boys really made it up? Clarence made a gesture with his hand as if brushing away the horrors that assailed his imagination.

"What are you forging?" he asked Diallo.

"An axe."

"Another one?"

"Yes. But this one . . . This one . . ."

"Will you ever forge anything else?"

"I want to forge better and better ones," said Diallo. "And this one . . . Oh! I should like the king never to have seen a finer one, although I know well enough that it's impossible."

He went to the fire and took the axe out. It was in the shape of a crescent like all those he had made before.

"You always make them crescent-shaped," said Clarence.

"Yes, always! But just look at the curve on this one. I don't think I've ever made anything as fine."

"It is very fine," said Clarence. "I wouldn't swear that it's any finer than the ones you made before, but it is certainly very fine. It is like a crescent moon."

"Yes, like the moon," said Diallo dreamily. "It shall have the purity and brilliance of the moon."

"You'd better hurry up, if you're going to offer it to the king."

"Did Dioki tell you that I had to hurry?"

"She didn't tell me anything definite."

"Then why should I hurry? It's not the sort of work you can do in a hurry."

"I don't know," said Clarence, "I've the feeling that the king won't be long in coming now."

"The boys said you were of quite a different opinion a little while ago."

"A little while ago, yes," said Clarence. "But since then . . ."

"Year after year I've been waiting for him," said Diallo.

He was hitting the axe with sharp little blows, as if afraid that any more exuberant blow might destroy the sharpness of the blade.

"You as well," he went on, "you've been waiting."

"Waiting! Waiting!" cried Clarence. "Oh, how I've waited
for him! The king only knows just how long I've been waiting
for him! . . . But I haven't always waited for him with the
same ardent longing, with the same fervour. At times . . ."

He saw Akissi, or rather he saw everything that lay behind
Akissi and behind his stay in Aziana. He could see the frightful face of the darkness, the shadowy and midnight part, the
unmentionable part which lies at the back of all things: all
those women who had kept on visiting his bed at night, who
had kept going backwards and forwards between the harem
and his hut. And he was overwhelmed with disgust. Clarence
savoured this disgust for a moment; it was like a bitter weed
or the aftertaste of vomit . . . But he was not always chewing
that bitter weed; and he did not always have the taste of
vomit in his mouth. That weed did not taste bitter until
afterwards, and that nausea was only the sickening feeling
which follows on too rich a feast. There was the South: at
least what Clarence called "the South." There was the beast
inside him, the lustful frenzy of the beast, and an irresistible
appetite for the unmentionable . . .

"I have not always waited for him as I should have done,"
he said.

"No one waits for him as they ought to," said Diallo.

Clarence remained thoughtful. He thought that the odour,
the South . . . Yes, they existed, without doubt, the odour,
and the South. But had there been nothing else . . . Oh! if
there had only been the odour and the South, if there had
not been that secret complaisance, that secret compli-
city! . . .

"Clarence!" the boys suddenly cried. "Clarence! Diallo!"

They had leapt to their feet, and Diallo was standing with
his hammer in the air, as if turned to stone. They listened
hard.

"What is it?" said Clarence.

"The king! . . . It's the king!" shouted the boys.

"What do you say?" Clarence asked.

"The king is coming! The drums are announcing the arrival of the king!"

"The king!" exclaimed Clarence.

He rose to his feet. His eyes were burning. At last! . . . At last, the king was coming! . . . He was coming down the cavern's rocky wall . . . He was riding on his horse, and the great parasol, above his head, was swaying from side to side.

"The king!" he cried.

His face was shining with a radiance which certainly belonged more to the king than to himself.

"He is coming, and without any warning," said Diallo. "He is coming, just as I told you . . . I was waiting for him . . . Oh! I have never stopped waiting for him! . . . And he is coming without warning after all!"

He was looking at his axe, which was unfinished.

"I won't have time to finish it," he said.

"But you have other ones," said Clarence.

"Many others," said Diallo. "But this was the one I had set my hopes on."

He sighed. Why was he sad? Hadn't he made his choice long ago? But perhaps it's not as easy as all that, to make a choice. Perhaps . . .

"I shall choose the very finest," he said. "Or rather I'll offer them all. Then perhaps what is lacking in quality will be made up for in quantity."

"When will the king be here?" asked Clarence.

"To-morrow! He'll be here to-morrow, on the stroke of noon," the boys replied.

"Yes, on the stroke of noon," said Clarence softly.

And he seemed to see the arcade; he saw it looking as it did from the door of his hut.

"And in the afternoon," he said, "he will sit under the arcade. He will sit where the naba sits . . ."

His face still shone with rapture. He was glowing as if the king had already laid his eye upon him. Yes, as if another face, a loftier, greater gaze had already become part of his own . . .

2

THE KING

"Scrub my back, Akissi," said Clarence. "Scrub it well, scrub it better than you have ever done before. You know, a day like to-day . . ."

"Don't you worry," she said. "I'll give it a thorough scrub . . . Have you seen the carpets?"

"The courtyard is covered with them," he said. "There are even some on the square. They are all along the palace wall. I did not know the naba had all those carpets."

"That's why you always laughed at his chests."

"I used to laugh at them without really laughing. I used to laugh because the naba made such a fuss of them, and then out would jump a lot of rats."

"But didn't I tell you there was more than rats in them?
. . . Bend down a little, will you? I can't get the back of your
neck washed properly."

"Get the stool," he said. "It will be easier for you . . . But
he didn't keep all those carpets rolled up in his chests, did
he?"

"He had them rolled up in his hut . . . Not all of them, of
course; but he kept the most expensive ones rolled up."

She lifted the earthenware jar and poured a little water
down Clarence's back.

"Don't pour too much over me at once," he said, "or the
hut will be flooded."

"I can't do it any other way."

"No, you mustn't, not with all these carpets about. I
wonder why they set them out at daybreak. The king isn't
coming until the stroke of noon."

"When I've finished washing you, I'll mop up the water,"
she said.

"Rub me hard. I don't want to have the slightest speck of
dirt on me."

"When I've scrubbed you with the pumice-stone, you'll be
as bright as a new pin."

"Have you noticed the master of ceremonies? He keeps
coming and going, running here, running there . . ."

"He really seems to be everywhere at once," she laughed.

"He is everywhere and nowhere!"

"You shouldn't say such things. On a day like this, it is he
who sees that everything is done properly."

"I can't bear him."

"Well, you're not the only one!"

She started to laugh.

"He thinks he's the naba!" Clarence said. "He imagines
that everyone is at his beck and call."

"May the king preserve me from ever taking *you* into my services," said the master of ceremonies, entering at that moment. "I couldn't imagine any more disgraceful . . ."

"But you're not above listening at doors."

"I don't listen at doors, or at windows," said the master of ceremonies. "Not even at the tiny window of the court-room, as some people do . . . If I happened to hear what you were saying, it was because I couldn't help it. Besides you may be sure I don't attach the slightest importance to what you say about me."

"I see that," said Clarence. "You are above all that; you are the master of ceremonies! . . . Don't forget, you used to wear a cold compress on your backside!"

"I have not forgotten. It was only a token compress, but I have not forgotten. I never forget anything!"

"Then next time don't forget to knock before you come in. My hut is not a public thoroughfare."

"Admitted. Provisionally, at any rate. But tell me this: does the naba knock before entering a hut?"

"You are not the naba. You *think* you're the naba! . . . You allow yourself too much latitude."

"Not as much as you think, Clarence. I have come as a messenger from the naba, and on the naba's orders. Inas-much as I am the official message-bearer, I am entitled to all the privileges due to him who sent me. In the circumstances, I could command you to put on your clothes to hear the message I bring. However, I shall relieve you of the necessity to clothe yourself as befits the occasion; primarily because I am a person without pride, even though I have reason to be proud of myself, and the right to be proud of all I do; and also because everyone knows that you take all your clothes off on the slightest pretext . . ."

"You make me sick!" said Clarence. "Come to the point!"

"I am coming to it," said the master of ceremonies. "The naba has given orders that you are under no circumstances to leave your hut to-day."

"What!" cried Clarence.

He took a step forward and looked defiantly at the master of ceremonies.

"Have you gone mad?" asked Clarence.

"The naba cannot be mad. The naba . . ."

"The naba ought to know that on a day like this I can't stay shut up in my hut."

"Why can't you? It doesn't mean that because you may not leave your hut you will not take part in the day's festivities. From your hut you will be able to see everything; you'll be able to see the dancing on the square through the left-hand porthole; and by looking through the right-hand porthole you will see the reception under the arcade even better than you would if you were on the square."

"I understand. I understand perfectly," said Clarence. "I shall see everything. In a way, I shall see everything. But the king—the king will not see *me!*"

"The king? . . . Why should the king see *you?* Do you think the king is coming just to see you?"

"The king . . ." Clarence stammered.

And he stopped short. No, the king would certainly not come to Aziana just to see Clarence. The king . . . The king was coming to make a visitation to the naba, and . . .

"I have conveyed to you the naba's exact words," said the master of ceremonies.

"His 'words'?" cried Clarence. "The naba's 'words'? . . . You've given yourself away this time! Since when has the naba started using words? . . . I shall believe what you say only when I've had a talk with the naba myself, and not before. Go and tell the naba that I request an audience with him."

"I am sorry—there will be no audiences to-day. You must understand that on a day like this the naba hasn't a moment to himself. Every minute of his time is taken . . ."

"Well, then, one second would be long enough to . . ."

"Even a second would be too much. The naba could not possibly free himself from his commitments—not even for a second."

"Did you contrive all this?"

"I have drawn up the day's programme of ceremonies, and I have done no more than I always do on such occasions, for the ceremonials are always the same. Consequently I have not overstepped the mark in any way, but have simply performed my usual duties. If you care to see in this some sort of contrivance, you are welcome to do so! . . . But enough of that. Such a discussion is not only quite unnecessary, but also most inconvenient. It is not for me, nor for you either, to question the naba's orders. Moreover, I am not bound to give you an account of my actions, still less to make excuses for myself, when I have not been guilty of any dereliction of duty. And now I've spent far too much time in a hut where I can see my presence is found to be undesirable, and where, in consequence, I have suffered offence to my own person . . . I would desire you to ponder well what I have said, and get it firmly fixed in your head, even though that head should be the most brainless on the face of the earth!"

He did not wait for his host to reply, but at once gave a curt parting bow—either because he really felt offended or because he really had no more time to spare. In any case, it would have been useless for him to stay any longer: Clarence had no intention of replying to such a vain and pompous speech. He was like a man who has been hit on the head with a heavy club.

"I can't understand it . . . can *you?*" he asked Akissi when he had recovered from the shock.

"What can you make of that kind of talk?" she asked. "The man is just an old windbag."

"I wish Baloum would come."

"Perhaps the naba is afraid you might soil his carpets."

"Well, after all, they are there to be walked on! But he need not have feared . . . I would have taken my shoes off."

"He must have said to himself: 'He's a white man . . .' "

"Look, go and get Baloum."

"I was just going to dry you."

"No! Go at once! I'll dry myself."

"Here is the towel," she said.

"All right," he said impatiently. "Now, go quickly!"

He began to dry himself, but stopped almost at once and began pacing up and down. What a blow! . . . Was the naba really going to stop him from showing himself to the king? . . . If only he knew what went on in the naba's head! But who could tell him? The naba talked with his beard, and everybody claimed they knew what he meant when he wagged the beard. But perhaps the movements of the beard meant nothing at all, perhaps it wagged for no reason at all: and because it could not express anything, because the things it wagged for were trivial things like shaking off a fly or easing the muscles of the lower jaw, everyone could draw his own conclusions, everyone could interpret the movements of the beard to suit his own ends, and, of course, always to his own advantage. The master of ceremonies . . . "Why didn't I let them go on flogging him?" thought Clarence bitterly. "That would have been the end of the master of ceremonies!"

Oh! if they ever flogged him again, he would not intervene, and the master of ceremonies' backside could go on swelling, could swell to ten times its normal size, till it was ready to burst, and he still wouldn't stop them! Certainly the spectators would no longer have cause to be displeased; they would have their money's worth, and their cruelty, their sense of justice, and anything else they cared to name, would be satisfied—anything else their folly and their eternal baseness might suggest . . .

"What's this I hear?" said Samba Baloum.

"Baloum!" cried Clarence, running towards him. "Has Akissi told you?"

"She told me what the naba said, and . . ."

"Well, then, hurry up and tell the naba I simply cannot stay shut up in my hut on a day like this. Go on! Don't dawdle!"

Lord! how slow Baloum could be! Clarence shoved him from behind.

"Go on!"

"Don't shove me like that!" said Samba Baloum. "You can see I'm going."

"Quickly!" said Clarence. "Don't take such tiny steps. Go as fast as you can!"

He watched him going over to the naba's palace. He was quivering with impatience. When the master of ceremonies had made for the door, Clarence had been stunned; now he was all on edge. He could not imagine why Baloum was swaying along with such tiny, tripping steps. Was this the moment to sway one's hips?

"You haven't dried yourself," Akissi said.

"I haven't time to dry myself!" he cried.

"I shall dry you," she said, taking the towel from him.

"Don't touch me. I shall not dry myself until I've had an answer from the naba," he cried.

"I don't see the connection," she said.

"If I had to stay cooped up in here all day, I don't see any need to dry myself."

"That's not reasonable."

"It's stupid," he admitted.

He sat down on the bed, then got up at once and went on pacing up and down the hut.

"If only Baloum would get a move on!" he exclaimed. "He's always so slow!"

He told himself he really never had any luck, and that he had never had any. How was it other people were always so lucky? Things just fell in their lap, that was it. They just took what they wanted. But whenever *he* tried to get his hands on anything, they closed on air—the bird had flown!

"Here's Baloum coming back," said Akissi.

Clarence ran to the door.

"Baloum!" he shouted.

"Don't get worked up like that!" said Samba Baloum. "It makes me hot to look at you, and you're making yourself hot, too . . . Everything's arranged. The naba merely requests you not to walk on the carpets."

"Oh, Baloum, you're a real friend!"

"Yes, I know, but in future don't make me bustle about so. I'm sweating all over."

"If you hadn't . . ." began Clarence, almost speechless with joy.

"He didn't want me to wipe him dry," said Akissi.

"What a child you are," said Samba Baloum. "Let Akissi dry you, and hurry up and put your *boubou* on. The ceremonies are about to begin . . . Well, I'm going now; I've got so much to do, I don't know how I'll ever get through it."

He sighed.

"Watch out for the carpets," he said as he went out. "Remember to take your shoes off."

Akissi came up to Clarence to dry him.

"Akissi," said Clarence, "do you realise how happy I am?"

"You are getting worked up about nothing," she said.

"Don't you see that to me it's a . . . a question of life and death?"

"But you never give me a thought."

"I *was* thinking about you. I was worried about you."

"Were you really?"

She stopped wiping him for a moment and stood in front of him with the towel in her hand.

"Don't you believe me?" he asked.

"I don't know."

She kept twisting the towel in her hands.

"But of course the king comes first in my thoughts."

"Yes," she said.

And she sniffed tearfully.

"You're not going to cry, are you?"

"No."

"I didn't intend to be cooped up in Aziana for the rest of my life."

"No. You came here to wait for the king. And then . . ."

She could not finish what she was saying.

"What?" he asked.

"Nothing."

She was still twisting the towel in her hands.

"I shall be wearing the green *boubou* with the white flowers," he said.

"When the master of ceremonies sees you . . ."

"Call him over here," he said. "And give him his full title. You just watch how I handle him!"

"Your excellency the master of ceremonies!" Akissi shouted.

"He's coming," she said. "You might have put on your *boubou* to receive him in."

"Leave it where it is. I'll receive him in whatever way I please."

"Did you call me?" the master of ceremonies asked.

"I had someone call you," said Clarence. "I would have called you myself, but I still haven't had time to put my *boubou* on, and I could not decently expose myself at the door of my hut without my *boubou*."

"But I thought . . ." said the master of ceremonies.

"Yes, usually I do. But I cannot allow myself the freedom I usually enjoy when I am with you . . . I have been thinking over what you told me just now."

"You mean you've finally got it knocked into that thick skull of yours . . ."

"Exactly," Clarence interrupted him. "You are a wise man, full of good counsels. And that is why I called you over . . . You'll share a calabash with me, won't you? . . . Akissi!"

Akissi unrolled the mat, and Clarence sat down on it beside the master of ceremonies.

"I shan't take up too much of your valuable time," he went on, knocking his calabash against the master of ceremonies'. "I know that to-day you are overwhelmed with work which anyone less diligent and less intelligent than you would never be able to bring to a successful conclusion."

"You are too kind," said the master of ceremonies gravely.

"Do you think," asked Clarence, "that my green *boubou* with the white flowers would be suitable for today's ceremonies?"

"Green with white flowers?" the master of ceremonies said in a thoughtful voice, looking at his calabash.

"Yes: olive green with white flowers."

"But what does it matter what you wear?" cried the master of ceremonies. "Hasn't the naba forbidden you to appear at the reception?"

"That *was* his intention, so I am told. But things have changed: Baloum has spoken to the naba."

"Is that why you are so nice all of a sudden?" asked the master of ceremonies.

"Have not our relationships always been of the utmost cordiality? If, on the day when the naba had your backside flogged with your own rod, you got away with nothing worse than a cold compress on your behind—a token compress, as you so admirably and elegantly put it—did you not owe your escape to my own affectionate intervention?"

"I have already manifested my gratitude to you for what you did."

"You have manifested your gratitude with such generosity and spontaneity that this morning, this very morning, you were trying to move heaven and earth to stop me from meeting the king!"

"I did it for your own good."

"No?" said Clarence. "Heaven is my witness—I never realised that . . . Akissi, did *you* realise that . . ."

And he began to laugh in a particularly insulting fashion. He felt he now had the master of ceremonies tied up in knots—he had him tied hand and foot, as on the day when he was flogged. He wished Noaga and Nagoa could have been present to witness the discomfiture of this malevolent creature.

"Do not laugh too loud, or too long," said the master of ceremonies. "It's nothing to laugh about, and you may soon be laughing on the other side of your face. Why should you meet the king, anyhow? Have you done anything to deserve such an honour?"

"I have been waiting for him."

"And kicking your heels at the same time."

"I wanted to work," said Clarence.

"But you were careful to avoid doing anything. On the other hand, if you had continued your journey through the forest . . ."

"A fool's errand."

"There's no such thing as a fool's errand," said the master of ceremonies. "Everything depends upon the spirit in which a thing is approached. If you had continued your journey, you would have something to show for it to-day—feet bruised with treacherous roots, and hands torn by cruel thorns. Nothing much, I grant you; these are small things. But you haven't even *that* to show—not the smallest scratch or bruise: you have no claim to any kind of merit."

"No claim at all, that's true. But perhaps the king will give me credit for my good-will."

"*Your* good-will! . . . Don't make me laugh!"

"That's all I have," said Clarence.

"What use is your good-will to you if you never make use of it? Only those who deserve it are allowed to have access to the king!"

"Yes, I see that. But if I have done nothing good—for perhaps I *have* done nothing good, however much I've wanted to—neither have I done anything really reprehensible."

"You haven't done anything reprehensible?" said the master of ceremonies. "Really? Do you mean to stand there and tell me you've done nothing reprehensible?"

He struck the ground with his rod.

"Oh, no, *you've* done nothing reprehensible!" He had adopted a rather unpleasantly familiar tone; and he suddenly sniggered very provocatively.

"You've done nothing reprehensible, only got the whole harem with child!"

"How was I to know?" said Clarence. "The king is my witness that for long enough I didn't know what was going on."

"But you found out eventually. You soon realised that the little half-caste brats didn't come from nowhere."

"Don't talk to me like that!" cried Clarence. "I find your familiarity offensive. I don't know what right you have to talk to me like that."

"I'll talk to you as I please!" said the master of ceremonies. "I'm not here to spare your feelings. There is a time for everything, and this is no time to spare your feelings. I'm going to tell you once and for all what's on my mind, and to hell with my backside. I'm going to let you have a piece of my mind, whether you like it or not; I'm going to reckon up what you've been doing and how you've been doing it while you've been kicking your heels here in Aziana . . . It's been nothing but idle chatter with any Tom, Dick or Harry; it's been nothing but guzzling and wine-bibbing and pinching the naba's calabashes, foolish escapades with those two scamps and long idle hours gossiping at the forge; you took months to weave a horrible little towel; you performed your ablutions naked in full view of the passers-by; you . . . But what did it all amount to? . . . Your house became like a public flour mill, open to all and everyone. And what sort of flour did you grind? The unmentionable things that went on here! . . . Every night, you were with someone different, like two snails out on a filthy crawl!"

"Shut up!" Clarence shouted.

"Why should I shut up? Have I said anything you don't know already? Doesn't it speak for itself? Even if I were to shut up, the odour of your hut would speak for itself. Can't you smell that odour? . . . No, you can't even smell it any longer! It has entered into your flesh and bones, and you can't smell it any more! . . . And do you think you'll ever get rid of it? You won't get rid of it by making Akissi scrub your back with pumice-stone; nothing will ever wash it away! The king will smell it from the arcade; as soon as you go near him, he'll smell it!"

"Will you shut up when I tell you?" shouted Clarence.

He had stood up and was now holding his hands out in front of him, as if to ward off this flow of venom.

"I'll say no more," said the master of ceremonies. "I haven't told you a hundredth part of what I had to tell you; but I'll say no more. I've said enough."

He gazed at Clarence for a moment.

"A cock! that's all you are, a great cock!" he said. "It was for a cock the beggar sold you to the naba, and it is as a cock you've behaved."

"He sold me?" said Clarence incredulously.

"Yes, sold you! Bartered you, if you like. Bartered you for an ass and a woman past her first youth."

He too rose to his feet and pounded the earth with his rod.

"Have you the effrontery to tell me that you didn't know about that either? There's a lot of things you know nothing about! Perhaps there are one or two things that you really

don't know anything about, but there are too many things
that you simply pretend not to know anything about. Perhaps you didn't know that you are no longer your own master, that you belong body and soul to the naba; well, now you
know: you know that even if you wanted to serve the king,
you could not possibly do so. But what right have you to
serve the king? Even if the naba consented to let you go
. . . and there is no reason to suspect that he would give up
what belongs to him . . . that he would be able to overcome
his miserliness . . . what would the king want with such
a cock? . . . Can you imagine the naba presenting you to
the king? Can you imagine the naba saying: 'This is my
cock? . . .' Or, 'I should like you to meet my cock? . . .' Or,
'Would you care for this cock? . . .' Oh, you may count
yourself fortunate that such things will never be said about
you in the king's presence!"

"A cock . . ." said Clarence in a wretched voice.

"A cock is not worthy to appear in front of the king," said
the master of ceremonies. "A great cock like you . . ."

He spat.

"Foul as you are, you are good for nothing but the harem!"

Turning his back on Clarence, he walked towards the door.
On reaching the threshold, he shook himself, brushed his
boubou with the back of his hand, as if to shake off some dirt
or blow away some unpleasant odour. Then he went off as if
he was running away from the plague. He went off with his
own pestilential odour in his heart and mind; a pestilence
more virulent than the plague itself.

With his departure, a great peace should have descended.
In fact, the hut seemed just as noisy as before. All those
accusations the master of ceremonies had hurled at Clarence's head and at the walls of the hut continued to echo and
re-echo like the noise of the sea in an ocean-shell. Clarence

seemed to hear them reverberating like the noise of a mighty ocean. He could hear each one, each particular wave; he could hear them all, confounded in the same furious roaring: they were like a stormy sea.

A cock! . . . Yes, that was just what he was; a great cock, that was all he was! Others had told him so before, but they had said it jokingly. But it was nothing to joke about; now that the king was drawing near to Aziana, it was nothing to joke about any more! Besides, it had never been a very funny or witty joke—in fact it had been a very indelicate one! It was not the sort of thing that lent itself to good jokes; and the master of ceremonies had certainly not treated the subject in a joking fashion.

"Why don't you say anything?" asked Akissi.

She came up to him and took his hand.

"You're trembling," she said.

"I know I'm trembling."

"Do you feel cold?"

"It's not that. The cold is in my heart."

"You shouldn't tremble like this," she said. "The master of ceremonies is always shouting and making loud speeches; but no one pays any attention."

"Don't you understand?" he said. "I'm . . . impure."

"Impure?" she echoed. "What do you mean? . . . No, I do not understand. I don't see anything impure about you."

"Why did you always leave the hut at nights?"

"The naba used to ask for me. Was there anything wrong in that?"

He freed his hand from her grasp.

"No, you do not understand," he said. "I don't think you will ever understand."

"Well, *that* is something I don't understand. I . . ."

She stopped suddenly.

"The drums!" she cried. "Can you hear the drums? . . . Quick, put your *boubou* on!"

"Leave my *boubou* where it is."

"You're not going out, to-day of all days, without your *boubou?*"

"I don't want to go out."

"But you *did* a little while ago. You were dying to go out. You . . ."

"I still want to," he said. "I expressed myself badly. With all my heart, I want to go out. Oh! you can't imagine how much I want to! . . . But I can't now, I can't go out any more . . ."

The shameful accusations made by the master of ceremonies still reverberated in Clarence's ears, with the same fury and the same roaring sound as a tempestuous ocean. It does not matter when you take from the sea those great sea-shells in which the ocean sounds—on a calm day or a stormy one—or when you bring them to your ear—on a calm day or a stormy one—for within them always there is the ocean that goes on roaring with the same intolerable monotony.

"You go, Akissi," he said. "Yes, you go . . . Leave me alone."

"I shall stay beside you," she said.

"No, go away . . . I'll be better alone."

"How do I know how much longer I shall see you?"

"You shall see me every day and every hour. From now on, you shall always see me. It no longer depends on me whether I see you or whether I don't see you . . . Go now! I need to be alone . . . Later . . . Later on, when I've thought a little about it all, I shall call you."

He pushed her gently towards the door. The drums were beating louder and louder.

"The king is entering Aziana," she said.

"I know," he said. "Hurry! . . ."

He went back and sat on the bed.

"The drums . . ." he said softly to himself.

But it was not the drums he could hear. He heard the noise of the sea; and he saw once again the reef, the terrible race of water that protects the shore of Africa; and cutting through this noise of rolling waves, at intervals the master of ceremonies' accusations came to him like an even louder roaring. The rolling of the drums was probably not absent from this greater roaring; yet it was not the drums that Clarence heard; and neither was it the royal progress which he saw coming towards him: it was the rolling waves he saw!

Each time the rolling wave was about to reach the shore, it was lifted up; it would lift its head, and glimpse, for a second, the red earth of Africa; then it would fall back and spread out in furious fans of foam. It would lift its head and look, but it was careful not to look too long or to approach too closely to the shore! As soon as its curiosity was satisfied, it relaxed again. And if in its wild dash to the shore it bore on its foaming crest a brittle bark, it would know quite well that the crew of the bark wanted to glimpse the red earth too; it would lift the bark and for the space of a second hoist it high on its shawling crest, and then, flowing swiftly back on itself, it would carry the bark out to the open sea again. It did not forget to draw the bark away from the shore, for it knew that once their curiosity was satisfied, the crew of the bark had nothing more to expect from the red earth of Africa. It knew, with age-old wisdom, that it would be their undoing if they were to learn any more.

But the crew of the bark would by no means be content with this one far-off glimpse. They would have neither the wisdom, nor the age-old experience of the great, rolling ocean-wave; and so they would want to touch that shore, to

tread that deep-red earth. The rolling wave would try in vain
to dissuade them and though it would take them again and
again towards the open sea, they would ignore its counsels;
they would bend to their oars with greater force and stronger
determination: and finally, they would triumph over the reef,
and touch land!

For a few hours or days, and sometimes for as long as a few
weeks, the crew of the bark would not know how to contain
their rapture. They would really believe they had won a great
victory. But what a defeat it would prove! And they would
learn how much better it would have been if the bark had
never reached the land, how much better it would have been
if the ocean had swallowed them up for ever! But this last
stroke of luck, this supreme stroke of luck, which the crew
of the bark would have looked on as a great misfortune, was
rarely granted.

"Luck . . ." sighed Clarence.

He sat a long while thinking of nothing. He had thought
about luck so much—chance, good luck, bad luck—that he
no longer knew what to think. He did not come back to earth
until he heard cries which were so piercing that every other
sound—and the Lord knows the uproar of the drums and
trumpets was deafening enough—was drowned by them. But
these cries doubtless only appeared so piercing to Clarence
because they were so familiar, because he seemed to recognise the voices of the two boys. He ran to the left-hand oval
window, which gave on to the square.

He recognised the two boys at once. Nagoa and Noaga
were in the centre of the square, and the crowd had made a
wide circle round them. The boys were wearing head-dresses
crowned with long, pointed antelope horns. They were kneeling down, and bending so that their elbows rested on the

ground. They looked like crouching beasts with great loads
on their backs.

The load seemed to weigh upon them a long time. The
crowd was silent. Then suddenly the boys lifted their behinds
and ran away like baboons, uttering animal cries.

Clarence sat down on the bed again. He knew well what
that dance had been—the two boys had repeated it often
enough for him to know the meaning of every step; it was a
fecundity mime. Would he always have to witness such inde-
cent orgies? And would the odour of the South follow him,
haunt him for ever? . . . Clarence felt a blush of shame flood
his cheeks and make them flame . . . But had he really any
right to blush? Was he so very pure?

"Did I blush at night in the hut?" he asked himself.

No, he did not blush then. At such times, he was himself
the chief actor in that mime and he felt no shame, no revulsion: he was that beast, and he was the load that weighed
upon . . . But why had they chosen to present this particular
mime to the king? Would it not be offensive to him, be an
insult to his purity? Or did the presence of the king take
away the ignominy of the display? . . . Perhaps it did . . .
Perhaps when the king was present, everything was pure!
. . . Oh! if only everything could be purified by the royal
presence! . . . No, there were impurities which nothing could
wash clean, and nothing restore . . . Probably no one could
really be offensive to the king, because the king was above
all offence. But the offence would be there. And all the waters
of the earth, all the tears and all the blood of the earth were
powerless to wash it clean . . . No, there were some things
which could not be purified.

The sound of panting breath roused Clarence from his
thoughts. The boys were standing before him. They were

breathing raucously. They must have run like the wind from the dancing space to the hut; they hadn't even waited to take off their costumes.

"Why are you wearing those antelope head-dresses?" Clarence asked them. "Take them off! Throw away those antelope horns and those animal skins!"

"Didn't you see us dancing?"

"I saw the last part only. I saw more than I wanted . . . When you started shouting, I went to look out of the window."

"You should have come on to the square," said Nagoa.

"And let the king see me?" said Clarence bitterly.

"You would have seen the whole of the mime," said Noaga. "The last part was . . ."

"The last part of it is pure filth!" said Clarence.

"Why didn't you watch the beginning?" Nagoa asked.

"I don't like that mime at all," said Clarence. "Even the costume I find distasteful."

"We were wearing it for the last time," said Noaga.

And he threw his head-dress in a corner.

"To-morrow, we are going with the king," he said.

"To-morrow!" said Clarence.

He looked at the antelope head-dress. Noaga was kicking it around.

"You should come, too," said Nagoa, throwing his head-dress down in turn. "Why will you not be coming?"

"Haven't I always wanted to come?" said Clarence.

"I don't know," said Noaga. "Before you started living in the hut, before all that . . . Well, *before*, you wanted to come, you certainly wanted to come then. But afterwards . . ."

"One does not always know quite what you want," said Nagoa.

"Have I ever wanted anything else?" Clarence asked.

"Yet if I had been firm, and strong-willed," he thought, "would these children be doubting my sincerity?"

"I have always wanted to come," he repeated.

But had he really wanted, always wanted to? "In the end one gives up hoping for anything," he had said. He had said that, and in the end he had given up hope of ever seeing the king. There had been moments when the arrival of the king had seemed to him incredible, impossible; moments when he had really begun to doubt everything and when everything had filled him with despair. And he heard the voice of the master of ceremonies echoing through his brain: "Of what use is your good-will, if you have no intention of using it?"

"Haven't I always wanted to come?" he cried.

He looked anxiously at the boys. He was expecting them to acknowledge his good-will; he was looking at them now as if his whole life depended on what they said, or their testimony. But what testimony could he expect from others that could not already be found within himself?

"Then why have you not presented yourself to the king?" Nagoa asked.

"Can you not smell the odour that clings to me?"

"What odour?" said Noaga. "Put on your *boubou*. When the king passes in front of your hut, you will present yourself."

He had taken off his animal skin and was rolling it into a ball; then he threw it to the other end of the hut.

"I cannot present myself now," said Clarence.

He looked at the two head-dresses, and the two animal skins at the back of the hut, and thought that his place would be there, henceforth, with those cast-off skins.

"It is too late," he said.

"Too late," said a voice from outside. "Too late for what?"

Diallo entered the hut.

"*You* know," said Clarence. "You certainly know better than I do; though it's still not too late, for you."

"It is always too late," said Diallo. "We have barely finished being born, before it's already too late for something or other. But the king knows that, and that is why there is always time."

"Is that what you said yesterday?" Clarence asked.

"Yesterday?" said Diallo. "What's yesterday got to do with to-day? It is only this day and hour that count."

"Can't you smell the odour?" said Clarence.

"What odour?" said Diallo.

"Put on your *boubou* and come with us," said Nagoa.

"No," said Clarence. "Everyone according to his merit. Everyone has the fate he deserves."

"An axe, Clarence, a simple axe, that is all I possess," said Diallo. "Do you think that's anything to brag about?"

"But you *possess* that axe," said Clarence. "That simple axe is *yours* ... I haven't anything. Or rather ... Oh, if I *did* have nothing, if it were only possible for me to have nothing! ... But I have this odour, this ineradicable odour. Can't you smell it?"

"I don't know what you're talking about," said Diallo. "There is always some slight odour ..."

"Of course, I also have my good-will," said Clarence.

And he sniggered.

"Only now I know just what it's worth, good-will. And my own good-will in particular. It's ..."

"It's what?" asked Samba Baloum, tripping lightly in and swaying his hips, as was his wont.

"It's the good-will ... of a great cock, Baloum!"

"Where did you get that from?" said Samba Baloum.

"The master of ceremonies has opened my eyes at last."

"The master of ceremonies! Do you take any notice of what *he* says? I thought you knew what to expect from these so-called 'just' men."

"Don't *you* ever take any notice of him?"

"Only in order to be able to say the exact opposite to what he says himself. That's all! That's how *you* should treat that whited sepulchre!"

"I thought so, too . . . once upon a time," said Clarence.

"Then think so again. And more than ever before. You should be out rejoicing on the square, instead of skulking in your hut. But if I leave you for a second you begin to get the queerest notions . . . Come on, put your *boubou* on and come with us!"

"And what about the odour? Do you think the odour will go away when I've put my *boubou* on?"

"Don't talk rubbish!" said Samba Baloum.

"No, Baloum, I can't show myself to the king after the life I've led here."

"So that's it! That's all that's stopping you? You are as worthy of being presented to the king as anyone else. If all those who present themselves to the king had to be worthy of him, the king would live alone in the desert. You ask Diallo."

"But *I* . . ."

"What?" said Samba Baloum.

"You've told me often enough that I'm just a great cock."

"What harm is there in that? You forget that the naba is an old man. Do you think he wasn't a cuckold long before you came?"

"But listen, Baloum. Does what you say excuse in any way what I have done? Does it alter my case at all? . . . And even if it were to alter my case completely, you know quite well that the naba would never part with me."

"I'll wager that's another of the master of ceremonies' fairy tales."

"A fairy tale? Do you call that a fairy tale?" said Clarence. "Is it a fairy tale that the naba is rather close with his money, and that this cock you see before you—this cock bought like a pig in a poke, as you said—cost him an ass and a woman past her first youth?"

"The next time I meet the master of ceremonies," said Samba Baloum, "I'll strangle him with my two bare hands!"

"You see!" said Clarence.

"No, I don't see. All I know is that the naba will do exactly as the king commands him. That's what *I* see."

"And do you know what the king will command him to do?"

"No, I don't know. I can't even guess. But you know no more than I do, and your guess is as good as mine, no better, no worse. And it is not for you, or for me either, to put yourself in his place and try to guess what he will say. If you don't try your luck, no one will do it for you."

"Luck!" said Clarence . . . "If I had the heart to laugh, I would split my sides. Luck . . ."

"Call it whatever you like; that's the name I give it. Perhaps it doesn't mean anything; and perhaps it means a great deal. Who can tell? All I know is—and I'm absolutely sure of this—that if it exists, it won't be handed to you on a silver platter; you'll get out of it only as much as you are able to get out of it. He who expects nothing must not be surprised if he comes back with empty hands. And finally, if no one is favoured all the time, no one is frustrated all the time. That's something the master of ceremonies doesn't know. Luck . . . You see now what I mean. You see what I mean by 'luck,' and what others mean when they talk of 'merit.' "

"The beggar used to call it 'favour.' "

"I call it 'pity,' " said Diallo.

"Give it whatever name you like," said Samba Baloum, "but don't be like the master of ceremonies, who is always only too ready to talk about it. And allow me to call it 'luck.' The word suits me—it suits my girth. But bumpkin that I am, I am not so rustic that I believe this 'luck' comes only to the cleverest person. It doesn't require any sleight-of-hand, and you, Clarence, are unfortunately not very good with your hands. I believe even less that it is simply calculation, something to do with the words 'right' and 'just.' And there again, Clarence, fortunately you don't know how to calculate, and you are not one of the 'just.' That is why I am telling you to seize your chance, for it is within your reach. But seize it now, put out your hands to it, for if you don't make the effort, you will never do it."

"I've never done it," said Clarence.

"Perhaps you've never tried."

"I *have* tried."

"Then what are you afraid of?" said Diallo. "You won't be asked to do anything beyond your powers."

"The naba won't allow me to seize my chance," said Clarence.

"Leave the naba out of this!" said Samba Baloum. "Nabas are two a penny. The king is here, and the naba is nobody, the naba is less than cat's piss. Why do you fret yourself so much about the naba? One would think you were scared of his beard, the way you talk about it. Yet—note this well—today he will not make one sign with his beard, and not one hair will dare move in it unless the king gives the word. Goats, too, you know, have goatee beards. Are you bothered about an old goat? I can't help wondering why you are so fearful of authority all of a sudden. If it's not the master of ceremonies, it's the naba! . . . Why don't you take a tip from

the boys? Stop working yourself up and put on your *boubou*.
The king will soon be passing in front of your hut."

"He will sit under the arcade . . ." Clarence said.

And the moment he said those words he fell into a kind of
faint—he was, one might say, incapacitated. That would be
more exact. The others all round him talked and fussed; and
perhaps he replied to their questions. Perhaps he was not
altogether unaware of what they were saying. And he even
sensed that he was answering them, and moving about, but
he was not conscious either of what he was saying or of what
he was doing; it had all become a confused noise, a babbling
of words, and movements without meaning. "Something like
life," he thought vaguely. "Something which is perhaps life
itself—utter folly—a saraband of noisy fools! . . ." Then a
great cry suddenly was heard: "The king!" He felt that they
were trying to put his *boubou* on by force, but he struggled
against them: he didn't want them to put his *boubou* on at all,
he didn't want the king to recoil in horror . . .

When he regained consciousness, he was alone, utterly
alone. A great silence, a dense silence, reigned in the hut.

"Is this the way one dies?" he whispered to himself.

Obviously it was—one entered a padded silence, a thickly-
feathered silence; one light in a diffused radiance, a soft,
strong radiance, a radiance . . . But where was this radiance
coming from? Clarence got up and went to the right-hand
window, from which this radiance seemed to be streaming.
And then . . .

He saw the king. He saw him sitting under the arcade at
the naba's side, he saw him sitting in all his glory. And then
he knew where the extraordinary radiance was coming from.

It seemed that he had been waiting all his life for this
moment. Now that he saw this longed-for scene, he did not
know if it was real, or if it was some mirage, some hallucina-

tion, an image projected by his own eyes upon the courtyard
wall; an image that had taken shape so long ago, and that had
been conjured up so often that the eyes finally seem to see
it, divorced from all reality.

No, the scene was real enough. An endless procession of
servants was bringing presents and casting them down at the
king's feet. Yet the king's eye never once rested on these
presents that were piling up in front of him; he was looking
straight ahead; and perhaps he saw nothing. Perhaps his eyes,
as in Dioki's cavern, were simply turned in upon himself;
perhaps that look which he bent upon a distant point was a
purely outward show, the result of a distracted and almost
disdainful condescension or amiability . . . What else could
it have been? There was nothing upon which the king could
rest his eye in this ignoble country of the South. This condescension was already a great favour, whatever the secret
scorn that lay behind it.

Behind the king, among his dancing pages, among that
great crowd of people who in truth were the only ones who
were saved, stood Nagoa and Noaga. Their eyes kept looking
from Clarence to the king and back again. Their eyes seemed
to be saying to Clarence:

"But what are you waiting for? . . . Don't you see it's the
time for the presents? Don't you see it's time to present
yourself? . . . Hurry up, Clarence! Don't let the moment slip
by. Don't lose a second!"

Yes, that was the sort of things the boys were saying; but
it must have been sheer effrontery urging them on to say
these things. For the more Clarence looked at the king, the
more he realised what courage, what audacity would be
needed to go up to him.

And it was not just his nakedness, it was not just his
vileness which prevented Clarence from going up to him; it

was something else—many other things. It was the fragility—the fragility as well as the great strength of the king—the same adorable fragility, the same formidable strength that Clarence had observed on the esplanade; the same smile, too, the same far-off smile which, like the look in his eyes, could be taken for disdain, that could almost certainly be taken for disdain, and which really seemed to float round his lips rather than be an actual part of them. And probably his garments, too—the immaculate whiteness of the mantle, the gold of the twisted rope tied like a heavy turban round his head; so many other things, too, so many other things that would have taken a lifetime to enumerate . . . But above all, so much purity, so much blazing purity. All these prevented Clarence from going up to him.

"Those are the things I am losing for ever . . ." said Clarence.

And he had the feeling that all was lost. But had he not already lost everything? . . . The boys could give him as many pregnant looks as they liked, he would not go near the royal presence; he had the measure of his own unworthiness. He would remain for ever chained to the South, chained to his hut, chained to the naba and to the harem, chained to everything he had so thoughtlessly abandoned himself to. Oh! if only he could have his life again! . . . But can one ever go back and start again? Can one ever wipe out what has been? . . . His solitude seemed to him so heavy, it burdened him with such a great weight of sorrow that his heart seemed about to break.

"And yet . . . My good-will . . ." he thought. "It's not true that I was lacking in good-will . . . I was weak, no one has ever been as weak as I am; and at nights, I was like a lustful beast . . . Yet, I did not enjoy my weakness, I did not love

the beast that was inside me; I should have liked to throw
off that weakness, and I should have liked not to be that
beast . . . No, it's not true that I was lacking in good-will."

But of what use was this good-will? Clarence was about to
curse it, curse it for its failure to help him. And the tears
sprang to his eyes.

But at that very moment the king turned his head, turned
it imperceptibly, and his glance fell upon Clarence. That look
was neither cold, nor hostile. That look . . . Did it not seem
to call to him?

"Alas, lord, I have only my good-will," murmured Clarence, "and it is very weak! But you cannot accept it. My
good-will condemns me: there is no virtue in it."

Still the king did not turn his eyes away. And his eyes
. . . In spite of everything, his eyes seemed to be calling
. . . Then, suddenly, Clarence went up to him. He ought to
have bumped into the outer wall, but as he approached it the
wall melted away, the hut behind him melted away, and he
walked on.

He went forward and he had no garment upon his nakedness. But the thought did not enter his head that he ought
first of all to have put his *boubou* on; the king was looking at
him, and nothing, nothing had any more meaning beside that
look. It was so luminous a look, one in which there was so
much sweetness that hope, a foolish hope, woke in Clarence's
heart. Yes, hope now strove with fear within him, and hope
was growing stronger than fear. And though the sense of his
impurity seemed to be holding him back, at the same time
Clarence was going forward. He went on with stumbling
steps; he stumbled as he trod on the rich carpet; every moment it seemed to him as if his legs or the ground beneath
him were going to disappear. But he kept moving forward,

forward all the time, and his legs did not betray him, nor did the ground open up under him. And that look . . . That look still did not turn away from him. "My lord! My lord!" Clarence kept whispering, "is it true that you are calling me? Is it true that the odour which is upon me does not offend you and does not make you turn away in horror?"

And because that look still calmly rested upon him, because the call was still going out to him, he was pierced as if by a tongue of fire.

"Yes no one is as base as I, as naked as I," he thought. "And you, lord, you are willing to rest your eyes upon me!" Or was it because of his very nakedness? . . . "Because of your very nakedness!" the look seemed to say. "That terrifying void that is within you and which opens to receive me; your hunger which calls to my hunger; your very baseness which did not exist until I gave it leave; and the great shame you feel . . ."

When he had come before the king, when he stood in the great radiance of the king, still ravaged by the tongue of fire, but alive still, and living only through the touch of that fire, Clarence fell upon his knees, for it seemed to him that he was finally at the end of his seeking, and at the end of all seekings.

But presumably he had still not come quite near enough; probably he was still too timid, for the king opened his arms to him. And as he opened his arms his mantle fell away from him, and revealed his slender adolescent torso. On this torso, in the midnight of this slender body there appeared—at the centre, but not quite at the centre . . . a little to the right—there appeared a faint beating that was making the flesh tremble. It was this beating, this faintly-beating pulse which was calling! It was this fire that sent its tongue of flame into his limbs, and this radiance that blazed upon him. It was this love that enveloped him.

"Did you not know that I was waiting for you?" asked the king.

And Clarence placed his lips upon the faint and yet tremendous beating of that heart. Then the king slowly closed his arms around him, and his great mantle swept about him, and enveloped him for ever.

Camara Laye was born in Guinea in 1924. A child of intellectual promise, he went first to the technical college at Conakry, the capital of Guinea, and later to France to study engineering. In Paris he found a totally different culture and, lonely and unhappy, wrote his first book, *The African Child*. This largely autobiographical work tells the story of his childhood among the Malinké tribe, surrounded by ritual magic and superstition, and his emergence into manhood and independence.

Twelve years later, having returned to his native land, Camara Laye wrote *A Dream of Africa*. In this sequel to *The African Child*, the narrator—now influenced by his experiences in Europe—sees an Africa on the violent brink of independence.

He is also the author of *The Guardian of the Word*, which was cited by the Académie Française, France's foremost literary institution, in May 1979.

In poor health for many years, Camara Laye died in 1980 in Senegal, where he had lived in exile for thirteen years.

VINTAGE INTERNATIONAL

VINTAGE INTERNATIONAL

Now at your bookstore or call toll-free to order: 1-800-733-3000
(credit cards only).